# Before The Devil Knows You're Dead

## Owen Mullen

*For*
*Devon and Harrison*
*My biggest supporters*

Colin McMillan sat in the car outside the flat and stared at the window. More than once he started to get out and changed his mind. The light was on. She was there; he'd seen the curtain move an hour ago. Since then there had been nothing. For two months he had tried and failed to have a conversation with his estranged wife. Joyce didn't want to speak to him and hung up as soon as she heard his voice.

Without her, the house in Bearsden where they had lived for fifteen years, was just bricks and mortar; rooms filled only with memories of them as Colin and Joyce: The McMillans.

On their last night together they'd made love in the dark. And in the dark, Joyce was more demanding than he had ever known her. She devoured him, scratching his back and beating her fists on his chest, like a trapped animal trying to escape. When it was over she turned away, sobbing quietly into the pillow. Because she had known.

The following evening, McMillan returned to find his wife gone, leaving him confused and unhappy and alone to wonder what he had done wrong.

Since then, he had drifted through days that became weeks then months, paralysed with sorrow; unable to come to terms with it. He had been here on other nights, hoping she would talk to him and at least tell him why.

The edge of the curtain drew back a fraction. For a couple of seconds, a face peered down at him. Or did it? He couldn't be sure. It had been a long and difficult day in theatre dealing with a series of complicated deliveries; the surgeon was exhausted. Seeing what he wanted to see, maybe. So he waited, afraid of causing a scene, knowing it wouldn't help. After twenty minutes, he came to a decision. Whatever the problem was it could be put right. He had to have one last go at saving his marriage.

McMillan got out of the car.

*His footsteps echoed in the stairwell. A lonely sound. At the top he stopped. The door of the flat was open. He called. 'Joyce! Joyce! Joyce it's me!'*

*McMillan went inside, along the hall and into the lounge at the end. There was no sign of his wife. He tried a bedroom. Nobody there. Not in the kitchen either. In the second bedroom he found her and his world fell apart.*

*Joyce was hanging from a cupboard door. She had cut an electrical cable off something and used it as a makeshift noose. Her features were distorted by the agony endured in the minutes before she died. Saliva trickled from her mouth and a viscous strand of mucous hung from her chin, like the beginning of a spider's web. The tip of her tongue poked from between her teeth above bulging eyes that didn't see.*

*The books she'd been standing on lay scattered on the floor and her arms were by her side, pushed tight inside the belt she had been wearing so she wouldn't be able change her mind. Joyce McMillan hadn't wanted to save herself.*

*Colin McMillan ran to his wife and threw himself around her waist, sobbing like a child. He eased her lifeless body off the door and carried it into the lounge. On the couch he placed a pillow beneath her head and ran his fingers tenderly through her hair.*

*What kind of hell had she been in to do this?*

*The answer was on the coffee table. Three crisp pages slipped under a half-finished cup of tea, still warm. Joyce's small unhurried hand explained all her husband hadn't understood, and more.*

*At the end she had written 'I'm so sorry. Forgive me. Please.'*

*Reading it broke McMillan's heart. It hadn't been passion that final night – it was despair. When he finished, he was crying. He turned off the light and sat staring into the darkness, drained of every emotion except hate. Joyce's face, horribly twisted in her final moments, would be with him for as long as he lived. He loosened his tie with a trembling hand. Eventually, he folded the sheets of paper and put them in his jacket pocket, reached for the telephone and dialed 999.*

# Chapter One

4.30. Hogmanay
**Francis Fallon Hospital, Glasgow**

The car drifted into the path of a bus headed for Springburn. Just in time, Gavin Law caught the flash of headlights and realised his mistake. He swerved back to his own side of the road and felt the wheels lose traction on the icy road. If he didn't get a grip, there would be no new year for him. Fat snowflakes landed on the windscreen. He didn't see them. The shocking turn of events had made him blind. He'd been a fool and he knew that now. His mistake had been to believe he was the one dropping the bomb. Wrong. They were ahead of him.

Half an hour earlier, he had taken the lift to the seventh floor of the private hospital and barged into the director's office. Jimmy Hambley was alone. He looked up from behind his desk; if he was surprised, he didn't show it. Law launched his ultimatum, boiling with righteous indignation.

'I complained months ago about Wallace Maitland. You know what he did to Mrs Cooper yet he's still operating. Your inquiry disregarded my evidence, and cleared him, for Christ's sake. The family has asked me to testify on their behalf in their legal action and I'm going to. I'll be the star witness.'

He leaned across the table.

'You're covering for Maitland because he's your wife's brother, but you won't get away with it. Francis Fallon will be on the front page of every newspaper in the country, and it won't stop there; the GMC will get involved. This is your last chance to do the

1

right thing – admit liability and settle with the Coopers. After that, I expect you to deal with Maitland.'

The response was unexpected and more ruthless than anything Gavin Law could have foreseen. The director listened to the outburst, then calmly reversed the roles.

'Mr Law. I was going to send for you. You've saved me the trouble. An allegation of misconduct has been made against you. Serious misconduct.'

Gavin Law sneered. 'What is this? What the hell is this?'

'A letter informing you of the process and your rights is on its way. You may wish to consider representation. That would be my advice. It may well be a matter for the police. As of now, you're suspended from all duties. Please leave the premises.'

'Allegation? Of what?'

Hambley told him and watched the colour drain from Law's face.

The accuser had become the accused.

# Chapter Two

**4.30. Hogmanay**
**City Centre, Glasgow**

Three days after I agreed to try to find him, Dougie Bell passed within a yard of me on the street. He walked quickly, shoulders hunched, hands buried in the pockets of his Parka, as if he had somewhere he needed to be. And indeed he did, though he didn't know it. His mother was in a coma in the Royal Infirmary and not expected to recover. If someone didn't tell the boy soon it would be too late; he would never see her alive again.

It was late in the afternoon: dark and bloody freezing. The morning forecast of heavy snow by evening looked a safe bet; the road was already covered in a frosty glaze.

I was standing on the pavement outside the Italian Centre, opposite the old sheriff court, listening to Patrick Logue rant about Auld Lang Syne, waiting for a break in his monologue so I could make my excuses and get out of the cold. Bell's eyes met mine. He half-nodded to me in one of those odd reflex moments when strangers mistake each other for someone they know. Patrick's passionate defence of Scotland's national poet kept me from recognising him immediately, and lost precious seconds in what would happen next.

Pat's breath came in smoky clouds. 'There's an excuse for a Sassenach like yourself, Charlie.'

I'd been born in Edinburgh – as he well knew.

'Don't expect you to know better. But when people on STV and the like sing "For the sake of auld lang syne…" I want to kick their ignorant arses. Robert Burns was a genius. The idiots…'

I cut him off. 'It's him!'

Bell must have heard because he took to his heels and raced towards Royal Exchange Square with me and Pat Logue behind him.

In my office, his father had studied his hands and admitted the two men, constantly arguing, may have contributed to the massive stroke which would probably take a wife from a husband and a mother from a son. The last head-butting session on Christmas Day ended with the boy running out of the house with his new mobile – a present from his mum and dad. Bell Senior couldn't remember what had started the row. How sad was that? But he told me this wasn't the first time young Dougie had pulled a disappearing act, though he had always come back home when he calmed down. Not this time. And he wasn't answering his phone, either. Stressed out of her mind and worried sick about her son, his mother collapsed on the kitchen floor on Boxing Day and hadn't regained consciousness.

A sorry story any way you looked at it. The irony didn't escape me. My relationship with my own father, although better now than it had been, remained uneasy; being in the same room for any length of time was still a trial for both of us.

From his picture, Dougie seemed no different than a thousand sixteen year olds in Glasgow; smiling and acned, eager and immature; into music and football. Beyond that, I knew little about him, apart from something that suddenly became very clear.

This guy could run.

Patrick had distracted me just long enough to give him a ten-yard start. That, plus a couple of decades, might be the difference between catching him or losing him. I considered myself pretty fit, but I wasn't sixteen. Bell raced along Ingram Street, twisting through the traffic without slowing down. One car skidded on the icy surface and missed hitting him by inches. People stood aside to let him pass, astonishment on their faces. Nobody tried to stop him. I could hear Pat Logue somewhere close. It would be a mistake to depend on him bringing the boy down; his entire lifestyle was against it.

Dougie charged across Queen Street into Royal Exchange Square, past the statue of the Duke of Wellington, with the old soldier, as usual, wearing an orange traffic cone on his head – a Glasgow tradition.

Bell looked over his shoulder, the hood fell away and I saw his young face stretched tight with fear.

Why was he running?

Who did he think we were?

What had he done to react like this?

He was pulling away from me. Winning. Through the arch at the far side of the square I gained a little ground when he collided with a group of women coming out of the Rogano. He stumbled, almost fell, and re-gained his balance.

Dougie swerved right, into Buchanan Street. My legs wouldn't carry me and my chest was on fire. I didn't have any more to give. I wasn't going to catch him; twenty-odd-years was just too big an advantage. Pat Logue came round the corner, puffing and blowing like an old man, his face the colour of ash. We stood together, watching the boy glide between pedestrians, like the teenager he was, still full of energy.

He must have sensed we had given up because he stopped and looked back at us, grinning. Then, with all the arrogance of youth, he held up his middle finger.

Patrick said, 'Cheeky as well as fast.'

I didn't see it like that. This young man was about to lose his mother. His future wasn't what it used to be. There was a guilt trip coming that might never let him go. I felt for him. At sixteen, you could do things older people couldn't do – like run – that left a helluva downside; the best part of a lifetime to regret. And everybody makes mistakes.

The boy threw a last victory wave at us, grinning like the cat that got the cream. From where we were, it was too far to be certain what exactly happened next. Tripped or slipped, I couldn't say, but Bell went over and didn't get back up.

We started running. When we got there Dougie was sitting on the ground, holding his ankle, blood oozing from his nose, his trousers torn at the knee. He looked through the crowd gathered round him, saw us, and blurted an unaskedfor confession.

'It wasn't me. I had nothing to do with it.'

'Not sure I believe you, Dougie. Even if I had the foggiest idea what you're talking about.'

His expression creased in confusion. 'So why're you chasing me?'

'Why're you running? Your father needs to speak to you.'

He realised we weren't who he thought we were and assumed the surly default position his age group kept for adults; expressionless face; monotone voice. 'He can fuck right off. I'm not interested.'

'Yeah, you are. Can you stand?'

Patrick helped him to his feet. He winced, clearly in pain. My guess was a sprain rather than a break. Painful, not serious.

Pat said, 'Think you're out of the big game on Saturday, squire.'

Joseph Bell's number was unobtainable. Of course it was. He would be at the hospital with his wife. I sent a text and two minutes later he called me back, sounding relieved when I told him I had his son. The son glared defiance.

'If that's my father, I'm not talking to him.'

Patrick told him to shut it, and I spoke quietly into the phone. 'How are things, Mr Bell? Any change?'

'No,' he said. 'No change.'

We helped the boy walk to St Vincent Street, supporting him between us until a taxi stopped. Pat Logue and Bell got in the back. I spoke to the driver and paid the fare.

Dougie didn't ask where he was going. His father was waiting at the Royal Infirmary with news that would devastate him. Whatever the outcome, they would have to deal with it together, and it wouldn't be easy. Maybe it wouldn't even be possible.

Finding Joseph Bell's son was my last piece of work in what, in many respects, had been a good twelve months for me. Most of my cases had come out all right. Of course there were exceptions. Shit happens and that's a fact. Sometimes, there's just nothing you can do.

The door closed and the black cab drove away, leaving me on a pavement in the centre of Glasgow with the world turning to ice around me.

\*\*\*

I stood on the steps outside the Concert Hall, behind the statue of Donald Dewar, and followed the lights on Buchanan Street to St Enoch's Square in the distance. It was five minutes to five now, and the flagship department stores and up-market shops were closing. Most people had gone home to get ready for midnight; only stragglers remained. A lone piper in full Highland dress, stood at the entrance to the underground – known locally as the Clockwork Orange – a phantom in the snow that had started to fall, playing a lament that hung in the air. Bagpipes weren't my favourite instrument but their sound touched something in me. I closed my eyes for a moment and listened.

Scotland invented Hogmanay and tonight, all over this country, Scots would say goodbye to the old year and welcome the new with handshakes and songs, laughter and tears. Auld acquaintance would be forgot and never brought to mind as sadness gave way to hope, and the promise of a clean slate. A fresh start. A chance to try again.

Who didn't wish for that?

Pat Logue was right: Robert Burns was a genius.

Of course it wouldn't last. It wasn't supposed to last. But while it did, it was magic.

The piper was putting his pipes away – he'd been a brave man to stick it out so long. Later, he'd be in big demand. I wandered into Buchanan Galleries for a final few minutes of window shopping. When I came out, the brave man had gone, and the city was a white desert.

# Chapter Threee

**9.30. Hogmanay**
**West End of Glasgow**

Gavin Law felt better. Two stiff whiskies helped. He stepped out of the shower and padded through to the lounge, without bothering to cover himself. No need, he was the only one there. He poured another drink and imagined himself at the party with Caroline giving him a dressing down for being drunk and embarrassing her in front of her friends. She needn't worry. It wouldn't happen – he wasn't going. A pity, because he had invited a nurse called Alile, a twenty-eight-year-old stunner from Malawi, who wouldn't be out of place in the Miss World contest. But tonight, he wasn't in the mood.

Unusual for him.

He fished out his mobile and punched in her number. It went straight to voicemail.

'Alile. It's Gavin. Hate to cancel at the last minute. No luck, I've come down with something. Just came on this afternoon. I'll call you in a few days.'

He doubted she would be bothered one way or the other. When you were as good-looking as her, men were like corporation buses; there would be another one along in a minute.

The next call, to his sister, connected him to Caroline's recorded voice, asking him to leave a message. Everybody was busy.

'Sorry sis. Going to pass on the bells. Too tired. Speak to you tomorrow. Have a good one.'

That would go down like a lead balloon. Caroline was obsessed with what other people thought and would have mentioned he was coming. When he didn't show, people would talk. Tough titty. Her brother couldn't give a monkey's. Life really was too short.

But Hambley had rattled him, and the reaction since the complaint had gone way beyond anything he had expected. Colleagues Law worked alongside and shared coffee with closed ranks and snubbed him, as if he had something to be ashamed of. Nurses fell silent when he came into the room. Suddenly, he was on the outside looking in.

Nobody got it.

Nobody, except McMillan.

Law made his third telephone call in a row and listened to it ring out.

Colin McMillan had been through a rough time. His fifteen-year marriage had ended in tragedy. His wife moved out of the family home in Bearsden into a bedsit in Shawlands. Two months later, he found her dead; she had hanged herself. On his first day back, McMillan wrote his own letter, complaining about Wallace Maitland's incompetence, and delivered it by hand to the seventh floor. Twenty-four hours later, an un-named member of staff claimed he had confessed to being suicidal. McMillan denied saying anything of the kind, but his personal circumstances played against him. He was suspended, his name removed from the operating list and he was told he would be advised about the date of the inquiry in due course. It hardly mattered because whatever the finding, his reputation was in rags. He was finished.

The two surgeons weren't friends; in fact, they didn't get on. But together they had blown the whistle and one of them – McMillan – had paid the price.

A weary voice answered. Law didn't introduce himself. 'Those bastards! Those bastards!'

'…Law? What's wrong?'

'They did it to you. Now they're trying it with me. I could go to prison.'

'I don't know what you're saying.'

'I've been suspended.'

'Why?'

'An allegation's been made about me.'

'An allegation of what?'

'Rape.'

There was silence at the other end of the line before McMillan whispered 'Christ.'

'It never happened.'

'…Of course not. Of course it didn't.'

Law heard uncertainty in the other man's voice, and forced insistence into his own.

'Colin. It never happened. They were afraid I'd testify for the Coopers and want to discredit me.'

'And will you testify?'

'Yes. Yes, I will.'

'Where are you now?'

'At home.'

'You must be feeling like shit.'

'Yeah. My sister's invited me to her place but I can't face it. I'm not going.'

'No, you should. Tomorrow, call Hambley and withdraw your complaint.'

'Too late for that. The notification's already been sent.'

'Then start looking for a new job.'

'Done that. Got an interview at St Joseph's Hospital Health Centre in Syracuse.'

'Great reputation for obstetrics. When?'

'Fourth of January. Flying over on the second.'

'If they offer it to you, take it. Forget you ever heard of Francis Fallon.'

'And what about the Coopers? What about that poor woman? Should I just forget about her?'

McMillan was pragmatic. 'Only fight the battles you can win.'

'But without somebody to say what exactly went wrong, the hospital might never settle, or if they do, it'll take years.'

The surgeon's opinion didn't alter. 'Do yourself a favour. Make peace with the hospital and the rape thing will go away. It's over; they've won. Accept it. I have.'

Law stood in the middle of the room, feeling the slow burn of the alcohol at the back of his throat. McMillan hadn't any doubts about what he ought to do. Don't be their enemy, he'd said, and who would know better? Going up against them had cost him his career. Law didn't have to make the same mistake. At the end of the day, Wallace Maitland wasn't his problem. If the hospital was happy with a surgeon who was likely to kill as many patients as he helped, it was no business of his. He'd been a damned fool to get involved. It was time to get uninvolved. Tomorrow, he would call Hambley and withdraw his statement. After that – do his homework for the American post, polish his answers on the plane, and shine at the interview. The allegation would evaporate, and by spring, he'd be thousands of miles away from Glasgow and Francis Fallon, and fuck the lot of them.

He'd told his sister about his concerns with Maitland; something he regretted now. Caroline had been horrified and urged him to do the right thing. Predictable. She saw things in black and white; his personal life was an example. Everything would be better if only he found a nice girl and settled down. No need to get married, not these days, she accepted that, but having someone you could depend on made a difference. Tied to one woman, when there were so many, wasn't for him. Hospitals were full of them, walking around in those prim uniforms and cute hats. Every man's fantasy. Not something you got used to, and maybe, subconsciously, the reason he had been drawn to medicine. It certainly wasn't a disincentive.

He pulled on a black polo neck and smiled a whisky smile at his reflection in the wardrobe mirror. All right, considering. Tall, dark, and not especially handsome. Though it hadn't held him back.

Caroline enjoyed introducing him as "my brother, Doctor Law". "Mr" would've been more appropriate but then whoever she was trying to impress might not get it. Law didn't mind. "Doctor" was the magic leg-spreader.

When he met a female who interested him he usually let a couple of minutes go by before admitting that, actually, he wasn't just a doctor – he was a surgeon. To a bored housewife, with her very own Dean and a few too many drinks in her, that was exciting. Or a dissatisfied spouse. Plenty of those, thank God. The married ones were the best because they knew what they wanted and weren't slow to go after it.

No strings. No romantic nonsense with them.

Of course, if they forgot the rules, it could get messy.

He spoke to the empty room, imitating his sister's nasal Kelvin side accent.

'This is my brother, Doctor Law. Yes, a doctor. We're all very proud of him.'

Three cheers for Caroline. The party was starting to seem like a good idea. Then the mellow buzz faded, the whisky soured in his stomach and he collapsed into an armchair with his hands over his face.

*Rape, for Christ's sake.*

On the telephone with McMillan, he'd sworn the accusation was bogus; the truth was, he wasn't sure. There had been so many. The perks of the job. And somebody at Francis Fallon – probably Hambley – had made it their business to get hold of one of them.

Law tried to think. A relationship with a woman in cardiology had run its course and finished in tears. Whenever their paths crossed, she made a point of ignoring him. More recently, there had been a one-night stand with a midwife he'd met in a pub near the hospital. *June? Jan? Geraldine?* He couldn't remember the name. If he was being honest, the sister from the fourth floor could be a contender. He hadn't felt good about doing her – too much booze. Drunk females were better avoided, however tempting. No telling how they would react the next morning. Or maybe the blonde gynae nurse with the tight little arse; she'd put up a fight in this very room, though in the end, she'd been well into it. And come back for seconds, as he recalled. Not her. *So who?*

Law poured another drink. Winding up like Colin McMillan wasn't an option. He would definitely call Hambley. Let some other mug take them on if they liked; it wouldn't be him.

The phone rang. Caroline's opening line lacked festive cheer.

'What do you mean you're giving it a miss? You can't. I want you here.'

Law held the receiver away from his mouth and sighed. He didn't need this. 'Yeah, sis, I know. Gutted about it. Really am. But I'm not fit.'

Silence.

'It's Dean, isn't it?'

'Nothing to do with Dean, or anybody else. I can hardly keep my eyes open. And the day after tomorrow I'm off to the US. The interview. I told you about it, remember?'

She wouldn't be soft-soaped. 'That's ages away. You can easily come here.'

'I'm shattered, Caroline. Give me a break.'

'I'm the only family you've got, Gavin.'

Law felt his patience slipping; his hand tightened around the telephone. Of course, she couldn't know what had happened in Hambley's office and assumed ducking out of the party was about her.

'The one night. The one and only night of the year. People travel from all over the world just to be together. But not us. Not the Laws. You're twenty minutes away, yet you can't make it. And after I've gone to so much trouble.'

'You have no idea what I've been through today, Caroline. Sorry to disappoint but, hand on heart, it isn't about you.'

'You don't like my friends. You'll do anything to avoid them.'

Law couldn't hold on to himself any longer. 'Since you mention it, yeah, your friends are a bunch of tossers. But that's got nothing to do...'

'They're nice people. A lot nicer than you.'

'Glad you think so.'

*Rape, for Christ's sake* .

Caroline went quiet at the end of the line. When she spoke, she was near to tears. 'I blame myself. After Mum passed, I was worried how you would cope, so I spoiled you. You grew up selfish.'

'I'm not being selfish. I'm wiped. Barely have the energy to drag myself to bed.'

'Why don't you have a shower and see if you feel any better.'

'I've already had a shower.'

His sister lost her temper. 'Oh, give yourself a shake, please. What about the girl you wanted to bring – Alile, wasn't it?'

'Alile understands. I'm not coming, Caroline. I'm too tired.'

'Well, we'll be here all day tomorrow.'

'I won't promise. I'll see how it goes.'

'What..? You'll see how it goes? I'm your sister you pompous clown. And I'm trying to be nice to you. Have you any idea how up your own backside you are? No to tonight. Won't promise tomorrow. Then you're off to America the day after that. Aren't you at all bothered about me? Is that the thanks I get?'

Law threw the phone across the room. It landed on the sofa. Emotional blackmail was Caroline's specialty; he'd had a lifetime of it. She had to be in control, didn't she? For a moment, it occurred to him that maybe Dean hadn't always been such a wuss. Living with Caroline would grind the spirit out of anybody. Law slumped onto the couch, depressed. He swallowed what was left of the amber drink, feeling its effect, unable to escape the black thoughts it had failed to banish.

*Rape, for Christ's sake.*

All very well for McMillan to suggest he withdraw his complaint. What if it was too late? Hambley could then claim that once the process was in motion, it couldn't be stopped. Where would that leave him? Law knew the answer – America wouldn't be happening. No matter how much he impressed at the interview, any job offer would be dependent on satisfactory references. Something he hadn't considered before he'd started rocking the boat. Obvious, when you thought about it. Stay or go, those fuckers at Francis Fallon had him where they wanted him.

Law noticed he was holding an empty glass. He picked the bottle up by the neck, brought it beside him and carelessly splashed alcohol into the tumbler. Some of it spilled. He tried to think but wasn't able to concentrate; his head swam. *Who the hell was it?* His gut still said the gynae blonde although, when he'd given her money for a taxi to take her home, she'd made a joke about payment for services and they'd laughed. She seemed fine at the hospital, too; whenever they passed each other, she smiled.

So? Somebody else.

The phone rang again. Law let it and poured himself another whisky; it would be Caroline. After a while, it stopped. He lay on the couch, closed his eyes and fell asleep. In his head, he could hear Colin McMillan telling him the same thing, over and over.

*Don't be their enemy*
*Don't be their enemy*
*Don't be their enemy*

# Chapter Four

**9.30. Hogmanay**
**Bothwell. 9 miles from Glasgow**

Sean Rafferty spent most of his life on the phone, and even as the last few hours of the old year wound down, that didn't change. On the desk, a photograph of his daughter sat in a gold frame. Rosie had only been days old when the picture was taken; pink and wizened like all new babies. Rafferty had lost hours gazing at it, appreciating how fortunate they'd been. Rosie was almost a year old now, born prematurely and still small. The East End gangster didn't believe in God. Who to thank was already arranged.

He balanced the receiver between his ear and shoulder while he jotted columns of figures on a pad and totalled them in his head. Listening. Liking what he was hearing. Against the far wall, a model of Riverside sat on a table. The project had been Sean's idea and it was ambitious – a marina, casino, hotel, restaurant and retail development – the jewel in the crown of the Waterfront Regeneration plan. Two hundred projects on both sides of the river that would transform the Clyde. If it was approved, whatever benefits it brought to Glasgow, Riverside would help achieve two things for Sean Rafferty: cement his relationship with Emil Rocha, the foreign backer, and give Rafferty what he craved: respectability.

The door opened. From the terrace, the low hum of the band playing nineties pop reached him and Kim's beautiful face appeared in the frame. She didn't come inside. This was her husband's space; the rest of the house on the hill above the River Clyde was hers to do with as she wished.

Rafferty hung up. 'Are they here?'

His wife hesitated. Sean was bad at bad news. 'One of them is.'

'Lachie Thompson?'

'No.'

'So who?'

'Rutherford.'

'And he's on his own?'

Kim's expression answered for her.

Rafferty hid his anger with a tight smile. He'd met Kim in the Radisson Blu Hotel at the final of the Miss Scotland contest. A month later, he had taken her on holiday to Antigua, and during the second week, hand-in-hand on the beach beneath a crescent moon in a black sky, he'd proposed. Walking bare-foot over the still-warm sand that night, Rafferty had told the twenty-one-year-old history student he loved her.

He didn't. It was something he'd said because she needed to hear it. For him, it was unimportant; he liked her. More than enough to build the life he had in mind. She'd stand at his side: a flawless symbol of the re-invention of Jimmy's son as a respected member of the business community. Kim would be the mother of his children. And she would obey him in everything. Under the skin, Sean was not so very different from the father he'd feared or the brother he'd despised.

He came to the door and slipped his arms around her waist. 'You smell wonderful. What is it?'

'I can't remember.'

'Nice. Did Rosie go down all right?'

'Yes. Not a murmur out of her.'

'I'll go up in a minute.'

'What about our guests?'

'Fill them with drink. Free booze is the only reason they're here, isn't it?'

Not the only reason. They were afraid to turn Sean Rafferty down. Except Lachie Thompson; he wasn't afraid. The others had taken their courage from him and stayed away.

Rafferty closed the study door and locked it. Upstairs, he tip-toed into the nursery where his daughter was asleep. Sean had barely had a father, let alone a nursery, when he was a baby. Growing up with Jimmy was a loveless experience he would never get over. Rosie wasn't going to know anything like that. Her childhood would be very different; she would have everything money could buy from a man prepared to sacrifice his life to keep her safe.

The pink covers lay crumpled at the bottom of the cot; she had already managed to kick them off. Rafferty gazed at the little face – totally and completely at peace – and the long blonde eyelashes she had inherited from her mother. He gently pulled the blankets back over her, and went down to greet his guests.

***

Roland Kirkwood was at Sean Rafferty's elbow, grinning at him through a sunbed tan and designer stubble. 'Great party, Sean. Thanks for asking me.'

He was wearing jeans and a white kaftan trimmed with blue. The guy was a dick. His girlfriend was the reason he'd been invited.

'Where's Marie?'

'Over there.'

He pointed to a tall redhead who had three middle-aged men in suits eating out of her hand. Marie waved. Rafferty waved back.

'She's dying to meet you.'

'Tell her I'll catch her later.'

Through the crowd, someone Rafferty wanted to meet even more than Marie was sitting in an armchair by the fire. Sandy Rutherford wasn't drinking; this wasn't social. Rafferty eased past his guests and made his way towards him. The councillor stood and pulled himself to his full six feet.

Rutherford's reputation as a straight talker made him the obvious choice to bring the East End gangster to heel. That reputation was well-founded. In a public career spanning three decades, opponents had discovered he was capable of being more ruthless than they had ever imagined.

He played the part of a rough diamond – a down-to-earth hard man who could be trusted – and used it to his advantage. Like many convincing deceptions, it was based on a fragment of truth; he had been a welder, and during the Upper Clyde Shipbuilders work-in in 1971, spent lunch-hours listening to Jimmy Airlie's coarse rhetoric. Its potency had mesmerised the young apprentice and inspired him to join the Communist Party. At twenty-eight, he became a shop steward. Ten years on, he was a Labour Party fire-brand and elected to the city council. Sandy Rutherford was politically savvy but chose to hide his sophistication behind the joined-up shouting style which had so impressed him as a youth, standing shoulder-to-shoulder with his workmates at union meetings on the banks of the Clyde, with the ghosts of the Queens in the cold winter air.

He adopted the style and the language though not the principles. His real commitment was to himself. In fact, Rutherford and Rafferty were the same animal.

Neither man offered to shake hands. Rutherford came straight to the point. 'They won't go for it.'

'Who, exactly?

The councillor avoided answering.

'Who won't go for it?'

'Cards on the table, Sean. It's not the project, per se; it's who's behind it. People remember what doing business with Jimmy was like.'

'Jimmy's dead.'

Rutherford sighed; this was always going to be a difficult conversation. 'Even so.'

'Even so... what?'

'Jimmy. Kevin. You. It's still the family. Understandably, they aren't keen.'

'Who isn't?'

'Lachie Thompson isn't a fan. Tony Daly. Between them, they control half the votes. These men are public figures. They don't want to wake up and find their picture next to yours on the front of the Herald. Need to keep your name out of the papers for a while.'

On the other side of the room, Marie was watching; she was interested. Rafferty turned his attention back to the councillor. He had despised his father but he'd learned something valuable from him.

Never take a no from somebody who can give you a yes.

Violence had worked for the old man. With some people it was the only thing that did. Jimmy hadn't taken no. Ever. Neither would his son.

'I'm disappointed, Sandy. Very disappointed.'

Rutherford held his ground. 'It's early days, Sean. We're still feeling each other out. You have to appreciate what you're asking takes time.'

'We haven't got time.'

The councillor shook his head. 'You know, when you took over, I was hoping for progress. A new era if you will. But...' *Did this idiot realise who he was talking to?*

'...face facts. You're famous. These people don't do famous.'

Rafferty toyed with his water glass. 'So I'm the problem? But for more money, they'll take a chance, am I right?'

The councillor considered the question. 'They might.'

He put an avuncular hand on Rafferty's arm, as if he was schooling a boy in an important lesson he would do well to learn. 'You need to understand the value of patience.'

Rafferty pushed the hand away. 'And here's what you need to understand. What you did in the past didn't end with Jimmy. You worked for him. Now you work for me. You've got seven days to show me we're going in the right direction. Seven days.'

*Never take a no from somebody who can give you a yes.*

He looked at his watch. 'Starting in sixty minutes. Now get out of my house.'

# Chapter Five

**11.00 p.m. New York Blue**

Byres Road was awash with people on their way to the street party in Ashton Lane. Three girls – no older than sixteen – in short skirts and high-heels came out of Hillhead underground and laughed their way through the crowds. Outside Starbucks, one of them slipped and crashed to the ground. Luck was with her; the wine and the cider and the God knows what else she'd drunk, broke her fall; the bottle in her hand landed upright in the snow without spilling a drop. The girls giggled. Her friends pulled her to her feet and on they went: kids pretending to be adults. These ladies would be lucky to see the bells in. The taxi driver shook his head and spoke to me over his shoulder.

'Don't get it, do they?'

'Unfortunately.'

'Could ruin their whole lives and they're too stupid to realise it.'

Fifteen minutes later, the car drew into the kerb to the whisper of snow crushing under the wheels and came to a stop. In the background, barely loud enough to hear, the radio played hit songs reminding me I wasn't young anymore. I passed money though the grill to the driver who took it without bothering to check how much was there and pointed to the frozen world I was about to enter.

'All the best when it comes.'

'You too, mate.'

In spite of the cold, Alex was waiting for me at the door; he seemed agitated. 'Beginning to think you'd decided to give it a miss.'

'A party on Hogmanay? I was always going to be here.'

I followed him downstairs to a table by the side of the stage, where Jackie, the Logues, and Andrew and Sandra had already made inroads on the bar our host had set up for us. Outside, the temperature was below zero; in the club, it was hot: Africa hot.

The DJ kept the music going non-stop. Conversation wouldn't be easy. I squeezed in between Patrick and Andrew. Alex pushed a bottle of Black Label at me.

'Got a bit of catching-up to do, Charlie. Get started.'

Patrick had a low-strength lager in his hand.

'What's this?'

'New Year resolution.'

'You're joking.'

He whispered. 'Wish I was. Nearly didn't make it.'

'How so?'

'Gail didn't want to come. Not after last night.'

'What happened?'

'Young Patrick decided to celebrate early. Fell in the door.'

'Drunk?'

'Manky. Nine-point-seven on the Mankometer. Came home last week with his eyes double-glazed. Dope. Gail went mental. Really freaked. Said I'd speak to him.'

'And did you?'

'Yeah, gave him a right bollockin' for upsettin' his mother. I mean, smokin' Mara Joanna. Who hasn't done that? Told him to box clever.'

'Was he listening?'

'He's a teenager, what do you think?'

'How old is he?'

'Not old enough. It was sore for Gail to see him like that. Worse than the whacky baccy. Cried her eyes out. Twice in the same week means he isn't her wee boy anymore. She worries he'll end up a junkie or maybe have inherited the family problem. Gail's connection's knee-deep in alcoholics.'

'Lucky you came along to save her.'

Straight over his head.

'Exactly, Charlie. She's insisting I set a good example.' He tapped the beer. 'Picked a great night. Free bar.'

'And Hogmanay.'

'Not bothered about that. Never liked it.'

This was a surprise. 'You don't like Hogmanay? Thought you'd be well into it.'

He shook his head. 'For amateurs. Scrap it if it was down to me. Scrap the whole maudlin malarkey.'

I disagreed. Drawing a line and starting over again was an idea that appealed and, looking around, it wasn't just my opinion.

At eleven-thirty, Big River came on and rocked the house. At a minute to midnight, Alan Sneddon got up from behind the drums and did the countdown. Everybody joined in.

'...Four! Three! Two! One! Happy New Year!'

"Auld Lang Syne" blasted out, balloons fell from the ceiling, and if it had been loud before, it was deafening now. Strangers hugged each other and shook hands. Pat Logue didn't move until Gail threw her arms round his neck and kissed him like a teenager. After twenty-odd years together, not bad.

Alan held his hands in the air and called for quiet. I didn't fancy his chances but I was wrong. 'We promised you a surprise guest star, and we weren't exaggerating. The person coming on is both a star and an old friend of Big River. Currently in the middle of a world tour with North Wind. Give it up for NYB's favourite lady – Kate Calder!'

Every morning for months I'd passed a poster outside boasting about a Hogmanay "Special Guest," without giving it a second thought. And now, why Alex had invited me was obvious. If I'd known it was Kate I probably wouldn't have come. We'd been lovers; for a while, marriage was on the cards. North Wind – one of the biggest stadium bands around – offered her a job; she'd turned it down to be with me. Then, as suddenly as it began, it was over. A week after we split, Kate left Glasgow and joined North Wind.

Getting over her was still a work in progress, and for a while, I'd spent my nights Googling the band's web site. Eventually, I gave up. There had been women since, but the relationships were short-lived: they weren't Kate and never could be.

She picked her way to the front of the stage and waved. The crowd went wild. Kate Calder was one of their own and always would be. She checked the settings on the white Telecaster strapped round her neck, shaking the shoulder-length red hair that reminded me so much of a young Bonny Raitt. Kate had had a rock-chick thing going on from the beginning; her blue jeans and snake skin boots were a particular favourite of mine. Tonight, I was out of luck; they'd been replaced by leather trousers and black trainers with the Nike swoosh on the side. Cool, though not in the same class as the boots. Not even close.

The first number was a journey back in time for me – to two years ago when this wonderful talented lady had been mine. The guys in Big River lay back and grooved; wherever Kate took it was all right with them. This was a small Glasgow club – a far cry from the venues she was used to – and she played like she'd come home.

I heard a voice in my ear. 'Sensational, isn't she?'

It was Alex.

'She certainly is.'

One of us was talking about the music.

Towards the end of the show, Kate took the guitar off, sat on a stool, and sang the beautiful haunting Richard Thompson tune, "Dimming of the Day." I would've liked to believe she was talking to me. In my dreams. That ship had sailed. Some lucky guy would hear those intimate lyrics and know they were about him.

And Alex Gilby was right: she was sensational. The crowd wouldn't let her go. A quick discussion produced a shit-kicking jam of "Roll Over Beethoven," and when the final chord faded, the band held hands and took a bow at the front of the stage to an ovation that threatened to take the roof off.

Pat Logue was beside me, whistling and applauding. His dislike of fake beer and amateur drinkers hadn't stopped him enjoying himself. He shouted his verdict at me. 'Two words, Charlie! Su perb!'

'Thought you disapproved?'

'This is me disapprovin''

He finished his lager, twisting his face against the taste, and slipped an arm round his wife. It had been a brave effort from a guy who lived to drink. Gail smiled and kissed him. The Logues' marriage wasn't plain sailing – their bouts of domestic disharmony were well known – yet, they were together; even if the rest of the world couldn't see it, and at times they lost sight of it themselves. They were doing something right.

Patrick winked, and turned to Alex Gilby. NYB'S best customer had seen the old year out and the New Year in on kid-on beer in an uncharacteristic display of moderation; his good example was coming to an end. Normal service was about to be resumed. 'And now a word from our sponsor. Any chance of one for the road, Alex?'

'Every chance, Pat. Upstairs.'

We made our way out of the club. I glanced back at the stage, hoping Kate would appear. She didn't.

The restaurant was in darkness. Alex opened the door, switched on the lights and went behind the bar. 'So? What're we after?'

Geddes answered. 'A wee goldie wouldn't go amiss.'

It was unusual to see him so relaxed; a lot of that was down to Sandra. His ex-wife, Elspeth, better known as the Wicked Witch of the North, hadn't been the warmest person I'd ever met. Sandra was light years away from her, and the reason they were here. Left to himself, Geddes would be in bed.

To prove my point, he started dancing with her; waltzing to music nobody else could hear. Very un-Andrew. DS Geddes was a glass-half-empty guy. A stocky, black and white moralist, with little faith in people beyond their ability to hurt each other. Dour was his default position, re-enforced by a job he was one hundred and ten percent committed to. The result was a great detective who could be a difficult companion. In a city like Glasgow, he often found himself face-to-face with dark forces which, inevitably, soured his view of the human race, and took him closer to the grumpy old man he was destined to become.

But he had a good heart and was a friend who had helped me many times.

The wee goldies he'd already had were doing their work.

Alex gave everyone a drink and handed him a whisky. He hid his gratitude with a question showing it would take more than booze to eradicate the pessimist in him. 'Think you'll be able to drive? Coming in, it didn't look good.'

Alex held up his hands. 'Andrew. It's snow. Even if we have to spend the next couple of days here, so what?'

Alan Sneddon appeared to a round of applause from Sandra and Gail. He made an exaggerated bow – obviously pleased with himself – then shook their hands. Jackie got more than a handshake. With me he just nodded. Now the identity of the special guest star was out, I guessed he was uncomfortable.

Alex Gilby took me aside. 'Hope you aren't angry, Charlie. I wanted it to be a surprise.'

'It was certainly that.'

'Been advertising for months but we only knew for sure two weeks ago. North Wind's American tour broke for the holiday on the twentieth of December and picks up again on the fourth of January. Kate called me two weeks ago, just before she went on stage in Tulsa, to say she would definitely be here. Guessed you wouldn't want to miss it, given the history.'

Unfortunately, tonight reminded me history was all that was left.

'A good thought, Alex. Appreciate it.'

I made small-talk with Alan Sneddon about the difficulties of putting a set together in such a short time. He was pleased with himself and keen to discuss it. We were still talking when Kate came in. She hugged Gail and Jackie. I was last. Although our break-up had been friendly we hadn't seen each other in two years. She shook my hand – a strange experience.

I said, 'You look great.'

'So do you.'

'What's it like being a big star?'

She laughed. 'No idea.'

'How long are you here?'

'Just a couple of days. We kick-off again in Chicago on the fourth. I'm going back on the second.'

Someone with a blunt knife could've cut a slice out of the awkwardness and taken it home in a cake-box. Jackie and Alan chose that moment to interrupt and I caught Jackie glance anxiously to see my reaction. I hung around for a while on the edge of the conversation and eventually drifted away to speak to Patrick and Gail.

Gail pointed to Kate. 'Looking great, isn't she?'

'Yes, she is.'

'Hard to believe not so long ago she was playing here every week.'

Not for me it wasn't

'Still fancies you, you know.'

Patrick tried to save me. 'Gail, don't start your women's intuition stuff. Please.'

His wife ignored him. 'Telling you.'

I borrowed from Alex Gilby. 'Ancient history, Gail. Water under the bridge.'

She allowed herself a self-satisfied smile. 'Want to bet on it, Charlie? You'll lose.'

I would be more than happy to lose.

Alan Sneddon held up his hands. 'Just want to thank Alex for getting Kate back, even if it is only for tonight. Great to see her again and an honour to be on stage with her.'

Alex and Kate looked suitably modest as everybody cheered.

I moved across to the Rock-Ola and pretended to study the playlist. I sensed someone beside me. It was Kate. She ran a finger down the chrome edge of the jukebox and took us on a stroll down memory lane.

'This was where we spoke the very first time.'

I didn't need her to remind me.

'Robbie Ward had left the band. I was the new kid in town.'

'And you were nervous.'

'Terrified. You told me it was going to be great and not to worry.'

'I got that right.'

Kate laughed. 'I thought Robbie couldn't be replaced. You said...'

'...Robbie who? I remember.'

She turned to face me and took my hands in hers. 'Happy New Year, Charlie.'

'When did you get here?' was all I managed to get out.

'Late this afternoon. Alex was ready to smuggle me in but you'd just left with Pat.'

And ended up chasing Dougie Bell round Glasgow.

I studied her face; nothing had changed. She realised what I was doing and smiled. 'The road takes its toll. Too many late nights and not enough sleep. In a couple of years. I'll look a hundred and ten.'

That wouldn't happen.

'Which hotel are you in?'

Kate pursed her lips. 'Don't have one. Was kind of hoping I might stay with you.'

Over her shoulder, Alex Gilby was grinning.

He wasn't the only one.

# Chapter Six

**Bothwell, 9 miles from Glasgow. After the bells**

The people in her house were unknown to Kim, although she had no problem recognising them as sycophants and hangers-on. Star fuckers and false-faces. None of them were friends; Sean had no friends. They ignored her, while he took their adulation in his stride, enjoying the role of king of the hill.

They chanted his name like the idiots they were. Sean! Sean! Sean! Sean!

He stood on a chair in the middle of the room, swaying; acting drunk. He wasn't. That would mean being out of control, and Sean Rafferty had to be in control. Sean smiled down on them, called for silence, and raised his glass.

'May you be half an hour in heaven before the devil knows you're dead.'

They roared their approval.

Kim went upstairs and sat in the rocking chair beside the cot, watching Rosie sleep, listening to the steady rise and fall of her breathing. This was the miracle they had created. Eventually, she made her way back down and started looking for Sean. No sign. Perhaps he was in the study, on the phone, as usual. It wasn't fair to dump a bunch of strangers on her and just disappear. That said, she doubted any of the toadying bastards had noticed. So long as the booze kept flowing, they would be happy.

The hall was deserted. She stopped outside the door and turned the handle, expecting it to be locked, surprised when it opened. He stood with his back to her; trousers round his ankles, grunting like an animal. A woman was spread across the desk beneath him. She was naked, her bare legs wrapped round his waist, binding him to her. One high-heeled Bionda Castana hung from her foot; the other had landed beside her dress and underwear.

Everything on the desk had been violently swept away – even the photograph of Rosie was broken. It lay on the floor, the glass in the gold frame cracked from top to bottom. In future, no matter how hard Kim Rafferty tried to erase the scene from her mind, that image would not delete.

Rafferty bent forward, his open mouth searching and finding one erect nipple then the other. His partner moaned, her thighs tightening as her lover pounded her.

Kim neither needed, nor expected, her husband to be faithful. She wasn't hurt or jealous. He could have as many whores as he pleased and service them as often as he liked for all she cared. Except not in their house while their daughter slept upstairs.

Rafferty lifted the woman's legs over his shoulders and thrust into her more deeply than before. She arched her back and climaxed, long and loud.

It was almost over, and if Sean turned around he would see her. Kim edged out of the room, carefully closing the door. There were tears in her eyes, not of sorrow but of anger. When the assured, well-dressed stranger introduced himself at the Miss Scotland final, Kim had known exactly who she was talking to, and accepted his dinner invitation with full knowledge of where it might lead, and what it might mean. On the beach in Antigua, he'd told her he cared for her because he thought it was something she needed to hear him say. Sean Rafferty was wrong. Kim's mind was already made up; he would ask her to marry him. She would say yes and take the comfortable life on offer.

Love hadn't come into it, yet there was a moment under the moon and the stars when she'd almost believed she loved him. It passed, as it was always going to. This was the reality, and the thieves and liars cheering him and chanting his name – begging to be bought, or already paid for – understood. Kim would never speak of what she'd seen tonight. She would go on smiling into his eyes, even as she shuddered at his touch.

Not forever; for now.

In the lounge, a man with dull eyes came towards her, shaking an empty wine bottle. He turned it upside down and spoke to Kim in a slurred voice, heavy with disappointment and disbelief.

'Champagne's run out.'

'Has it? That means it's time for you to leave.'

# Chapter Seven

**Peebles, 50 miles from Glasgow. After the bells**

Colin McMillan wasn't sure what had wakened him, or for that matter, if he had ever been asleep. He had no idea what time it was. Not unusual these days. Some nights he didn't make it to bed and came to in the chair at the fire, cold and confused, with another bleak twenty-four hours in front of him. At some point, church bells and fireworks told him it was midnight and he was living in a new year. Since then, he had drifted, not asleep though not fully conscious, through unfamiliar landscapes which brought no peace. McMillan doubted he would ever know peace again. That was all right. Peace wasn't what he craved. Joyce's death had left him on fire with anger and the inferno inside him would never be extinguished. The moment he walked into that room, his life ended. She had been a beautiful person but the woman hanging from the door frame was twisted and ugly.

Voices from a passing car, kids probably, loud and laughing, no doubt on their way to a party in Innerleithen, broke his train of thought. McMillan envied them; they had their whole lives still to live. He got up and went to the window. The snow had stopped and the featureless scene was surreal.

He padded in the dark to the main room and wondered about having a whisky. Johnnie Walker was his only friend; recently, they'd become very good friends, indeed. Trouble was – and he couldn't deny it – one wasn't enough anymore.

When his wife was alive, Colin McMillan rarely bothered with alcohol. His work required a clear mind and a steady hand.

Joyce had had to scold him to take her out, even as far as the pub. When they got there, they'd sit side-by-side, staring into space with nothing to say to each other. What he wouldn't give to be able to speak to her now.

She would like it here; she'd loved the Borders.

McMillan's mother left the cottage to him in her will. Somehow, he hadn't got round to selling the house in Bearsden, though he had no plans to return – even to visit. That was Joyce's house. How excited she'd been when they bought it and over the years, filled it with love. There wasn't a corner of the place that didn't have her mark on it.

He would find her dressed in one of his old shirts – miles too big – painting the kitchen, or sanding the floor; what a mess she'd made. McMillan suggested they get somebody in. Joyce wouldn't hear of it. Bearsden had more memories than Colin McMillan could handle; he wouldn't go back. Not ever.

He ran his finger up and down the bottle on the sideboard and lifted a glass. His only friend in the world. Then, he remembered the telephone call, and put the glass down.

***

He nursed the coffee between his hands, feeling its warmth against his palms. Dawn was breaking on the first day of a new year and through the window, something caught his eye. A fox: cautiously picking a path across the lawn, heading for the woods at the bottom of the garden, its body a vibrant orange against the virgin snow. The sweeping tail obliterated its tracks leaving no sign it had ever passed this way.

Left unchecked, a fox would ravage a chicken coop and go on to the next one to do the same again. Clever and cunning and probably rabid. What alternative did a farmer have except to put it down?

Harsh. Like the coffee.

McMillan ought to be aching with guilt and drowning out the horror of his wife's suicide with booze and tears. Yet, he was sober and calm. Sipping Nescafe without sugar or milk because he hadn't stepped over the door in days.

The letter from Joyce was under a floorboard in the bedroom. He brought it through and re-read it from the first line to the last heart-breaking word. Usually, he cried. Not this time. The sheets went back in their hiding place but the story they told stayed with him; there would be no return to sleep for him.

He hardly noticed the bitterness of the coffee, still thinking about the letter and the animal creeping through the snow, un-noticed; unseen.

# Chapter Eight

**Milngavie, Glasgow. After the bells.**

At first, James Hambley didn't understand what was happening; it sounded like somebody was taking a sledge hammer to the front door. Beside him, Martha came awake and sat up.

'What the hell is that?'

'Christ knows.'

'What time is it?'

Hambley switched the bed-side light on and got out. 'Ten past two.'

He pulled the curtain back and looked into the street. Every house was in darkness. The banging started again. He tried to sound calm, although he felt anything but.

'Stay here. Probably some doped-up kids. I'm going down.'

Martha shook her head. 'Not by yourself you're not.'

She reached for the phone. 'I'm calling the police. Let them deal with it.'

Her husband was already on the landing. The pounding came again, louder than before, and a hoarse voice cried 'Jimmy! Jimmy!'

Martha grabbed her husband's arm. 'Don't you even think about opening the door.'

'What about the police?'

'Line's engaged. Can't get through.'

Hambley shouted. 'The police will be here any minute! They're on their way!'

'Jimmy! Jimmy!'

Martha said, 'That's... That's...'

'I know who it is.'

Hambley opened the door and gasped. Wallace Maitland stared at them. His coat was gone and the white shirt was torn and covered in blood. He fell forward. Hambley caught him and eased him inside. Maitland was crying.

'In God's name, man. What's happened to you?'

Maitland lips moved but nothing came out. He started to tremble; he was going into shock. Hambley barked at his wife. 'Martha! Stop blubbering and get some brandy. And try the police again.'

'No...no...no,' Maitland said. 'Not the police. Just... help me.'

# Chapter Nine

**Central Glasgow. After the bells.**

We said our goodbyes to Alan and Jackie and Andrew and Sandra, and waited on the icy pavement for Alex to bring the car. Kate slipped her arm in mine. I pretended not to notice. Pat Logue had recovered the ground he'd lost. The temperature would affect him less than the rest of us but his wife seemed satisfied: her husband was never going to be a shining example of sobriety. Still, he'd made the effort. Short-lived though it was.

I got into the back with Kate and Gail; Patrick took the passenger seat.

'Drop us first, could you, Alex? Might be in time to prevent the boys from burnin' the house down.'

Gail reacted. 'I warned the two of them before we left. Any nonsense and they'll be looking for new digs. We don't do raves.'

Patrick corrected her from the front seat. 'Nobody does raves anymore, Gail. That was the nineties. Faded out when they stopped being a secret.'

'You know what I mean. They better be in bed or they'll hear me.'

We travelled through the deserted city with Alex hunched over the wheel, driving in the tracks of vehicles that had already come this way. He spoke without taking his eyes from the road. 'So long as I stick to the main drag we'll be okay. Slow going but we'll get there. They reckon it's El Nino.'

Patrick said, 'El Nino. Plays for Barcelona, doesn't he?'

At the Broomielaw, the lights were red but we didn't stop. Beneath us, the Clyde was a black chasm cut between the snow-covered banks.

Kate said, 'I wonder how long somebody would last in that.'

Alex answered. 'Minutes at most.'

Pat Logue didn't agree. He turned in his seat to speak to us. 'Depends.'

'On what?'

'Heard a story once about a man who wanted to join a tribe that lived miles above the Arctic Circle. To be accepted he had to pass three initiation tests no one had ever survived.'

'Is this a true story?'

'Do you want to hear it or not?'

We settled down and let Patrick speak.

'He had to walk twenty miles barefoot across the frozen tundra, wrestle a polar bear, and make love to an Eskimo woman. For eight days there was no sign of him and they were certain he must have perished. But, on the ninth day, a look-out spotted a speck on the horizon, crawlin' through the snow. When he was close enough they could see he'd been through hell. Deep wounds raked his flesh; one of his arms was almost severed. His clothes were in tatters and he'd lost a lot of blood. Delirious – probably near death – he raised his one good arm and spoke to the chief.

"Right,' he said. 'Where's this Eskimo woman you want me to wrestle?"'

Everybody laughed.

Patrick smiled a drunken smile. 'End of the street'll do us. And thanks. For everythin'.'

The Logues got out and we drove back across Glasgow. Nobody spoke until Alex voiced what we were all thinking.

'How does Gail put up with him?'

I said, 'She puts up with him because he's a good guy. He goes his own way and he's unreliable, but if you need a friend, Pat Logue won't be hard to find. Apart from that, she loves him.'

We stopped outside the Devonshire Hotel, near Anniesland Cross, on one of the city's main arteries. Tonight – or more accurately, this morning – it seemed alien.

'This do you?'

'Absolutely. Will you be all right?'

'Never died a winter yet, Charlie. I'll be fine.'

We watched him do a u-turn that normally wouldn't be possible on this part of Great Western Road and drive away. Kate took my arm again and we picked our way carefully towards my flat on Cleveden Drive. It felt colder than earlier; the air burned our lungs and nipped our skin. I slipped and almost fell. Kate rescued me. A few steps further on, we both went down, and lay in the snow, laughing.

Kate said, 'I'm having fun, Charlie.'

I helped her to her feet. 'Glad somebody is.'

She pulled me to her and kissed me. Her lips were warm. 'Somebody is.'

In Cleveden, the parties had ended or moved on. I made coffee, adding a generous measure of brandy to take the edge off, while Kate dumped her stuff in the spare bedroom. Her guitar was safely locked away downstairs at NYB; we'd collect it on our way to the airport.

I hadn't seen this coming. Our affair had been over for two years and at the time we'd agreed it was for the best. Now Kate Calder was in my flat and I still wasn't sure what it all meant until she called my name and I turned round.

She was standing in the doorway, one hand leaning against the frame, red hair falling across her pale shoulders onto her bare breasts. The night hadn't been short of surprises but nothing matched this. Her body was as smooth and lean as I remembered. Flawless, and for a moment I struggled to breathe.

'Think I'd come all this way without these?'

I didn't reply. I couldn't. Kate saw the look on my face and walked towards me, arms outstretched – naked apart from the snake skin boots.

She smiled a slow smile. 'Let's try that again. Happy New Year, Charlie.'

'For Auld Lang Syne?'

'For whatever.'

# Chapter Ten

**New Year's Day**

Martha's question wakened him. 'What's going on, James?'

He opened his eyes and sighed. 'I have no idea.'

'Don't lie to me. I'm not stupid.'

'I'm not lying to you.'

'I think he's been in an accident. Or a fight. We should call the police.'

Hambley forced a laugh. 'A fight? Who would Wallace be fighting with? Relax. I'll speak to him.'

Thank God she couldn't see his face.

He was exhausted and angry. Martha was expecting answers about where Maitland had been. Last night was a disaster, whatever way he looked at it. A bad situation had suddenly got worse – much worse – and Hambley had no idea what to do about it. Everything he'd worked for could be ruined. And there were other possibilities, too serious to dwell on; he might go to prison. What they'd done was coming back to haunt them.

After a series of miscarriages, Margaret Cooper and her husband, David, were desperate to have a child. During Margaret's fourth pregnancy, she started to suffer severe back pain and began to bleed. David brought her to Francis Fallon where partial placental abruption was diagnosed. When the bleeding became heavier, this was upgraded to complete separation. Wallace Maitland performed an emergency caesarean section but the baby was stillborn. His next move ought to have been to carry out a hysterectomy. Instead, he elected to try to save the womb. Maitland couldn't get the bleeding to stop and, deprived of oxygen and Margaret Cooper suffered brain damage.

Neither Francis Fallon nor Wallace Maitland accepted responsibility. Hambley chaired the internal review of the case which concluded Maitland had acted in the best interests of the patient, and while the hospital regretted what had happened to Mrs Cooper, everything possible had been done to save her and her child. Gavin Law was the assisting surgeon. His testimony was disregarded. Soon after, he submitted a letter of complaint about his colleague.

Hambley strode into the bedroom and threw back the curtains. He opened a window. Bright daylight and cold air flooded in. Under the duvet Maitland drew in on himself like a frightened child.

'Get up. Get up!'

Maitland didn't move.

'Stop hiding, and get up.'

Maitland's head emerged from under the clothes. Martha had cleaned him up but his face was still a mess: both eyes were black; one of them was closed and his nose looked as if it might be broken. Hambley ignored the pain Maitland had to be in and got straight to the point.

'What the fuck happened to you?'

'I don't know.'

Hambley answered his own question. 'You went to find Law, didn't you?'

'Yes, I think so.'

'Did he do this?'

Maitland started to cry.

Hambley was unmoved. 'You can cut that out for a start. Feeling sorry for yourself won't change anything. Tell me what you did.'

The words came out thick, mangled by the swollen lips. 'All I remember is being in the street, shouting for him to come out.'

'That's miles from here. You must've got a taxi.'

Wallace Maitland shook his head. Hambley didn't try to hide his disbelief. 'You drove? You fucking moron. So you went to his flat and there was a fight.'

'I honestly don't remember. I think I was hammering on his door… it's a blank.'

'But you got as far as his door?'

'I'm not sure. I'm not sure of anything.'

'How did you know where he lives?'

'His personnel file was open on your desk. I memorised the address.'

Hambley grabbed Maitland's arm and dragged him up. 'So you can remember getting his address but not what you did to him. Don't believe you.'

'It's the truth.'

'You bloody fool. Don't you understand the trouble we're already in?'

'I wanted to teach him a lesson.'

'For what? Blowing the whistle on you?'

'I didn't do anything wrong.'

Hambley struggled to keep his voice down. 'No? Margaret Cooper's a fucking vegetable. You were the surgeon in charge and I covered for you.'

Maitland hit back. 'To protect your precious hospital.'

Hambley ran a hand through his hair. This was getting them nowhere. He pulled the bedclothes away; there was blood on the sheets. Maitland's body was covered in ugly bruises; yellow and purple. Perhaps he had been in an accident. A hit and run the drunk bastard had been too far gone to recall. His clothes – what was left of them – suggested something else; the torn shirt was already in the bin.

Even in this vulnerable state, Hambley had to resist an urge to beat some sense into him for the mess he'd made of everything. Except the director knew he had contributed to this disaster. It would have been wiser to have forced Maitland to admit responsibility and paid the compensation which would make the

Coopers' life more comfortable. Margaret Cooper was paraplegic, and after all, wasn't that why hospitals had insurance? Surgeons were human. Sometimes they didn't get it right. Wallace would've been demoted with a recommendation he undergo re-training. In a couple of years – having gone as far as he could go professionally – he would retire and they could all have moved on. David and Margaret Cooper wouldn't move on, but Hambley didn't dwell on that.

Maitland gathered the bedclothes around him; in a single night he'd aged twenty years. Hambley spoke sounding more in control than he felt. 'Take a shower. I'll get you trousers and a shirt. You better get home and tell Shona something she can believe.'

'Like what?'

'The hospital called. An emergency. On the way back, you stopped to give a lift to a couple of teenagers, who thought it was fun to beat up a stranger. They dragged you out of the car and mugged you. That's your story. You don't remember anything else.'

'Shona will want to tell the police.'

'Remind her you were over the limit.'

Maitland nodded. 'I took the car because I was in a hurry.'

Hambley stopped at the door. 'You realise we're still in trouble, don't you? Getting mugged. Driving the car drunk. It isn't about that.'

Maitland looked away. 'I know.'

'By the way, where is the car?'

'I'm not sure. Think I left it at my place. I didn't want Shona to see me like this.'

His brother-in-law didn't hold back. 'You're a fucking idiot, Wallace. A dangerous fucking idiot.'

# Chapter Eleven

Kate had intended to fly out on the second of January to re-join the North Wind tour. Too soon; much too soon for me. It didn't happen. The whole north-east of the United States had ground to a halt. In Chicago, minus twelve degree temperatures had the city buried under six feet of snow. Flights in and out were cancelled. So was the show. I didn't even pretend to be unhappy about it. We stayed in bed for five days. As Patrick Logue might say, su perb.

And I fell in love with Kate Calder all over again.

Glasgow Airport had changed since the last time I'd been there; it was bigger. A sallow-skinned Emirates cabin crew, I guessed had just arrived from Dubai, passed in front of us wearing cute little pill box hats and wheeling well-travelled bags behind them. They were young and slim and female with beautiful teeth that showed when they smiled at each other. None of them had a coat. They were in for an unpleasant surprise when the terminal doors slid open and the freezing air hit them.

Kate was on an early evening BA flight to London, connecting to Chicago. I carried her luggage – a single bag she wouldn't be checking-in – she hauled her guitar case, and started a serious conversation with the girl at the ticket desk about protecting her instrument. Halfway into it, the girl interrupted. 'I recognise you.'

'Do you?'

'Yes, I do. You're the singer in Big River. Saw you on Hogmanay. Fantastic.'

Kate could've put the record straight about being on a world tour with one of the biggest bands around but didn't and I liked her for it.

'I'm really glad you had a good time.' She glanced at me. 'So did I.'

We had almost an hour to kill. I assumed we would get ourselves a drink and talk. That wasn't her plan. Kate busied herself re-arranging the contents of her bag then went to the toilets, leaving me to stare at the departure board wishing I was going with her. Except her life was somewhere else. Mine was here, in Glasgow.

It was a different Kate who came back; this Kate was distant and all business.

'I'll go through now.'

'Don't you want to sit down and have some coffee?'

She brushed the suggestion away. 'No. I'll pick-up something in the departure lounge. That way, I'll avoid a last-minute dash to catch the flight. You know how we are when we get started.'

Indeed I did, but I played my part. 'All right. It was great to see you. Stay in touch.'

We were on the point of shaking hands when she threw her arms around me and held me tight. She whispered in my ear. 'I'm sorry. I'm so sorry.'

'I'm sorry, too.'

'I love you, Charlie.'

'I know. I know.'

I kissed her forehead and the tip of her nose. Then I kissed her properly. For a long time. At domestic departures, she waved, and I waved back. Before I lost sight of her she waved again. And she was crying.

In the car, driving to the city, the last five days ran through my head. Seeing Kate again had been the biggest and best surprise. I wished it had turned out differently for us, though in my heart, I knew the timing just wasn't right. A call from Dougie Bell's father brought some much needed perspective. On Hogmanay, Dougie had arrived at the Royal Infirmary, moments too late to speak to his mother. It wasn't hard to guess how he felt about that.

They say life's a bitch and then you die.

No argument from me.

***

The shrill ring of the internal phone broke the silence in the office. I swung my legs off the desk and answered it. Jackie's voice was spiked with her usual sarcasm.

'You still in business?'

'Not so you'd notice. Why?'

'Somebody asking for you.'

'Send them up.'

Saying goodbye to Kate had left me in a bad place. A case would've taken my mind off her. I didn't have one. Or maybe I did.

A minute later the door opened and a couple came in. The woman glanced nervously behind making sure the man hadn't deserted her on the way up the stairs. She was in her early forties with blonde hair tied up above a pleasant face aged with concern. He was bald and serious and ten years older. I watched him hold the chair for her and started to like him. She shot a weak smile and turned to me.

'I'm Caroline Law, and this is my partner, Dean. We need your help, Mr Cameron.'

She tried to speak and couldn't. He placed a comforting arm on her shoulder. I'd only just met them and already had the impression that Dean was a man she could depend on.

'Her brother has disappeared. She's convinced something's happened to him.'

I listened and made notes while they shared the story between them. Gavin Law was the common link, though their descriptions of him were so at odds they might have been speaking about two different people. The sister was clearly infatuated by her successful young brother; her partner was less enthusiastic. Caroline was too tightly wound to notice but by the end, she seemed to have relaxed. Talking about her fear had helped – it always did. I started with the obvious question.

'Have you spoken to the police?'

Her answer came from deep in her throat; a sound I'd heard more times than I could count whenever the police were mentioned in a missing person case – a mix of anger and contempt. 'Of course. First thing I thought of. It was a waste of time.'

'What did they find?'

'Nothing. Absolutely nothing. Came back the next day and told me there was no reason to believe Gavin had come to harm.'

The police had a duty to investigate. That said, without something to suggest a crime had been committed, there wasn't much they could do. Dropping out of sight wasn't against the law. Most of my clients found their way to me after the police had drawn a blank.

'Was your brother depressed or in any kind of trouble that you know of?'

She shook her head.

'I take it you've phoned his mobile?'

'Twice a day every day. He doesn't pick up.'

'Is there anything you could point to that might possibly explain his disappearance – if indeed he has disappeared?'

More head shaking.

'You say you've been to his flat.'

'Yes. On New Year's Day. He wasn't there.'

'He wasn't there or you didn't see him there?'

She bristled. 'The next day I contacted his cleaner and used her key to get in.'

'You don't have a key?'

'No. Gavin had the interview on the fourth and was flying out on the second. So I wasn't surprised when he wasn't there. My worry was he might be sick or something.'

'You assumed he was on his way to America.'

'Yes.'

'There's been a white-out over there. He may not have made it.'

I consulted my notes. 'You went back to the flat two days ago.'

'And again today.'

'Expecting him to have had his interview and be at home. What did you find?'

'The flat was empty. The bed hasn't been slept in. I called Francis Fallon and asked to speak to him. They were unhelpful. All they would say was he wasn't there.'

'And you believe something has happened to him?'

Caroline Law sighed. 'Why don't the police do something?'

'Ms…Caroline…without at least the suspicion of a crime, the police can't act. To expect anything else isn't realistic.'

She lost patience with me. 'I'm not interested in being realistic. My brother told me he'd be back at work today. The hospital doesn't know where he is. I don't know where he is. The last time I spoke to him was on Hogmanay. Seven days ago. And all you want to do is ask stupid questions.'

I spoke softly. 'Gavin had a job interview on the fourth in Syracuse. They may have wanted a second meeting with him. Or he might just have decided to have a holiday.'

'So why hasn't he called? Why hasn't he contacted Francis Fallon?'

'Maybe because he's been offered a new job.'

Her face was expressionless; she didn't accept a word of it.

I struggled to convince her. 'What if he met a woman?'

Dean had been quiet, now he seized on the notion. 'That's possible. Gavin's partial to a pretty face.'

Caroline shrugged herself away from him, and vented her exasperation by pounding the table with her fist, her voice hoarse with emotion. 'You have no idea what you're on about. Nobody understands my brother like I understand him. He's proud of what he does. I'm proud of what he does. He takes his responsibilities seriously. His operating lists are arranged months in advance. For him to not show up means something's wrong.'

She was losing it again. Her partner whispered reassurance and patted her hand. Reluctantly, she let him. I needed more before getting involved.

'With respect, Caroline, you're assuming the worst. People often do strange things. Weird, out of character stuff. We think we know them, then…'

She leaned forward, wild-eyed, and I realised I was talking to myself.

'So you'll help us?'

I hesitated. 'I'm not certain there's anything to help you with. That's what I'm saying. Gavin might turn up with a suntan, a new job or a new girlfriend. Maybe all three. You could be jumping the gun.'

She fell back in her chair, defeated.

Dean spoke for both of them. 'Is that a no?'

I had one more shot at getting through to them.

'Look. I can agree to work on your behalf and do a convincing job of going through the motions, even if I say so myself. Except, taking money for doing nothing isn't my style. From what you've told me, Gavin has a good life and he's happy. He's got a lot going for him. What would make him want to run away from that?'

Caroline Law was nearing the end of the road. As far as she was concerned, her brother had come to harm, and she was the only one who could see it. The fact there was nothing concrete to support her certainty didn't matter. I was just one more disbeliever. She was right about that. Too many boxes hadn't been ticked and much as I needed something to take the focus off Kate Calder, I wasn't in the mood for a wild goose chase.

Law's sister couldn't contain her disappointment any longer. She stood with her hands on the desk and made a final appeal to me. 'Why won't you help?'

She broke down. Dean wrapped her in his arms and let her sob. Over her shoulder he mouthed "sorry." I waved it away; there was nothing to apologise for. In a few minutes, Caroline was wiping her eyes, and blowing into a handkerchief, courtesy of her partner.

'I'm sorry. Really, I am. Our parents died when he was twelve. I brought Gavin up. The thought of anything… bad happening …I can't stand it.'

'He's lucky to have someone who cares so much about him.'

She disagreed. 'No. He gives so much. And the work he does…'

Behind her, Dean stared at the floor.

'Leave it three or four days. Don't be surprised if he got the job and has been celebrating ever since.'

'Yes. Yes.' She smiled and dabbed at her eyes. 'Of course I'm over-reacting. Who would possibly hurt Gavin? He hasn't an enemy in the world.'

# Chapter Twelve

Sean Rafferty was having a bad day. He'd given Rutherford a week to come back to him with an answer he could use and so far, he'd heard nothing. An early morning telephone conversation with Emil Rocha in Spain hadn't helped. Rocha was a sleeping partner; the money to finance the project was his. For ten minutes he'd made small talk peppered with home-spun wisdom neither man believed. Women were honoured, God was praised and children valued above everything.

Of course it was an act. The Spaniard was anything but a God-fearing family man. He was a killer and a chameleon, able to assume whatever front best suited his purpose.

Sean's father, Jimmy, had been executed on the orders of this man for trying to double-cross him. Rocha could easily have taken over Jimmy's operation in the East End of Glasgow. Instead, he allowed Sean to fill the void without ever reminding him where his power had come from.

But Rafferty knew.

Two thousand miles away, Emil Rocha laughed. 'The woman is the centre of the universe. When she is happy the world is happy. Am I right?'

Rafferty played his part in the bullshit; Rocha would get to business in his own time. 'As usual, Emil. Right as usual.'

Rocha paused, considering his next question. 'How is your wife? Is she happy?'

'Kim is very happy, Emil.'

'And very beautiful.'

'Yes she is.'

This man was a connoisseur of women.

'Your daughter was lucky to survive. How is she?'

Rafferty shifted in his seat at the other end of the phone. Hearing Rocha discuss Rosie made him uncomfortable. 'She's well, Emil. Rosie is well.'

'Let's hope she has her mother's looks and her father's brains and not the other way round, eh?'

Rafferty said nothing. Suddenly he understood where the conversation was going. Where it had always been going. Rocha was threatening him. The laughter died in the Spaniard's voice and was replaced by cold detachment; he changed the subject. Rafferty might have been talking to another person.

'I expected news.'

Sean Rafferty marked the difference, and chose his words carefully. 'Emil, when I brought the idea of the development to you, I didn't hide the difficulties. I admitted pulling it together would be complex and complicated.'

Rocha was unsympathetic. Excuses didn't interest him; he had no time for them. 'True. But you assured me they could be overcome and that you were the man to do it. I believe your fee – apart from the percentage you'll eventually own – reflects the scale of the obstacles and my faith in your ability to defeat them.'

'I have it in hand, Emil.'

Rocha seemed satisfied 'Good. Good.'

He returned to his philosophical tone. Rafferty relaxed at the other end of the line.

'In this life the weak must stand aside so the strong can create. Otherwise we would still be living in caves. I will hear from you very soon, I hope. Until then, kiss Rosie for me.'

'...I will.'

'Our children are a gift from the Almighty. It is our duty to protect them. Don't let me down.'

The phone went dead. Rafferty stared at it. The threat was unmistakable. Not once. Twice.

\*\*\*

Rutherford's instructions had been clear – he was to go to the car park in Elmbank Crescent, drive to the top level, and wait. Rafferty was more accustomed to giving orders; taking them didn't sit well with him. He edged the Audi forward, reached out, and pressed the button. The ticket appeared, the barrier lifted and he drove through.

On the open roof, he found a space next to a dark blue Mondeo, and turned off the engine. He was early. Sitting in the car gave him time to think about what a crap day it had been so far. Rocha, demanding results. Spouting his what-a-wonderful-world bollocks and, at the same time, trying to intimidate him. The Spaniard was out a shit-load of money; he wanted what he wanted. Fair enough. But where was the credit for what Sean had done? More than three quarters of the site ear-marked had been acquired albeit with Rocha's cash; the rest – along the banks of the river – was why he was here. The whole thing was Rafferty's idea. And he'd told Rocha it wouldn't be easy. Maybe wouldn't even be possible. They'd agreed it was a fantastic opportunity and decided to go ahead. So fuck him if he wasn't happy! Fuck him, lying in the sun while Sean took instructions from bent councillors.

All morning, Kim had been in a funny mood. What the hell was up her nose? And now he came to think about it, it wasn't just this morning; she'd been avoiding him for days. Leaving the room when he came in. Pretending to be asleep. Walking around like a wet weekend and finding fault with him whenever he went near Rosie.

No problem. Whatever was wrong would right itself. Or she'd be gone; he'd trade her in for newer model, one who smiled once in a while. Rafferty had enough hassles in business without getting them at home. *Watch it, baby. Watch it.*

A black Mercedes soundlessly crawled into the light and, for a moment, Rafferty thought Rutherford had come in an official car. The Merc made two circuits before squeezing onto the end. Rafferty got out and walked to the limo. The door opened and he got in. Rutherford adjusted the rear-view mirror so he could see if somebody decided to join them. Sean Rafferty knew he wasn't going to be hearing anything good.

Rutherford shook his head. 'Sorry, Sean. I tried. They're not having any.'

'By "they," you mean..?'

'Thompson. Where Lachie goes, Daly follows. Buy one get one free, normally.'

'Apart from the obvious, what would make them change their minds?'

Rutherford blew air through his teeth. 'Don't think anything will.'

'Not even more money? You do surprise me.'

Rafferty gazed out over the city skyline. He didn't speak, sensing Rutherford had something more to say. After a long silence the councillor spat it out. 'It's Jimmy, Sean.'

Rafferty lost his temper. 'How many times do I have to say it? Jimmy's dead. There is no, Jimmy.'

'People remember.'

'They can remember what they like.'

'They're scared. More scared of the Raffertys than getting caught.'

'That's the past.'

'Not to them it isn't. Your old man was a bastard. You're his son.'

The conversation with Emil Rocha ran through Sean Rafferty's brain. He looked at Rutherford; his skin was grey. 'What about you? Where do you stand in all this given you've had your wedge? Should I be expecting a refund?'

Rutherford tried for a smile and failed. He bit his lip but didn't answer.

'That's what I thought. So now we do it my way.'

\*\*\*

From his office on the seventh-floor Jimmy Hambley looked out at the traffic racing along Great Western Road and wondered how it had come to this.

He blamed himself for not acting sooner. Maitland's drinking had been out of control for a long time; he'd seen it. Of course, Wallace didn't come to work under the influence – that would've been indefensible – but he'd become noticeably distant with colleagues and on occasion, his judgement, as Gavin Law had pointed out, was dangerously flawed, even reckless. Colin McMillan stated the same, citing instances where the senior consultant had avoided safer options and gone with an alternative procedure, increasing the risk to the patient or the baby, or both. Taken in isolation, it boiled down to one surgeon's opinion against another's but, added to the original complaint from Law, it was a scandal in the making which would irrevocably stain Francis Fallon's and James Hambley's reputations.

On Hogmanay in this office, Hambley had delivered his bombshell and watched the blood drain from Gavin Law's face. At that moment, with McMillan safely neutralised, he'd foolishly believed he had the situation under control. Hours later, Maitland – drunk again – trashed his efforts and raised the consequences to a new level.

This morning, Personnel had confirmed his worst fears. Law's sister had called, asking about him. HR refused to discuss a member of staff over the phone. It was clear Caroline Law didn't know her brother was suspended. Or why.

Hambley assumed the role of concerned employer, issuing instructions with a calmness he didn't feel. Inside, he was falling apart. 'Get hold of Mr Law and come back to me.'

Half an hour ago they had. The surgeon wasn't answering his landline or mobile; paging, email, and text had produced nothing. Hambley put the phone down, unable to speak, unable to think. When the initial shock subsided, he buzzed his secretary and told her to find Maitland and tell him to come to Hambley's office.

He was still waiting.

The telephone rang again. He picked it up. 'Yes.'

'Mr Hambley. HR here. We have Mr McMillan holding. He wants to know if a date has been set for his case. He's pretty insistent. I told him we had no information and he asked me to call you.'

A fresh wave of disquiet swept over the director. 'Please tell Mr McMillan to expect a letter from the hospital in due course giving a date for him to undergo psychiatric evaluation.'

'Indeed. But according to my file, the letter was sent on the twenty-seventh. It ought to have arrived by now.'

'Re-send it and apologise to Mr McMillan. It isn't in anyone's interest to prolong the process.'

Hambley put the phone down. Today of all days, this was the last thing he needed. It was odd for McMillan to want to force the pace because the evidence against him was conclusive; a witness was prepared to swear he'd told him he was suicidal. When that testimony became a matter of record, Colin McMillan's career would end. Francis Fallon would let him go and few, if any, hospitals would employ a man with a history of emotional instability. Perhaps he just needed it over.

The buzzer on his desk sounded. His secretary said, 'Mr Maitland is here.'

Hambley sat behind his desk and fought to control his anger. This bastard was responsible for the whole mess. He kept his voice even. 'Send him in.'

Maitland shut the door behind him. One look at his brother-in-law's face was enough to warn him. 'You want to see me? What's happened?'

Hambley resisted an urge to beat his stupid head against the wall until it was a bloody pulp. 'Sit down, Wallace. I think it would be better.'

Maitland did as he was asked without taking his eyes off Hambley. Their relationship had come about because Maitland married Martha's sister, Shona; the men had known each other for over twenty years. But they had never been friends. Now, they were a whole lot less than that. Hambley let Wallace Maitland wait, enjoying the anxiety on his face, taking pleasure in inflicting pain on the person who had probably ruined his life.

After a while he spoke. 'Law's gone missing.'

Maitland reacted like a frightened child. 'What does that mean?'

Underneath the table, Hambley balled his fists. 'Just as I say. His sister can't find him. She's already been on to us.'

'What did you tell her?'

'I haven't spoken to her, at least not yet. HR fobbed her off. For today, that'll do. Tomorrow, or the day after…'

Before Hambley's eyes Maitland shrank; suddenly his clothes seemed too big for him. He stared into space. What he was hearing was beyond his understanding. A barely remembered nightmare.

The silence was broken by the telephone ringing. Hambley lifted it. 'Not now.'

The person on the other end kept speaking. The director cut across them. 'I said not now.'

He put the phone down and folded his arms. 'You killed him, didn't you?'

'No. No…How can you say that?'

'Because it's true. I was there when you fell in the door. I saw you.'

'Jimmy, how long have we known each other?'

'Too fucking long.'

'I wouldn't hurt anybody.'

Hambley laughed a grim laugh and mimicked Maitland's terrified justification. '"I wouldn't hurt anybody". Really? Is what you tell yourself?'

Maitland shook his head; his heart pounded in his chest. He tried to defend himself; the words wouldn't come. Hambley despised Maitland and realised he always had.

'You murdered him. I don't know how but you did.'

'Surely you don't think that's true?'

'Why wouldn't it be true? Look what you did to Margaret Cooper. She would've been all right if she hadn't met you. Law was going to expose your incompetence, so you killed him. You stupid fucker. Why couldn't you leave well alone? I had it under control.'

'I couldn't. I was drunk. I would remember.'

'Except you don't. At least you say you don't.'

'Jimmy! Jimmy! This is crazy!'

Hambley stood up. 'Don't worry, Wallace, I won't shop you. I expect you'll do that yourself once it sinks in. Just know this. I'm not covering for you any longer. When they find his body – whatever you've done with it – it'll be only a matter of time before they come for you. And when they ask me I'll have to tell them, won't I? No choice. Pity about, Shona. She doesn't deserve this. She'll divorce you, of course. Should've done it years ago.'

'Jimmy! Jimmy, please!'

'You'll be on your own, Wallace. You already are.'

# Chapter Thirteen

Margaret had stopped whimpering and was staring into space with her mouth open. That morning, David had called the surgery and asked if someone would drop in and take a look at her. Around two o'clock, Doctor Bennet arrived. He did some tests and asked the same questions David had answered two dozen times before.

At the end, Cooper said, 'She's deteriorating, isn't she?'

The doctor wouldn't commit himself. 'I don't detect any major change since my last visit.'

'But there is. I can tell. Sometimes she can hardly breathe.'

'It may be Margaret's body hasn't yet found the level it will operate on, given what has happened. There may be some settling which can sometimes even look like improvements in the condition. Your wife may be experiencing stabilisation, in that sense.'

'Is that a medical term for sinking?'

'Every organ in the body gets instructions from the brain. Not just signals. Commands. If they aren't being sent…'

The doctor glanced at Margaret Cooper and, from force of habit, lowered his voice.

'I'm sorry to sound blunt. I don't mean to be. But you have to accept she isn't going to get better.'

'I do accept it. I have accepted it. My question is: is she getting worse?'

'There will come a time when it's no longer practical for you to look after your wife by yourself. She'll need more care than you'll be able to give. More than any one person could give. That time may be far away, or it may be soon. You understand what I'm saying, Mr Cooper?'

David Cooper understood.

# Chapter Fourteen

Caroline Law was back in two days, calmer and more certain than ever. She got straight to the point. 'He's disappeared. Gavin's disappeared. Definitely. I went back to his flat again. He keeps his passport in a drawer in the bedroom; it wasn't there. His suitcase wasn't there either.'

'So he's in America?'

She seized on my conclusion and beat me over the head with it. 'No, he isn't. Yesterday I called St Joseph's hospital in New York. They wouldn't say much but admitted Gavin hadn't been interviewed. Then I tried Francis Fallon again. Down-right unhelpful. Refused to discuss anything over the phone except to say he wasn't on the operating list.'

'I take it he still isn't answering his mobile.'

'The number's unobtainable.'

'Okay. The passport and suitcase say he's left the country but hasn't gone where he was supposed to. Maybe he decided against the interview.'

'Possible though unlikely. He said it was a tremendous opportunity. Why would he not turn up?'

I didn't have an answer for her.

'Did you contact his friends?'

The question didn't sit well with her. Some of the certainty left her voice. 'I don't know them.'

'Caroline didn't see as much of Gavin as she would've liked. His friends tended to be female. Nobody regular. '

'No guys?'

'None that he talked about.'

Dean rested a hand on his partner's shoulder. She didn't acknowledge it. I got the impression she wasn't pleased with him for speaking out and he knew it.

'Where did he meet these women?'

Caroline's expression was stone. Clearly her brother's love life wasn't somewhere she wanted to go. At least not with me. She had brought him up. In her own words she had been the only mother he'd ever had. Maybe she resented other females getting his attention.

Deep. Too deep.

Dean was either a very brave man or a very stupid one; he ploughed on, in spite of the warning signs. 'I think he worked with some of them. None were in the picture very long, so far as we could tell.'

'All right. Leave it with me.'

'You'll take the case? Thank you, Mr Cameron.'

'I'll want to see inside Gavin's flat.'

'What do you expect to find?'

'How would I know?'

'I mean, I've been there twice. Is that really the best place to start?'

Behind her, Dean rolled his eyes. Caroline would be a difficult client.

*Was there any other kind?*

Jackie watched Caroline Law sweep out like a ship under sail with Dean trailing after her. 'And so it begins, Charlie. Another adventure.'

I refused to take the bait. 'And so it begins, Jackie. Don't knock it.'

An hour later, I left NYB and stepped into a chilly wind. In summer, this was a suntrap where Glaswegians watched the world go by over lattes and flaky croissants. Today, it was deserted. I walked around aimlessly; killing time. In the West End, my flat would be in darkness. Kate wouldn't be waiting for me: there was nothing to hurry home for.

\*\*\*

Lachie Thompson came through the heavy doors of the City Chambers into George Square and ran a blue-veined hand through what was left of his hair. He couldn't remember the last time he'd seen the sun. It wouldn't be today; the sky was low enough to touch. Scotland in January. Bloody awful.

The snow from Hogmanay was long gone but the temperature hadn't climbed much above five degrees. Thompson shivered; he was seventy-one; too old to be cold. No, he was too old full stop.

The meeting he had just left challenged that theory. A discussion which should have lasted no more than an hour had run to three, without a decision being reached and it still wasn't finished. Not for the first time he realised the fundamental flaw in democracy: everybody got a vote. After thirty years in politics, Lachie should've been used to it. He wasn't and never would be. Most people were too thick and too lazy to merit an opinion; a view he shared only with his most trusted colleagues. The majority of councillors were sheep, easily frightened and easily led. Though even sheep had to be allowed to make a noise every now and then. Otherwise, they might realise no one was interested in them.

Across the Square, two Union Jacks drifted in the wind at the base of the Cenotaph – good men dead on the whims of elected idiots. A wise man made his own arrangements. Lachie Thompson was a wise man.

His watch told him what he already knew; he was late. He hated to do what he was going to do but there was nothing else for it. He stabbed his daughter's number into his mobile and waited for her to answer.

'Hello, Dad.'

Thompson drew a heavy breath. Joan's mother had been a strong woman and Joan was no different. She wasn't going to be pleased.

'Hi Joan. I'm sorry about this but I can't collect Annie from school. I know it's a bugger. The meeting has run over.'

'Again?'

The irritation was undisguised. 'I wish you'd told me sooner.'

'Yeah, sorry…'

Joan cut him off. '…look…Dad…I have to go. I can't leave Annie at the school gates with nobody to pick her up. She's only six. Why didn't you tell me you couldn't make it?'

'I didn't know.'

His daughter ended the call. Her father put the phone in his pocket and turned to go inside. Maybe it was time to call it a day. Glasgow wouldn't fall down without him. The next local round of elections was eighteen months away; perhaps he should retire – he'd had a good run. Rutherford was a competent politician, though not as competent as he thought he was. He could take his place and do a decent job. Scotland was changing. The whole country was changing. For the foreseeable future, the Labour Party was finished north of the border; its fifty-year influence was on the wane. Old warhorses, like himself, had had their day. Besides, there were more important things, like collecting his granddaughter from school. Let somebody else be the shepherd. Lachie was tired of it.

Fine talk, except the councillor didn't believe a word of it. At the moment, the bloody Scot Nats were doing well, but how long was that likely to last? Their appeal was too narrow and, when push came to shove, people baulked at stepping into the unknown. Labour, the party of Nye Bevin and Keir Hardie, would regain what had been lost. Men with his experience would be needed.

Thompson shivered and drew his coat to him.

No, he wasn't ready to go; there was still work to do. And if he was looking for a reason, he had one. For over thirty years, Jimmy Rafferty had been a stain on the face of the city, coercing and intimidating to get what he wanted. His son was set on going down the same road. Lachie Thompson was too old to be scared by another East End thug.

\*\*\*

Traffic was heavy. Annie's mother cursed at a moron in a white Vauxhall going slow enough to be following a hearse.

She took her frustration out on the horn. 'Come on! Come on! Move it, for Christ's sake!'

At the first opportunity, she passed the car with a final irate blast. She was going to have to speak to her father. It wasn't working. This was the second time he had let her down. On something else, she wouldn't have a problem. Annie wasn't something else, and Joan needed to be certain he would be there at three o'clock. Every day. Without fail. Last minute phone calls weren't on. The truth was, she hated the council. Growing up, she'd seen less of her father than other children. He was always at meetings or surgeries – something. Her mother had more or less raised the children on her own, while he was off doing "important things." And it hadn't changed. He was still at it, except this time it was her daughter who was suffering because of it. Annie deserved better, and she would have better. The world was full of crazy people. Kids needed to be protected. Now *that* was a job worth doing.

As soon as she came round the corner she saw her; blonde hair tied in a ponytail and carrying her tiny satchel. Usually, a crowd of adults gathered at the gates, waiting for their kids. Today there was no one.

Just Annie. And the man she was talking to.

Joan braked so suddenly she lurched forward and almost hit her head on the windscreen. Annie saw her and waved. Her mother ran to her and scooped her into her arms.

The stranger smiled. 'You have a lovely daughter. You must be very proud of her.'

Something in his eyes made her shiver. Joan backed away, blurting out apologies. 'I'm sorry. I'm sorry, baby. I'm sorry I'm late.'

'It's all right, Mum. This man knows granddad.'

The innocence of it made her mother want to cry. Later she would, but not now. Joan held her little girl tighter. The news was full of pervs and child molesters. Her father had no right putting his precious council before Annie's safety.

'Does he?'

'Yes. He knows all about him.'

The stranger made to walk away. He waved. Annie waved back. 'Remember what I told you to tell your mum?'

Annie nodded and rolled her eyes.

'You're supposed to tell Granddad.'

Joan hesitated; afraid to ask. Her voice trembled. 'Tell Granddad what?'

'Sean says hello.'

\*\*\*

Lachie Thompson wasn't surprised when Joan called and said she wanted to talk to him. Her tone told him all he needed to know: he was in the bad books.

He tried to sound casual. 'Okay, when?'

His daughter didn't mince her words. 'Right now.'

Collecting Annie from school was a serious responsibility. Calling off at the last minute was unacceptable. A tongue-lashing was on its way and he deserved it. Too often, when Joan was young, he hadn't been around. No outsider could appreciate how much they had sacrificed so he could attend a function or yet another meeting which – invariably – over-ran into the small hours. He returned to a house in darkness, his family asleep. Lachie remembered sitting downstairs, nursing a whisky, his mind still racing, too wired to go to bed.

In the beginning, Sally had been his biggest supporter but, in the end, even she couldn't take the loneliness that came with public office, and divorced him. Thompson understood: it was the price. Then Annie had come along. His second chance. And he was blowing it.

Joan was waiting for him in the kitchen and from the look on her face he could tell she was upset. More than upset: furious. Her voice trembled with an emotion her father thought was anger; it was fear.

He sat at the kitchen table. Joan stood with her back against the sink, gripping the edge so hard her knuckles poked white through the skin. Her father began with an apology. 'Look. Joan. About this afternoon. I'm very sorry. I...'

He didn't get further.

'Do you know what happened today? Do you have any idea?' She'd lost him.

Joan barked her questions at him. 'Who is Sean? Sean who? I want to know.'

'What're you saying? I don't get it.'

'Don't you? Don't you, really?'

She leaned across the table until her face was inches from his. 'A stranger gave Annie a message at the school gates. A message for her granddad.'

Thompson shook his head. 'What stranger? What message?'

'He told her to tell him "Sean says hello." So, I'm asking. Who the fuck is Sean?'

Thompson didn't answer; he was too stunned. Finally he got up and walked to the door. 'I'll take care of it,' he said. 'It won't happen again.'

His daughter looked at him, her expression a mixture of disbelief and contempt. 'What've you got us into, Dad?'

# Chapter Fifteen

I'd wanted a case to take my mind off Kate. Well, all right – I had one.

Caroline Law's problems hadn't started on Hogmanay. I'd only met her twice but it didn't take Billy Big Brain to realise she was a possessive over-protective woman, needy in the extreme, whose behaviour had probably driven her brother away. He was young when their parents died. No doubt his success in later life was largely due to his sister's love and sense of duty in those early years. Unfortunately for her, that time had come and gone and she couldn't see it. Gavin was thirty-three. A man. Not the vulnerable orphan he'd once been.

It wasn't hard to understand. In the aftermath of the car crash that had killed their parents, she must have set aside her own hopes and dreams to look after both of them. Admirable. Except Caroline's love wasn't unconditional; it came with the expectation of her staying front and centre in her brother's plans.

His non-appearance at the party was seen as a rejection – probably just the latest in a long line – and she'd over-reacted. When he wasn't at his flat, she'd jumped the gun.

But now we knew Gavin Law hadn't shown up for his interview, there were grounds to at least suspect Caroline's initial conclusion had some substance. Maybe. I wasn't convinced. Not yet. At this time of the year, Law could just be off on a bender.

My first phone call was to a contact at Glasgow Airport asking him to find out if Gavin Law had actually left the country. He said it would take a couple of days, and rang off. Next, I tried my luck with Andrew Geddes. His gruff voice growled down the line. 'Charlie, what an unexpected bummer. What do you want?'

I feigned injury. 'Can't a pal just give a pal a call without being accused of having a motive?'

'No, a pal can't. So what do you want, pal?'

I filled him in on the background, knowing he was bound to be unimpressed. In his world missing people weren't a priority. 'And before you ask the usual question, no. At this moment, there's still no evidence of a crime. Just a sudden disappearance that looks off.'

'There's your answer then. Anything else?'

Mr Awkward – the role he was born to play.

'Has anyone reported it?'

'The sister has. Nothing doing.'

Boredom and irritation met. 'Get to the point, Charlie. What is it you want?'

'Would you approach the hospital? Break through the red tape.'

'In my capacity as a DS?'

'Yes.'

'Without any suspicion of a crime?'

'Right.'

'In other words, impersonate a police officer. Over-step the mark because you occasionally buy me a coffee?'

He was winding me up to amuse himself. 'Got it on the screen in front of me. Car's gone. Passport's gone. And no sign of a struggle at his flat. Your man's done a runner. Understandable in the circumstances.'

'What circumstances?'

'Didn't the sister tell you?'

'Tell me what?'

'Her brother's been suspended from work. An allegation's been made against him.'

Andrew teased the information out; enjoying himself.

'An allegation of what?'

'Rape.'

I hid my surprise from him. 'Are the police involved?'

'Not yet. Might not happen. Ninety percent of sexual assaults aren't reported. Often the victims don't want the humiliation of a trial and let the attack go. Can't say I blame them. Who'd want to re-live an experience like that with no guarantee of getting a conviction? So, no, we aren't involved. Also, he withdrew money.'

'He took cash? How much?'

'Three grand from ATMs in the city – the first on Hogmanay – and another couple two days ago in London. Looks bad for him. Why bail on a successful career unless he knows it's coming to an end? Must be desperate. Won't get far on five grand.'

'Will the police monitor his credit cards?'

'Worry not. Good old Uncle Andrew will keep an eye on it.'

I could picture him at the other end of the line, shaking his head and smiling.

'You certainly know how to pick them, Charlie.'

I put the phone down and called Caroline Law. She answered on the third ring. I didn't bother with introductions. 'You didn't tell me Gavin was suspended.'

She didn't reply.

'I asked if he was in any kind of trouble. You said no. That was a lie?'

Caroline found her voice. 'It wasn't a lie. It's nonsense. They're trying to discredit him.'

'Who?'

'Francis Fallon.'

'Why would they do that?'

'Gavin and a colleague complained about one of the surgeons. Since then, their lives have been hell. They've already suspended the other guy.'

'What's his name?'

'Gavin didn't say but he told me that whatever way it went, he was ruined. They'd make sure of it.'

'You can't be serious.'

'I am serious. Reputation is everything to these people; they'll go to any lengths to protect it.'

Her story wasn't credible. Francis Fallon was a respected private hospital. She sensed my disbelief.

'Gavin was going out with a nurse. Would she be involved with him if there was any truth in it?'

'What's her name?'

She thought about it. 'Can't remember. A foreign girl. India. Africa. Somewhere like that. Ask her. Ask her about him.'

'Look, Caroline. He took money with him.'

'For his trip. That was why he was going to America. He knew there was no future for him here.'

'You're forgetting; the interview didn't happen. He didn't show up. Does he know anyone in London?'

'Why?'

'Withdrawals were made down there?'

Every instinct told me to dump the case. She realised what I was thinking. 'Does this mean you won't try to find him? I know my brother. He hasn't done anything wrong.'

'Then why is he missing, Caroline?'

'That's what I need you to find out.'

\*\*\*

She was waiting for me, and inside I caught her glance expectantly in my direction, willing me to seize immediately on some clue her untrained eyes had missed. Too much television.

The flat was typical Dowanhill. Large rooms, high ceilings with cornices, and an original fireplace in the lounge. Furniture was stylish – modern without being minimal – on top of parquet flooring. A Moroccan rug Law had probably rescued from the souk in Marrakech, and paid three times what it was worth, hung like an Old Master on a wall catching the eye, just as it was supposed to. The gleaming stainless steel kitchen continued the theme. All the appliances matched.

Seeing where somebody lived gave a sense of who they were, and for me, this was a show house rather than a home. Whoever stayed here was trying to impress.

'When was Gavin's cleaner last in?'

Caroline's face fell as her notion of me as Sherlock Holmes faded. 'Yesterday, I think.'

'But definitely in the last week?'

A reluctant "yes."

I went into the bedroom and opened a drawer. A folder, lying on its side, took up most of the space. I lifted it out and let the loose plastic sleeves run through my fingers: Bank of Scotland. Santander. MBNA.

Law's sister supplied the background. 'Gavin keeps his business affairs in it. Credit card statements and insurance policies. His passport was the first thing I looked for. When it wasn't there I assumed he'd gone to his interview. Then I noticed he'd left his PC. Gavin would never do that.'

'May I take it?'

'If you want.'

Caroline Law was right; he hadn't been here recently. I left her on the steps outside and drove to the office. Before we went our separate ways, she put her hand on my arm.

'I'm sorry I didn't tell you the truth about the police. I was scared you wouldn't want to help, and I was sure my brother didn't assault anybody. You don't know him; he's not like that.'

I didn't share her certainty. That didn't make her wrong, but it did make her an unreliable witness.

*\*\**

The computer taken from the flat didn't have a password. It didn't need one; there was nothing of interest on it. Mid-morning, my contact at Glasgow Airport called and what he said made me reconsider my opinion. Caroline Law was wrong about her brother.

'Hasn't left from here or any other UK port or airport, Charlie.'

'What about the tunnel?'

'Checked that as well. No record.'

Gavin Law was still in the country.

# Chapter Sixteen

Wallace Maitland slumped into the chair across from his brother-in-law. Hambley didn't acknowledge his presence; he kept writing. Maitland spoke, his voice husky with fear. 'Have the police been back?'

Hambley made his signature with a flourish at the bottom of the page and looked up. 'They haven't and they won't unless somebody tells them what you did.'

Maitland maintained his innocence. 'I didn't do anything. How can you believe I did?'

Hambley's tone was brittle. 'Easy. You're a functioning alcoholic who doesn't function as well as you used to. Most of the time you don't know what you're doing. Law was right. You shouldn't be operating. Take a holiday. I'll find somebody to cover for you. That's an order. By the end of today I want you off the premises.'

He lifted another letter from his in-tray and scanned it as if the conversation was over.

Maitland pleaded. 'I don't need a holiday.'

Hambley's response was harsh. 'Then take a handful of Xanax. But do it far away from Francis Fallon, will you? You've caused this hospital enough trouble.'

'Look. Jimmy. I'm sorry for what's happened but… you can't seriously think I killed him.'

The director put the pen down. 'You're forgetting, Wallace, I was there. I saw you out of your head and covered in blood.'

He stood up and came round the desk. 'Let's be clear. Shona's the only reason you still have a job. We both know you botched the op. And Gavin Law knew. That's why he complained.'

'It was a judgement call. How many times?'

Hambley towered over him. 'Stop lying. You fucked up and caused a disaster – for the Coopers and for the hospital. I should've let you get what was coming to you instead of brushing it under the carpet. Law's dead and you killed him!'

James Hambley lifted a quivering finger and pointed it at the other man. 'Here's what's going to happen. You'll take extended leave. In a couple of months you'll tender your resignation on doctor's orders. Stress. In the meantime I'll keep doing what I've been doing. Cleaning up your mess. Now, get out of my sight.'

At the door, Maitland turned. 'What'll I tell Shona?'

Hambley bared his teeth. 'Tell her any bloody thing. I couldn't care less.'

When Maitland had gone, Hambley sat down; he was shaking with anger. Wallace was a pathetic fool and always had been, but he couldn't avoid responsibility for letting it get as bad as this. Unlike Law, Colin McMillan wasn't present when Maitland bungled the operation and left Margaret Cooper a brain-damaged paraplegic. His letter questioned Wallace's ability and cited instances of alleged incompetence. Those charges hadn't been pursued because of the doubts that emerged over McMillan's state of mind. In a matter of months his life had come apart and, in due course, it seemed likely Francis Fallon would terminate his contract on medical grounds.

To lose three surgeons in such a short space of time – whatever the reasons – didn't reflect well on Hambley or the hospital. Eventually Law's body would be recovered from wherever Wallace had hidden it. McMillan was unstable and Maitland was slowly unravelling; he had to go. Hambley was in the middle of a shit storm. Regrets wouldn't help. All he could do was carry on.

The buzzer on his desk sounded. His PA said, 'There's somebody to see you, Mr Hambley. I've told him he needs an appointment but he insists.

'Who is it?'

'A Mr Cameron.'

Hambley didn't recognise the name and was about to refuse to see him. The next words changed his mind.

'He's a private investigator.'

The director straightened his tie and pulled himself together.

'Give me five minutes then send him in.'

\*\*\*

I'd assumed – wrongly as it turned out – getting to speak to Gavin Law's boss would be difficult. The woman on reception was anything but the loyal Rottweiler I'd anticipated: mid-thirties, attractive and perfectly civil even when she told me it wouldn't be possible to see the director without an appointment. Once upon a time a younger keener me had had cards printed: a thousand of them. There couldn't be more than nine hundred and ninety-seven of them left.

Nine hundred and ninety-six, as of today.

She read the words, eyes moving between them and me.

Charlie Cameron

Private Investigator

It must have impressed because she asked me to take a seat. Five minutes later I was in. The man behind the desk rose and shook my hand. Unlike the receptionist, he was everything I expected: three-piece suit; blue and white striped shirt and a serious face. Seeing him unannounced shouldn't have been so easy, yet it had been. I wondered why.

'Take a seat, Mr...'

'Cameron.'

'I don't get many of you people in my office. What can I do for you?'

Friendly and condescending at the same time. A rare skill set.

'I'm representing Caroline Law, Gavin Law's sister. Gavin hasn't been heard of since the thirty-first of December. Ms Law spoke to one of your people and was told he wasn't here. Can you add anything to that?'

'Unfortunately, no. Francis Fallon has a duty to protect the privacy of our employees. Without written permission from

Mr Law, I can't discuss his circumstances. It would be wrong, though I'd be obliged if you would pass on our support to Ms Law.'

His fingers flicked through the in-tray until he found what he was looking for. He placed it in front of him and studied it. I was forgotten; he had dismissed me.

'Can I assume those circumstances include an allegation of rape?'

Hambley was an old hand. He didn't react. 'You're free to assume anything you wish, Mr Cameron.'

It had taken less than a minute to hit a brick wall. As far as the director was concerned, the meeting was already over. I ignored the signs and soldiered on.

'Ms Law is worried about her brother. On top of everything else this allegation has come as a shock. She'd like to know who made it.'

He spread his arms in mock powerlessness – a master class in fakery. 'I'm afraid that won't be possible, Mr…'

'Cameron.'

'It may go further – I couldn't say – but at this stage it's purely an internal matter.'

'The police aren't involved?'

'Not yet. Whether that changes is a decision for the victim.'

'Alleged victim, surely?'

Annoyance shadowed his eyes. He got it under control and quoted the hospital's induction manual at me. Payback for daring to correct him.

'Confidentiality is the cornerstone of employer/employee relations. Everyone who works at Francis Fallon is treated fairly and equally.'

There was plenty more where that came from and he'd prove it if I carried on. He paused and put me in my place with a final flash of sarcasm. 'Inconvenient though it may be.'

Hambley picked up a pen and gave his attention to his papers. He'd owned the meeting from the beginning. He wasn't obligated to tell me a damned thing and hadn't. I was leaving with exactly nothing. At the door I gave it one last try.

'Where am I likely to find the surgeon Mr Law made his complaint about?'

Hambley stopped writing; the pen froze between his fingers and his eyes locked on mine. 'Mr Maitland is on leave.'

'Is that his idea or the hospital's?'

His lips pressed together; he was rattled. But give him his due – he recovered to throw another insult at me. 'You're a slow learner, Mr Cameron. Confidentiality is…'

I held up my hand. 'Yeah… the cornerstone of blah blah blah… you said.'

For most of the time he'd been in control, bossing the meeting from behind the force-field that came with authority. Until the end, when he had carelessly let slip something I hadn't known – the name of the man at the centre of Law's complaint.

Maitland.

In the lift on the way to the ground floor, my mobile rang. Caroline Law sounded out of breath. Her excitement bubbled down the line.

'I've remembered the name of the woman Gavin was supposed to be bringing to the party. It just came to me. Alile. From Malawi. She works at Francis Fallon.'

Good timing.

The hospital shop didn't have the best selection of flowers I'd ever seen but what they had would do. I bought a bunch of red and white carnations and watched an assistant with Sandra on her nametag wrap them.

'These are nice. I hope she likes them.'

'I hope so, too. A nurse was particularly kind to my wife. Flowers are the least I can do. Alile. Do you know her?'

'I don't. Sorry. Try Tracy on reception. She knows everybody.'

Tracy's reputation was well-earned.

I said, 'I'm looking for a nurse called, Alile. Sandra in the shop says you might know her.'

'Alile. Of course. From Malawi.'

'Any idea where she'll be?'

The receptionist checked her watch. 'Normally has lunch about now.'

'So the staff canteen?'

She made a face. 'This is a great place to have a baby. It isn't a great place to have something to eat. Unless you're a patient, that is. Most of us avoid the canteen. Don't know her shifts, but if she's on duty, you might catch Alile in the tearoom. Out the door and turn right. Can't miss it.'

I thanked her. Hospitals were one of the few places where a man carrying flowers wasn't an unusual sight. Nobody gave me a second glance. In the tearoom, eight or nine nurses sat in groups of twos and threes, chatting. The only black woman was at a table by herself, reading a book, and she had to be fifty. Not Gavin Law's type.

I got myself a coffee and waited. Five minutes later, a vision – black and beautiful – walked in and waved over to somebody. Law couldn't have been thinking straight to cancel on this. Caroline's concern seemed justified. Alile was slim and almost as tall as me. Shoulder-length hair framed soft features and smooth skin and when she reached for a tray, her uniform stretched against the perfect body underneath. I joined the queue and tapped her on the shoulder. She turned. Brown eyes smiled at me. Close up she was flawless.

'Excuse me. Alile?'

'... Yes.'

'Could we talk? I'd like to ask you a couple of questions.'

'Questions?'

'Do you mind if we sit down?'

'Questions about what?'

We were at an empty table near the door before I answered.

'Gavin Law. I'm working for his family. His sister told me you and Gavin are friends.'

She seemed puzzled. 'No. To tell the truth we hardly know each other. '

'Weren't you supposed to go to a party with him?'

'At New Year. That doesn't make us friends. And anyway, he cancelled.'

'Did he give a reason?'

She shrugged and managed to make it graceful. 'I got a message. He said he was tired.'

'Had you been out with him before?'

'The party would've been the first time.'

'Has he contacted you since?'

Alile looked me up and down. 'Who are you again?'

'Cameron. Charlie Cameron. Private investigator.'

I handed her my card. Nine hundred and ninety-five. At this rate I'd have to order a new print-run. She wasn't persuaded.

'I'm not sure I should be speaking to you. What's happened to Gavin?'

'He hasn't been heard of since Hogmanay. And if I can't find him the police will get involved. So it's really me or them, Alile.'

It wasn't intended to sound like a threat, though it did. Her reaction told me I was losing her. She handed the card back and those soft features hardened against me.

'Look,' she said, 'you'd do better to talk to somebody who worked with him. There isn't anything I can tell you. We were practically strangers.'

'Alile, his sister is out of her mind with worry. She hasn't spoken to him since New Year's Eve. She's convinced something's wrong. Did you know he'd been suspended?'

Her reply was unexpected. 'No, though it doesn't surprise me.'

'Why?'

'Mr McMillan had already been suspended for speaking out. Terrible for him with what he's been through.'

'What do you mean?'

'His wife killed herself. He was the one who found her. That didn't stop them going after him.'

'What's his first name?'

'Colin. He made the same mistake as Gavin and complained about the director's brother-in-law.'

'Maitland?'

'Yes. Blowing the whistle isn't done. There was a lot of gossip. People took sides. That was the reason I agreed to go out with Gavin, in spite of his reputation. I thought it was brave.'

'His reputation?'

Alile glanced away. 'A couple of the girls advised me to steer clear.'

I let her tell it her way.

'Said he was a chancer. Famous for it.'

It was strange to hear a woman from Malawi use a Glasgow expression.

'Alile, Gavin wasn't suspended by Francis Fallon as a reprisal. An accusation's been made by someone from here. Of rape.' I studied her lovely face and waited for it to sink in. 'You hadn't heard?'

She didn't respond; she had questions of her own. 'When is this supposed to have happened?'

'Can't tell you that.'

Because I didn't know.

'Who says he did it?'

'Can't tell you that, either.'

Alile struggled to come to terms with the news. Finally, she made up her mind and slowly shook her head. 'I don't believe it.'

'You seem very sure considering how little you know Gavin Law.'

'That's not what I mean. He wasn't exactly popular, although some of the staff thought he was right. But this. As I said, hospitals run on gossip. I would've heard.'

She had a point.

'Maybe. Maybe not.'

Alile got up. I held the card out a second time. She took it.

'You may remember something. If you do, call me.'

She didn't say she would but she didn't say she wouldn't.

Result.

# Chapter Seventeen

I walked down High Street in rain that had been falling, on and off, for the best part of a week. The guy Pat Logue mentioned, who played for Barcelona, might have something to do with it.

At NYB, the lunchtime biz was over. Most people had gone back to the snake pits and inside the scene was like a Jack Vettriano painting: Jackie Mallon behind the bar, polishing glasses; Pat Logue on a stool, switching his attention between the racing section of the Daily Record and the betting slip he was writing out; and Andrew Geddes, by himself at a table near the Rock-Ola. Andrew scowled and mouthed words that never came. The DS was having a conversation with somebody who wasn't there and, by the looks of it, it wasn't going well.

Jackie saw me and tried to smile but her heart wasn't in it.

'How're you doing, Jackie?'

Her pained expression said it for her. Patrick broke away from picking losers to add his tuppence worth. Bad decision.

'You want to watch that, Jackie. My mother always told me if God caught me making a sour face, it would stick and I'd be left ugly.'

She nailed him to the wall without missing a beat. 'So you can't say you weren't well warned.'

Jackie Mallon might be feeling low; she was still sharp.

I asked Patrick to meet me in the office.

'Give me twenty minutes, Charlie. Got to get these beauties on. Could be a game changer.'

I doubted anything very much would change apart from the amount of money in his pocket. Pat Logue was an optimist; the glass was always half-full. Andrew Geddes was the opposite, and today, the world was proving him right.

'Winning, Andrew?'

He turned his scowl in my direction and answered with a question. 'Ever feel you've been around too long?'

'Can't say I do, no. What's the problem?'

'I am.'

'How so?'

'I'm a dinosaur. Thinking of calling it a day.'

DS Geddes was always thinking about calling it a day.

'What's brought this on?'

Andrew blew through his teeth and toyed with the coffee he'd forgotten to drink. 'You remember I mentioned DI Baillie had put in for early retirement?'

'A while ago.'

'Well, he's gone. New guy's arrived and I can tell right now it isn't going to pan.'

'Relationships need time to gel. Look at you and me.'

He didn't laugh. 'He's come from a fast track programme. Quick promotion through the ranks. Not against it in principle. We should be encouraging good people to join.'

I waited for the "but."

'Candidates are moved around different departments and get a lot of experience in a short time. Usually promoted posts don't get near CID because of the level of legal responsibility and knowledge of investigative procedure demanded. But this guy.'

Andrew poked a finger at the ceiling 'Somebody up there likes him. Likes him *a lot*. He's been parachuted in and, of course, hasn't got a clue how to conduct an enquiry. Meanwhile, we have to hold his hand.'

'Surely it isn't too hard to steer him in the right direction?'

He made one of those faces Pat Logue's mother had warned about. 'I'm trying, Charlie. I'm trying. He's out of his depth and he won't listen. Why should he? He's the ranking officer. Got a degree in psychology from Edinburgh Uni, so that's all right. The fact he knows fuck-all isn't important.'

'You'll find a way to deal with it.'

'That's the thing. Don't know that I want to. Not with this one. On his very first morning, he brings out a tick sheet.Apparently, this is how he intends to stay in control. Then he says he'll expect a daily written report from every officer. Christ Almighty!'

Andrew's frustration wasn't difficult to understand.

'Joe Public doesn't get what solid police work involves. Fair enough. But when people higher-up act as if it's something you can just pick up, no wonder morale is low. I mean…' He sighed. 'If this is the future…'

'What's his name?'

'Adam Barr. He's thirty-three and already a DI. Can you believe it?'

I left him and went upstairs to the office. My meeting with James Hambley had been more than enough to convince me I wouldn't be getting any help from Francis Fallon, though unintentionally, he'd given me a name: Maitland. Alile had given me another: Colin McMillan; the obstetrician who had added his complaint to Gavin Law's and got suspended. I wanted to speak to him.

192.com offered a dozen C McMillans in the Glasgow area. Four under thirty – too young, and three over sixty – too old. Of the remaining five, one was a company director, three were female, and one was an obstetrician living in Bearsden. I wrote down the address then called the phone number. No reply.

Twenty minutes later Patrick appeared, noticeably less enthusiastic than he'd been.

'Is the game changer on?'

'Yeah, except it won't be changin' much. The favourite fell at the third and my next horse is still runnin'. What've you got for me, Charlie?'

The Malawian nurse's belief that hospitals ran on gossip stayed with me. When it came to getting information out of people,

Pat Logue was the best. I filled him in on the background. He listened; he didn't write anything down. If you wanted boxes ticked or a written report, then you didn't want Patrick.

'Ask yourself this: who knows everything that goes on in a hospital?'

'Pass.'

'The porters.'

'True.'

'Everybody talks to them. And what do they do when their shift finishes?'

'Go home?'

'Eventually. After they've been to the pub.'

'So use them to get the SP on Gavin Law and this other one, Colin McMillan?'

'Wallace Maitland, too. What's the word about this rape allegation against Law? Has to be big news. Only the nurse I spoke to couldn't tell me anything.'

Patrick rubbed the stubble on his chin. 'Could cost.'

'Really?'

'Yup. And since it doesn't look as if the gee-gees have pulled, I'll need expenses. Up front.'

Pat Logue never missed an opportunity for free booze. Alile would call him a chancer. I took three twenties from my wallet and handed them to him. He eyed the notes with contempt.

'Okay. That's tonight covered. What about tomorrow and the next night?'

'How do you know it'll be three nights?'

'An educated guess, Charlie. Might be more.'

He saw my reaction and defended himself.

'Have you any idea what it's like hanging about strange pubs, drinking dodgy beer?'

'Almost as bad as sitting at home listening to Gail on the phone to her sister. If you really do need more, I'll give it to you.'

He went away grumbling about not being appreciated. It could have been Andrew Geddes speaking. I followed him out, drove to St George's Cross and on to a busy Maryhill Road which brought me, four miles further, to Bearsden; at one time the seventh wealthiest area in Britain. Exactly where I would expect a successful Glasgow medical man to live. When I found it, the McMillan house was surprisingly modest: semi-detached, set above the road in a tree-lined avenue in Westerton Garden Suburb.

The street was quiet today; no doubt the weather had driven everyone indoors. I climbed the stairs and knocked on the front door. In the silence, the echo was like a gunshot. Across the road, a net curtain moved and, for a second, a face appeared at a window.

I knocked again and waited while rain drummed relentlessly around me. No answer. It wasn't the best day to judge, but the neglected look of the garden suggested the property might not be inhabited. I peered through the letterbox and saw envelopes on the carpet. McMillan wasn't here and hadn't been here in some time.

On the other side of the road, the curtain moved again: the watcher was back. I crossed over. A thin woman with a stern face eyed me up and down, uncertain whether she should even speak to me. I explained what I was doing and asked how well she knew the doctor, expecting somebody as interested as she was in other people's business to have plenty to say.

Wrong.

'Not well. Good neighbours. Wish there were more like them. Quiet. Tended to keep themselves to themselves. Didn't see them together much. Spoke to her the odd time but never him. Terrible how she ended up. He hasn't been here more than two or three times since. Can't say I blame him. Poor man.'

Sympathy but no facts.

She pointed back the way I'd come. 'Doreen Walters, two doors down, was on better terms with them. Think she has a key. I'd ask her.'

Doreen must have been doing her own share of hiding behind the curtains because she was waiting for me. Her hair was grey though she wasn't old, and from her expression, she was far from sure about me. I guessed she'd heard me knocking and decided to leave me to it. The vibe coming off her was low-level hostile. Odd, considering I hadn't opened my mouth. For some reason, strangers weren't welcome in this part of the city. Or maybe it was just me.

'I'm trying to contact Mr McMillan. There doesn't seem to be anyone in. Do you know when he'll be at home?'

She gave me the look I'd already had from the first woman and decided not to trust me. 'He isn't there, now.'

'So where is he?'

She drew up short of answering and repeated what I guessed was going to be her stock reply. At least as far as I was concerned. 'He isn't at home.'

'Yes, but where is he? It's important I speak to him.'

'Sorry, I can't help. Who are you anyway? Aren't from the newspapers, are you?'

'No. I'm a private investigator. The doctor may have information that could help a client of mine. It isn't about him. He isn't directly involved. The woman across the road says you have a key to the house, so I assume you know where he is.'

She wasn't having it. She shook her head. 'Doctor McMillan is one of the nicest men you could meet. What's happened to him…it's so sad.'

I didn't disagree.

'Surely you have a contact number? Would you call and let me speak to him? It's important or I wouldn't ask.'

She bit her bottom lip and thought about it. 'You're definitely not from the papers? He doesn't need any more upset.'

'I'm not, and I promise I won't upset him. I just have some questions.'

'Okay. Wait there.'

Scots pride themselves on their hospitality. Keeping me standing at the door in the rain showed it didn't always apply. I heard snatches of a one-sided conversation about me then Doreen returned for clarification.

'What's your name?'

'Cameron. Charlie Cameron. As I said, I'm a private investigator looking for somebody. Mr McMillan may be able to help.'

She disappeared again and came back with good news – although her face didn't think so. 'He'll speak to you.' She handed me the telephone.

I chose my words carefully. 'Mr McMillan. Hello. I'm Charlie Cameron.'

The voice at the other end was strong and assured. 'So I'm told. A private investigator.'

'That's right. A colleague of yours is missing.'

'Who?'

'Gavin Law.'

'Really. I'm sorry to hear it. How can I help?'

'I want to talk to you about him. Would that be possible?'

'Of course.'

'Where are you?'

'At my mother's house in Peebles. Had to get out of the city. It's peaceful down here. Much better than Glasgow.'

'I understand. When can we get together?'

'Anytime you like. I'm not exactly rushed off my feet. Bit of a long drive for you, I'm afraid. Not sure what I can tell you. Wouldn't want to waste your time.'

'That isn't a problem. How would next Tuesday suit?'

'Tuesday's fine. One o'clock in the Cross Keys hotel. Do you know Peebles?'

I told him I didn't.

'It's in Northgate. Anybody will give you directions.'

'All right. See you at one.'

Before he could hang up, I said, 'You and Law complained about a colleague. What case was that?'

'That was Law. Complications arose during an operation where he assisted. A woman called Margaret Cooper was left with brain damage. Law wasn't happy about the procedures adopted and put in a formal complaint against the obstetrician in charge. I wasn't involved.'

'It would be helpful to speak to them. Any idea where they live?'

'No, I don't. But give me your mobile number. I still have some contacts at the hospital. Call you back in ten minutes.'

# Chapter Eighteen

A line of black taxis were parked on Gordon Street, opposite the main entrance to Central Station. Lachie Thompson walked to the first and got in. The driver edged away from the kerb into the traffic. Over his shoulder he said, 'Where to?'

'Charing Cross.'

'Charing Cross, it is.'

They drove up Hope Street and stopped at the lights. Thompson loosened his tie and gazed out of the window, his face set hard; angrier than he'd ever been in his life. Almost as angry as Joan when he'd told her to pack a suitcase and be ready to go in twenty minutes. Her reaction had been predictable.

'You want me to leave my own home?'

'It's a precaution.'

'Against this Sean character?'

Thompson hadn't answered; he didn't want to explain. 'You'll be safer in Warrington with your aunt Agnes. Annie will be safer. Look on it as a wee holiday.'

In the station, Joan stopped under the faded black and white clock suspended from the roof and faced him. She kept her voice low so Annie wouldn't hear.

'When this is over, I never want to see you again. You don't have a family. You don't deserve one.'

'Joan…'

'Your bloody politics killed Mum. She died of loneliness and you were too busy to notice. I've come second to your precious Labour Party all my life, and here we are again. I don't understand what you're involved in and I don't want to, but this is the end.'

She spat the words from between clenched teeth.

'I never want to see you again. You're out of our lives. I hate you.'

Thompson didn't try to reason with her. Whether she believed him, what he was doing was in their best interests. This thing would be settled – he would make sure of it – and they would pick up from where they had been before an East End gangster over-stepped the mark. Joan would come round. In time.

He watched them board the train. Annie waved. He waved back then walked towards the main entrance with his daughter's rebuke ringing in his ears. And it was true; he had neglected them and he regretted it. Too late to change any of it. But not too late to save them from Sean Rafferty.

Lachie Thompson was married with a daughter and already set on the course he would follow for the next three decades the day the stranger had crossed his path.

At first glance, Jimmy Rafferty was just another hard man in a city full of hard men. His request – although it had never been a request – was for Thompson to have a word with the Licensing Board about a shop he was thinking of buying and turning into a pub – looking for a guarantee before any funds were committed. The councillor refused and forgot about the meeting until six weeks later when Rafferty returned. Their meeting was short. Jimmy did most of the talking, and at the end, Thompson had taken the first step down the long dark road he'd been on ever since.

Travelling along Bath Street, he remembered nervously weighing the envelope from Rafferty in his hand. The first of many.

Thicker envelopes. Heavier envelopes. Tenners became twenties, then hundreds. Now thousands.

The driver said, 'This do?' and pulled in at the King's Theatre. Thompson got out. On either side of the main door, billboards advertised the final weeks of *Aladdin*. A pang of guilt dug into him. He was supposed to take Annie to the pantomime – another broken promise to add to the list.

Further down the street, a wild-eyed beggar huddled under a shabby blanket next to a half-empty bottle of Buckfast wine. Thin fingers ingrained with dirt gripped a piece of cardboard with HUNGRY AND HOMELESS scrawled in red crayon, while on the wall behind him a woman in a bathing costume caught a brightly coloured ball on a Florida beach. The beggar lifted a plastic cup with two or three copper coins in the bottom, and held it up. Thompson, preoccupied, turned left towards his destination without giving him a second glance.

Inside Baby Grand, Tony Daly was on a stool at the bar, thumbing through a holiday brochure. Daly was in his fifties, unmarried and living with his sister. The councillors had known each other since he was first elected: a lot of years. Although never a star, he'd been a moderate voice that many found persuasive, and more than once a rebellion had been avoided because of his ability to find common ground between warring factions. Daly still had his supporters but his influence was on the wane. He was in the grip of alcoholism and spinning out of control. A recent meeting of the full council had been brought to an end prematurely because of his disruptive behaviour. He'd been drunk then and he was well on the way now.

Daly greeted his colleague with alcohol-driven enthusiasm. 'Lachie! It's yourself!'

Thompson shot disapproval at the glass at Daly's elbow and back to the drinker.

'Started early, haven't you?'

The criticism bounced off. 'Just a jag. No harm done.'

Thompson pointed to the brochure. 'Going somewhere?'

'Maybe. It's Cissie's birthday. Thought I might surprise her.'

'Then show up sober.'

Daly was beyond recognising a rebuke and ploughed on in expansive mood. 'Give my friend whatever he wants. On me.' He tugged Thompson's sleeve. 'This. This is a great man.'

The barmaid hid her discomfort with a smile.

Thomson said, 'Coffee. Black' and took a table in the window. Daly joined him.

'So, Lachie? What're we doing at the other end of the town?'

Thompson studied the flaking skin and purple veins in his colleague's face. In the last couple of years he had aged. The shirt he was wearing was grubby and frayed at the cuffs and a sprinkle of dandruff lay on his coat collar. No doubt his sister tried, but the man wasn't looking after himself and it showed. If you needed to depend on somebody, it wouldn't be him.

'What happened to you, Tony? What happened, eh?'

Daly was taken aback. 'Don't know what you're talking about. Nothing happened. What do you mean?'

'I mean, when exactly did you become an arsehole? Did it just arrive or is it something you worked on? Because that's what you are.'

'Hold on, Lachie…'

Thompson swept the glass off the table with his hand. It smashed against the wall. Rum ran in dark lines to the floor and for a second, conversation in the café/bar stopped.

'No, you hold on! You were a man worth listening to, once upon a time. Now you're a fucking waste of space. And if I didn't need to be talking to you I wouldn't see you in my road.'

The outburst startled Daly. He stared at Thompson and tried to understand what was going on. A girl appeared with a brush and shovel and swept up the shards. He mumbled an apology and offered a weak smile. His everybody's-pal-Jack-the-Lad act had come from a bottle and evaporated as quickly as the booze.

The barmaid said, 'Another rum?'

Thompson answered for him. 'No. He wants a black coffee, same as me. Preferably sometime today, if that's possible.'

Tony Daly realised Thompson was close to losing it. Not like him. Usually Lachie was a cool head. A strong character only Sandy Rutherford was able to stand up to. Between them they'd held the SNP at bay while other Labour councils the length and breadth of the country lost control in the rise of nationalism. Daly wasn't a match for his colleagues and didn't try to be. They were giants; the rest of the council – and he included himself – were pygmies. But giants weren't for everybody. He represented an alternative to Thompson and Rutherford. Given that, Lachie should be showing him more respect. He'd had a couple. So what? He was an elected member of Glasgow City Council and Thompson wasn't his boss, even if he thought he was.

Daly signalled to the barmaid.

'I'll take that rum whenever you've got a minute.'

Thompson was on the point of given him a mouthful when the door opened and Rutherford came in. He spoke to the barmaid. 'Just water, please.'

'Ice?'

'In this weather? You've got to be kidding.'

He brought a chair from another table and sat. Thompson let him settle before he got to the purpose of the meeting. The lunchtime crowd was arriving and Baby Grand was filling up. He lowered his voice. 'When Jimmy Rafferty died we agreed we wouldn't have anything else to do with the family, no matter who took over.'

Daly said, 'Sean's reckoned to be a different kettle of fish, maybe...'

Thompson cut across him and spoke to Rutherford. 'You were supposed to get him to back off.'

Rutherford waited while the waitress placed two black coffees, a rum and a glass of water with ice on the table. The councillor stuck his fingers in the glass, took out the cubes and put them in the ashtray. 'Nobody listens anymore.'

Thompson bit back his irritation.

Rutherford wiped his hand on a napkin. 'It's too late for that. The people he represents have already bought three-quarters of the land they intend to build on. They've invested millions. The last piece – the piece they need and don't have – is crucial to the project; a green belt backing on to the Clyde. It's owned by the city. Selling it will be strongly opposed. Even if they had the land, planning permission will be a nightmare. Without help, the project is dead in the water.'

Thompson was unsympathetic. 'Then they shouldn't have spent their money until they were sure.'

'Rafferty thought he could pull it off. Still does.'

'Well, he thought wrong.'

'Sean isn't his father, Lachie. We can work with him. At the end of the day, he's a Rafferty. We all understand what that means. But we don't have to marry him. Personalities aren't the issue. We're talking about a high-profile development that will bring a helluva lot of jobs to the city. Good for tourism and good for Glasgow, so why wouldn't we give it a push?'

Anger coloured Thompson's face; how quickly Rutherford forgot. 'Jimmy was a monkey on our backs. When he died we breathed a sigh of relief and swore we'd have nothing to do with whoever came after him because the whole family's poison.'

Rutherford was quick to disagree. 'In the past, maybe. Sure. Not now. Rafferty's getting out of the dodgy stuff and into legitimate business ventures. Like Riverside.'

Daly said, 'I can think of plenty who won't vote for it if a Rafferty's involved.'

Rutherford shot him a look. His input wasn't welcome. 'He's a sleeping partner. A bit like yourself, Tony.'

Putting Daly in his place was easy. Lachie was going to be harder to convince.

'Listen, Jimmy was a monster. And Kevin should've been in Carstairs. Absolutely. No argument. But Sean's on a different page. I spoke to him at his house on Hogmanay. He says he wants to put the bad old days behind him and go forward. I believe him.'

Thompson let Rutherford make the case, then spoke quietly. 'He threatened my family.'

After his last conversation with Rafferty, Rutherford expected something from him, but not this. This was too much. 'When?'

'Yesterday. Somebody at the school gates told Annie to give me a message.'

'What message?'

"Sean says hello." Daly was visibly stunned. He lifted his glass and emptied it.

Thompson kept his eyes on Rutherford. 'So much for putting the bad old days behind him, eh, Sandy? Bastard's trying to intimidate me. Me! And you're standing up for him.'

Rutherford shook his head. 'As I said, he's a Rafferty.'

Thompson poked him in the chest. 'So no matter what he's told you. No matter what you 'believe'. He isn't any different from his father. He's just the same. And Jimmy's son's coming for us where we live.'

Peddling the argument that Sean Rafferty was a reasonable man wasn't going to work. Lachie was incensed, and who could blame him?

'It isn't how we want it, no denying. Sean was always the sane voice. Violence wasn't how he dealt with things. He's a family man now. He wants a peaceful life.'

Daly called to the girl behind the bar for another rum and said what they were all thinking. 'In that case, he's changed, Sandy. Using Lachie's granddaughter is well out of order. Even Jimmy didn't go after kids. How can we trust him?'

Thompson answered the question. 'We can't. That's why we don't get involved. It won't end well. It didn't before.'

Rutherford imagined having to tell Sean Rafferty they weren't prepared to co-operate. Not something to look forward to. He toyed with his water glass and tried to salvage a solution.

'I understand how you feel. I feel the same. Except – and let's be realistic – this is going ahead, one way or the other. The people behind it are powerful. They expect a return on their investment. They'll get the land they need and planning permission, with or without us.'

'So you're saying…what, Sandy?'

Rutherford sighed. 'We go along or get left behind. There isn't a third option.'

'Yes there is. Crush Rafferty before he even gets started by opposing this development with everything we have. Give it to somebody already on the regeneration project.'

Rutherford bit the inside of his mouth. 'That wouldn't be wise, Lachie. Not wise at all.'

Thompson pressed his lips into a smile. 'Maybe not. But it's what I'm going to do. I don't work with people who would harm my family. When you speak to Rafferty, tell him that.'

This wasn't the result Rutherford wanted. He turned to Daly, already halfway through his latest drink and visible affected. 'What about you, Tony? What do you think?'

Daly didn't hesitate. Alcohol made him brave. 'I'm with Lachie. Fuck Rafferty. Fuck him.'

Just as he'd predicted: buy one get one free. Rutherford pushed his chair back and stood. So be it. He pitied them. If they'd looked into the East End gangster's eyes and seen what he had seen in them, they'd realise they were making a terrible mistake.

It was true. Sean Rafferty wasn't like his father. He was worse. And he would kill them all.

*** 

On the previous occasion, Sean Rafferty had been first to arrive at the car park in Elmbank Crescent. Not this time. Rutherford was already here. He got out of his car and walked towards the Audi without the usual confidence that had carried him from an apprentice in the shipyards to public office. He hadn't slept and it showed in his face. Fear was a new experience for the councillor. But today he was afraid.

Rafferty watched as he came towards him and realised he wasn't bringing good news. His hands balled into fists. His jaw tightened. He needed a result and he wasn't going to get one. Rutherford opened the door and slid into the passenger seat.

'You look tired, Sandy. Bad night?'

'You could say. I spoke to Thompso and Daly; they're not interested.'

'Really? Sorry to hear it.'

'That stunt with Lachie's granddaughter back-fired. He's angry. Thinks you over-stretched the mark.'

'Does he? What about you?'

Rutherford resisted the opportunity to criticise. Rafferty wouldn't appreciate it. He chose his words carefully and avoided answering the question.

'I can pull a fair number of votes together, though without the other two, not enough to guarantee a result. It needs to be just another decision nobody paid any attention to. Cut and dried. No opposition. No debate. Lachie can get controversial things through without a fuss.'

'Better than you?'

'Better than anybody. No surprise after thirty years on the council. People do what he says. Sorry, Sean. It's not what you want to hear. I tried.'

Rafferty's fingers drummed the steering wheel. 'Okay. Leave it with me.'

Rutherford breathed a sigh of relief. He had expected the gangster to go crazy and was pleased to be getting off so lightly.

'I'll come back to you,' Rafferty said.

'When?'

'Soon. Very soon.'

# Chapter Nineteen

Colin McMillan had given me a number to call and David Cooper was very keen to talk. I don't know what I was expecting but seeing the reality of Margaret Cooper's disability up close shocked me. The house the couple lived in was a bungalow in Knightswood, ironically not far from Francis Fallon. Cooper was standing in the doorway, waiting for me, wearing a wine cardigan over a light blue shirt and dark trousers. Heavy stubble covered his jaw and his hair looked as if it hadn't seen a comb in a while. As I came towards him I saw the strain he was under in the dark hollows of his eyes and the way his shoulders rounded. He stooped like an old man, bent beneath a burden that had fallen from a blue sky on a clear day and irrevocably changed his universe. I was witnessing the body language of the defeated.

He shook my hand and went inside. Before we got to the lounge he paused. 'Margaret's sleeping.'

The significance of the statement escaped me. 'Is she in bed?'

'No, she's in her chair. She falls asleep. I usually try to get some rest at the same time. At first I wanted her to stay awake; it felt better. More hopeful, you know? As if it was still the two of us. Now I just let her sleep. At least she isn't suffering.'

'Is she in pain?'

'Not physical pain, no. She cries a lot. We both do.'

I nodded as if I understood. I didn't. 'What happened to Margaret?'

'When the operation went wrong Maitland tried to save the womb so we would still be able to have children. He failed. He couldn't stop the bleeding and Margaret was deprived of oxygen for eight minutes. Our baby died – a boy; I called him

Thomas – and Margaret was left with severe brain damage. The medical term is anoxic injury. Everything she does is affected. She can't dress or feed herself. I have to do it. She has no control over her bodily functions. In almost every respect she's a child. Except a child grows and learns. My wife won't get any better.'

The operation had been in September. This was the end of January. These people had been given a life sentence and were serving it together.

'What age is she?'

'Thirty-four.'

'I'll keep my voice down.'

'No need.' He paused again. 'We can talk in the car if it's a bit much for you. Although I don't like to be too far away in case she wakes and needs me.'

His consideration was appreciated though, in the circumstances, impossible to accept.

'Of course not. Don't worry about me.'

'Sure? If you change your mind…'

He opened the door. Cooper's description of his wife and his offer to talk in the car should have prepared me for the tragedy on the other side. It didn't.

Margaret Cooper sat in the centre of the room, wearing a blue plastic bib on top of her blouse. Her head hung to one side and her tongue lolled from her open mouth. The second finger of her left hand tapped a silent beat on the wheelchair's metal frame – some involuntary muscle reflex perhaps – while her snoring filled the empty room like the sound of a muted trumpet. Thirty-four her husband had said. I would have put her at twice that and then some.

Cooper gave me a minute to come to terms with the scene in front of me. 'We can sit in the kitchen if you like.'

I liked.

He made coffee while I perched on a stool, imagining the excited conversations they must've had about the arrival of their first-born, over breakfast in this room.

Before.

The coffee was barely drinkable; too little sugar and too much milk. And it couldn't have mattered less. I began with where they were with their claim against Francis Fallon.

'There was an enquiry, wasn't there?'

Cooper laughed. 'It concluded no one was to blame. So the bastard who performed the operation walked away scot-free. The director took me aside and told me to let him know if there was anything the hospital could do to help. Then left me to make my own way home.'

'Did the surgeon speak to you after the operation?'

'Not him. Mr Law took me aside and went through what had gone wrong. He brought Thomas to me. I held him in my arms; he was so tiny. Maitland didn't appear until late on the following afternoon. He apologised and assured me he'd done everything in his power. Imagine it. The bastard apologised. How can you just apologise for taking away everything worthwhile?'

'Did you believe him?'

'At the time, of course. It didn't occur to me he'd made a mistake. A hospital – well you trust them, don't you? You just do.'

'When did you realise?'

'I think it was the day after. I started asking Maitland questions. Stupid questions about how long before Margaret improved. It must have been difficult for him knowing what he'd done and me, going on and on. Eventually he told me. This was it. "As good as it was going to get" was the phrase he used. Not in a cruel way. Just forceful enough to shake me out of my delusions. He succeeded.'

We'd both forgotten the coffee. Cooper remembered and took a sip from his cup. I left mine alone. Even if it had been the finest bean ever to come out of Colombia, I didn't have the stomach for it.

'And that's when I knew.'

'How?'

'I'm not sure. Something in his eyes. In his voice, maybe. But I knew.'

'What did you do?'

'I got hysterical. Shouting. Screaming. Two nurses calmed me down and he left. The hospital went through the motions, swept it under the carpet and we were sent home with Social Services buzzing around. Reeling. I still am.'

'And you haven't spoken to either Maitland or Law since?'

'I haven't. Our lawyer has. Alison Cummings. She contacted, Mr Law, and pleaded with him to testify against Maitland and Francis Fallon. He was there. He'd seen Maitland make the wrong decision.'

Cooper stared at the floor.

'At first he said he couldn't. It would be professional suicide for him. Later we heard he'd lodged a formal complaint. Then, before Christmas, he changed his mind and agreed to speak out if the hospital didn't re-open our case. We were delighted. Alison came round with a bottle of champagne. I poured a tiny drop for Margaret and helped her drink it. And now he's disappeared and we're back to square one.'

Words couldn't describe what these people were going through. Unfortunately, words were all I had. And promises that would probably turn out to be empty.

'If I hear anything I'll let you know.'

He half-nodded and I could see he was sinking.

I did my best to reassure him. 'I will. I understand what's at stake here. Can I have Alison's phone number?'

He took a card from a drawer under the table and handed it to me. A whining noise came from the lounge. Cooper jumped to his feet. 'She's waking up.'

'I better go.'

'Yes. Yes. You should.'

On my way out I said, 'Do you blame Law for not coming forward sooner?'

He wasn't bitter. 'I'm disappointed, though not surprised. Nobody really cares. They sympathise. Say the right things. Then they all go home, because at the end of the day, it isn't happening to them. It's happening to us.'

'What about Francis Fallon?'

David Cooper was distracted, anxious to see to his wife, yet the answer came easily and I knew he'd considered it many times.

'Those bastards. I'd burn their fucking hospital down and everybody in it. But who would look after, Margaret?'

# Chapter Twenty

I used the card David Cooper had given me and called Alison Cummings. She answered sounding young and serious. I told her who I was and what I wanted. 'As you know, Mr Law has disappeared. His sister has hired me to find her brother. Can I ask when you last spoke to him?'

She didn't bother to disguise her frustration and her disgust. 'We met two days before Christmas. An earlier approach from me was turned down. Said he wanted to give the hospital a chance to respond to a complaint he'd made. They didn't, and he made contact.'

'So he offered to get involved?'

'Yes. Just the best present I could've wished for. It meant the Coopers had someone credible to testify about what had gone wrong during Margaret's surgery. Someone who knew what he was talking about.'

'You must've been pleased.'

'Over the moon. We celebrated. That was a mistake. I raised David's hopes. Really, after my experiences with Francis Fallon, I ought to have been more cautious.'

'Don't be too hard on yourself. You thought you were on to a result.'

'And we would've been if…'

'…your star witness hadn't gone missing.'

She sighed. 'That was the thing. Mr Law offered us his support. Better late than never, but still.'

'You only actually met him once?'

'Yes. He seemed nice. Very anxious to help Margaret Cooper. I liked him. Then he spoiled it by asking me out.'

'Why did that spoil it?'

'I was wearing a wedding ring. But at least he was on our side.'

'Did he say anything about the hospital?'

'A lot. They'd had their chance to come clean and hadn't taken it. It was up to us to see to it they did.'

'"Us"? He actually said "us"?'

'Absolutely. He was off to America after New Year. We were going to agree a statement when he came back. His exact words were "We'll get them. We'll get the bastards." It was all so positive.'

Her voice changed.

'You can understand why David Cooper is so crushed. Without Mr Law they'll get nothing. Or, at the least, be tied up in litigation that'll take years to resolve.'

I thanked her for being so forthcoming.

'I hope you find him, Mr Cameron. Good people are depending on it.'

We ended the conversation on that note and I sat for a while, trying to make sense of what could have changed Gavin Law's mind although I suspected I already knew.

Rape.

I was considering going home when Pat Logue breezed into the office like a man on fire, and right away I saw he was pleased with himself. He began with a question.

'Ever dreamed about what you'd do if you won the lottery, Charlie?'

'Haven't given it too much thought, Patrick.'

He nodded as if he understood something that until then had passed him by.

'Well, of course you haven't. Never needed to. You're from money. You see it differently. It's just…there.'

He drew an arc in the air with his hand like a magician.

'My side was skint three hundred and sixty-five days a year. Should've married a well-fixed burd with big tits. Instead, I married Gail.'

'Good decision.'

'No argument. And one out of two's not bad. The point is her mob was even poorer than mine. Gail's an orphan same as me. Her parents didn't leave so much as a razoo. Not even enough to bury them. Fortunately they went within a couple of days of each other – did a deal with the undertaker.'

The pitiful sight of Margaret Cooper faded in my head. Patrick's patter was doing its work; he was on form.

'Treated me like one of the family from the off. Didn't understand it. Still can't. What had I ever done to them?'

I interrupted his act. 'I'm guessing you've got a result on the hospital.'

He grinned. 'When have I ever let you down, Charlie?'

I assumed it was a rhetorical question. He settled back to bask in his achievement.

'First thing you need to know is, it wasn't easy. Took hours to find where the porters drank. Tried the boozers nearest to the hospital. A dead loss. Not hard to understand why. Hole-in-the-wall joints. Piss poor beer. There's a hotel. Gave that a go as well. Nada.'

He pointed an admonishing finger at me. 'Hope you appreciate the sacrifice involved.'

Drinking and getting paid for it?

'I may be many things, Charlie, but when it comes to beer, I've got standards. High standards.'

'I've seen them, Patrick.'

He gave me a funny look and went on with his tale. 'Finally tracked them down in a pub half a mile from Francis Fallon. To you and me these porter guys just wheel sick people around. So what? We don't consider the responsibility involved. Drinking isn't cool so they do their bevvyin' a fair distance away.'

'And what's the story?'

He ran through the cast of characters on his fingers. 'The director and Maitland aren't popular though no surprise there; nobody likes the boss, do they? Present company excepted. Couldn't get much at first. Dour bunch of bastards. Not the cheeriest people you're ever goin' to meet. Even after I bought a few pints they still weren't sayin'. Eventually got pally with one of them. Probably an alki. Refused nothin' but blows. Cost you a few bob, Charlie. Sorry. Worth it though.'

'What did he tell you?'

'Accordin' to him, Maitland likes a drink. That makes him okay. The others thought he was an arrogant prick.'

'And Gavin Law?'

'Consensus is he's a bit of a pussy hound, but they like that. Banged everything that moved, apparently.'

'So the rape thing might be true?'

He shrugged. 'Not mentioned, Charlie. Unusual in a gossip shop, although it could be the hospital's managed to keep a lid on it. Sensitive stuff, after all.'

'Yeah, but a member of staff's been suspended on the strength of it, Patrick. Hard on the heels of another doctor. That can't be the norm. There has to be more than the big boss not being on anybody's Christmas card list and his arrogant brother-in-law too fond of a drink.'

'Agree with you. Got a hollow ring to it. Two suspensions in as many months should have the jungle drums at it.'

'So how come they aren't? What's the take on McMillan?'

'Again, not much. Plenty of sympathy. Decent guy who's had a rough time.'

'And is off the operating list because he told somebody he was suicidal.'

Patrick stroked his chin. 'Long faces when I asked about him. That said, no suggestions he wasn't.'

I stood up and paced the floor. 'Visited the Coopers this afternoon. You wouldn't wish what's happened to those people on your worst enemy. The wife – Margaret – she's still breathing. About all you can say for her. Gavin Law was going to testify for them against Maitland and the hospital. Without him they'll get nothing.'

'So what do you want me to do?'

For the moment, I wasn't sure.

'It all comes back to the hospital. The common factor linking Law and McMillan is Maitland. We need more.'

Patrick threw a piece of paper on the desk. On it, scribbled in pencil, was an address and a phone number.

'Wallace Maitland's?'

'The very same.'

'Good stuff, Patrick.'

He clapped his hands together and got to his feet. 'Now, where's this Eskimo woman you want me to wrestle?'

*** 

Wallace Maitland crossed the road at St Enoch's Square and made his way past House of Fraser at the bottom of Buchanan Street. An hour earlier he'd left Blackfriars pub in Merchant City – the last customer – where he'd spent most of the evening. For a change he was relatively sober. The steak and ale pie he'd eaten helped and anyway, he hadn't been in the mood. Glasgow wasn't short of watering holes but sitting at a bar wasn't the fun it had been.

Jimmy Hambley was right; his drinking was out of control and that worried him. A lot of things worried him: losing his wife; the end of his career; the nagging fear he might be a murderer. And, above all, getting found out.

Since New Year's Eve things between him and his wife hadn't been good. Wallace was to blame; he recognised that much. And turning up at Jimmy and Martha's covered in blood and unable to remember how he had come by his injuries was the last straw. They'd barely spoken since and he stayed away from the house; walking during the day and when night fell, walking some more. Anywhere he wouldn't have to look at the reproach in her eyes and know he was the one who put it there. By now, she would be asleep. Time to head home.

In his heart, he didn't believe he was capable of killing anyone and Law's accusation had come as a shock in more ways than one. Criticism from a fellow professional, especially one who was present at the operation, was difficult to take. Law should have understood. The Coopers were desperate to have a child. He'd acted to keep that dream alive.

With a complete abruption, an emergency caesarean and a hysterectomy was the obvious course. He'd chosen to do the bold thing. The brave thing. It wasn't his fault the bleeding wouldn't stop and her brain had been starved of oxygen.

He'd tried. God knows he'd tried.

Colin McMillan was a different story. Maitland hadn't a clue where he was coming from. Clearly the man was unstable. McMillan was a quiet individual who kept himself apart. Wallace didn't know him socially and couldn't have named anyone who did. As an obstetrician, he seemed first-class. As a colleague, he was an enigma.

Maitland had only met McMillan's wife once, at some cheese and wine do Jimmy insisted they attend and nobody wanted to be at. She'd been a looker, though he'd detected an intensity in her and marked her as the kind of female it was better to avoid. Too much like hard work.

They'd discussed poetry, of all things. She'd rattled on about Sylvia Plath. Wallace had switched off, satisfied his first impression was correct. His knowledge of modern poets could be written on the back of a beer mat yet he knew Plath had committed suicide and, later, so did Joyce McMillan.

How about that for irony?

A glance at his watch told him it was after midnight. Usually he'd be home by now. He turned right into Mitchell Street and quickened his pace. In the narrow passage, his echoing footsteps startled him. Maitland looked over his shoulder, nervous and uncertain, seeing nothing except blackened walls covered with posters advertising clubs, and a couple of out-sized rubbish bins, crammed to the brim with cardboard.

His nerves were shot; he cursed himself for being a jittery old woman. No surprise with the pressure he was under. At any moment, the police might discover Gavin Law's body and come for him. Law's complaint could end his career. That gave him motive. He'd be the prime suspect.

Christ!

A dosser, sleeping under newspapers and boxes, called out incoherently from a bad dream, and Wallace was struck by a terrifying thought. He might end-up like this: during the day, shuffling through the city scrounging cheap wine to get him through another freezing cold night, his comfortable life just a distant memory he wasn't sure had ever been real. Maitland followed the nightmare scenario through to its conclusion – dementia and death. He shuddered, more afraid than he'd ever been, and hurried on.

The car park was deserted. He put the ticket into the machine, paid the exorbitant charge and climbed the stone stairs with the sound of his own laboured breathing in his ears. At the second level, he stopped and listened. Somewhere behind him in the darkened stairwell he heard footsteps. Maitland fumbled for his keys and broke into a run. On level three, sweating and panting, he dragged the door open, fired the ignition and roared towards the exit. Out of the corner of his eye, he saw a figure draw into the shadows and his heart leapt in his chest.

It wasn't paranoia. Someone was following him.

\*\*\*

James Hambley lay in the dark going over the events for the hundredth time, starting with Margaret Cooper. Wallace wasn't the first surgeon to make the wrong decision; neither was he the first to refuse to accept responsibility. "The operation was a success but the patient died" wasn't a cliché for nothing. It happened. More often than people would believe. And when it did, doctors could be confident of the support of their peers. Quite right, too. The profession had to be protected otherwise they would be inundated with lawsuits, most of them without foundation.

Gavin Law's complaint, in itself, wasn't such a big problem. It could've been dealt with and contained. Threatening to add his weight to the other side took it to another level. Hambley had seen that coming and was concerned until the rape allegation effectively neutralised the righteous Law. From there, they had little to worry about, because with Law on the back foot, the case against Francis Fallon would certainly collapse.

As he'd told Wallace, these things had a way of resolving themselves so long as they kept cool heads. McMillan was a case in point. Look how easily that had gone away.

But that hadn't been good enough for the headstrong drunken idiot.

Hambley didn't know what his brother-in-law had actually done on Hogmanay. Wallace arrived with evidence of violence on him, and no one had seen Gavin Law since. Had Maitland killed Law, or had Law run rather than face his rape accuser?

As director, Hambley couldn't escape the consequences. A question had been tabled for the next hospital board meeting about the loss of two surgeons in such a short time. His management at Francis Fallon was coming under scrutiny. Not a problem. He could handle the board – most of them didn't have a clue – but if the police suddenly found a body, then that would change everything.

The phone rang. Hambley lifted it on the third ring, hoping it hadn't wakened Martha upstairs in bed.

'Jimmy? Jimmy, I'm being followed.'

Wallace.

'Calm down and tell me.'

'Tonight. Somebody was there.'

'Wait a minute. You're telling me…what, exactly?'

Maitland's voice was a savage whisper. Shona mustn't hear what he was saying. 'I was in a car park in town. There were footsteps behind me.'

'Did you actually see anybody?'

'No. But somebody was there. I swear. I didn't imagine it.'

'Wallace, have you been drinking?'

Maitland lost his temper. 'No…yes…no. Only a couple. That isn't the point.'

Hambley's tone hardened. 'I'm rather afraid it is, Wallace. Your lifestyle's catching up with you. It doesn't take much these days to set you off. We all saw that on Hogmanay. My advice is the same, except now you don't have a choice. Seek help.'

Maitland was close to tears. 'You're not listening. I heard him. He stayed in the shadows but he was there.'

Hambley sighed; he was tired of this. 'Who? Who was there?'

'I don't know.'

'Shit! I forgot. A private investigator was here asking about Gavin Law. Somebody called Cameron.'

Maitland froze. Fear crashed over him; he felt ill. The investigator hadn't known Maitland's name until Hambley let it slip. 'What should I do?'

Wallace really was pathetic. At the other end of the line, a cruel smile played at the corners of James Hambley's mouth. If he hadn't been Martha's brother, he would have sacked the bastard long ago. 'Better hope he's as good at his job as you are at yours. You could show him where you buried Law.'

'Jimmy. Don't joke. It isn't funny.'

'No it isn't, is it? Not funny at all. So listen you gutless fucker. I need you back here before this board meeting. I've got enough on my plate without having to explain your absence as well. Keep your head down and do your job. And if I so much as sniff drink on you I'll call the police myself and tell them what I should've told them on New Year's Eve. Got it?'

'All right. All right.'

'Assuming this investigator catches up with you, say nothing. Not a word. So long as you keep your mouth shut, you're in the clear.'

Maitland calmed down. 'I'm spooking myself. Sorry, Jimmy. And thanks. I feel better.'

'Good. Get Shona used to the idea of having you around the house more often. Like every day.'

'What d'you mean? I don't understand.'

'Perhaps you thought I wasn't serious. I am. Francis Fallon will be better off without you. As soon as the dust has settled on the mess you've caused, I want your resignation.'

# Chapter Twenty-One

In the black Lancia, Tony Daly sat beside someone he'd never seen before tonight. The two in the front were strangers as well. All of them acted as if he wasn't there, ignoring him when he spoke to them. At the lights at Charing Cross, he'd tried to get out and got punched in the stomach for his efforts. Now, strong hands pinned him to the seat and bile tasting of vanilla and molasses rose in his throat.

He'd expected to see Lachie and Rutherford at the City Chambers but there was no sign of them. As so often happened, the meeting went on longer than planned and Daly assumed the vehicle with the door open was a courtesy car laid on by the council to take him home. Too late he realised his mistake.

The driver turned right into Kelvin Way and carried on through Kelvingrove Park towards University Avenue. Even at this hour, cars lined either side. Daly glanced at one of his captors and in the harsh streetlight, saw the face of a killer and wanted to be sick.

They took a left into the darkened car park, behind Kelvingrove Museum and Art Gallery. A fresh stab of terror ran through him.

His voice trembled. 'Why're we here?'

His question went unanswered. The men got out, rubbing their hands together against the freezing air and shared cigarettes. Daly heard them talking. Their conversation was casual. None mentioned the petrified man in the back of the car or the awful thing they were about to do. One of them joked and the others laughed, while behind them, the ghostly outline of Glasgow University's tower pointed to a black sky.

They weren't in a hurry.

An hour later, the leader crushed the last of his smokes into the ground with the heel of his foot and barked an order. 'Let's do it. And remember: no marks.'

Daly saw them approach the car and felt warmth between his thighs. Without warning, his head was yanked back and thick fingers forced his mouth open. The guy in the front screwed the top off a bottle of whisky, straddled the seats until he was almost on top of him and poured the contents down Tony Daly's throat. Daly gagged and retched and struggled to escape. He couldn't breathe. Alcohol soaked his clothes.

The councillor pleaded for his life. He spluttered half-formed words and his eyes filled with whisky tears. He begged them. 'Please. Ple... I'll do... Tell, Sean. Tell him I...'

A choking fit brought temporary relief. His tormentors waited for it to pass – they didn't want him dead. Not yet.

Again, the gangsters prised their victim's lips apart and kept going. When the first bottle was empty a second took its place.

The driver started the car, drove along Kelvin Way and on to the heart of the West End. They crossed a deserted Great Western Road and pulled into the kerb close to the bridge on Queen Margaret Drive. From the boot, the thug who'd emptied the whisky down the councillor's throat got a length of rope that smelled like tar and ended in a noose. Daly was dragged from the car, moaning, and carried the few steps to the bridge just as a couple appeared. The girl's head rested against her boyfriend's shoulder; he whispered and she smiled.

Daly's persecutors threw their arms round him, pretending he was a pal who'd overdone the bevy. A hand pressed against his mouth prevented him from calling out, while another clapped his back in a show of support.

'You're all right. No problem. We'll get you home.'

An unnecessary performance; the lovers were blind to everything but each other. Daly tried to focus and couldn't. He knew he was going to die. In a final futile attempt to save himself he slurred and blubbered.

'I'll do it! I'll do it! Tell Sean I'll…Don't…'

Nobody was listening. They tied the rope to a lamp post and put the noose round his neck; he slumped, exhausted and defeated, against the wall, crying like a lost child. When they lifted him and rolled him over the concrete parapet, he screamed.

The rope tightened and the scream died.

Sean Rafferty was miles away, playing cards and winning, when Tony Daly went off the Queen Margaret Bridge.

But the message had been sent. It remained to be seen who heeded it.

\*\*\*

At one o'clock in the morning the temperatures dived and, for the first time since the New Year, rain became snow. For an hour it melted and vanished but, around two-thirty, it started to gather. By five, it was inches deep, coming down thick and fast. Glasgow was in for another day of train cancellations and traffic jams.

In the hours after dawn, the Kelvin Walkway was deserted. The Walkway was one of the city's best kept secrets. This early, the jogger had it to himself. Sometimes, especially in summer, he went as far as Milngavie. Today he didn't consider it. Beyond Maryhill, the narrow, muddy single-track would be rutted hard and dangerous. Even on the flat the soles of his shoes struggled to find traction. His friends already thought he was crazy. If they could see him now he would never live it down. They didn't understand what it was to feel you were the only person on the planet. Staying fit they got but missed the most important parts. The beauty. The peace.

He crossed the river behind the Botanic Gardens and headed into woodland just as the snow cleared. His footsteps padding the ground and the rasp of his breathing as cold air burned his lungs were the only sounds, apart from the rushing of the swollen river. The remains of the North Woodside Flint Mill distracted him; he slipped, almost fell, and decided that, however much he loved it, in the conditions, what he was doing wasn't wise. Tranquillity was one thing; a broken leg was something else. The chances of being found soon weren't good. He would freeze.

A bend in the path brought him in sight of the Queen Margaret Bridge.

The body hung motionless from the rope. Ridiculously, snow patched its head like a hat and lay on the shoulders like white epaulets. The face was grey. Grey and dead.

# Chapter Twenty-Two

The police car raced towards the scene, siren blaring and blue light flashing. In the passenger seat, DI Barr ran a hand over his dark hair and felt a thrill of excitement run through him. He had imagined how it would feel, and now it was happening he wasn't disappointed. This was what it was about, and he loved it.

On both Byers Road and Great Western, traffic was at a standstill. Cars sat bumper to bumper, unable to travel in any direction. And it wouldn't get much better until the crime scene manager was satisfied and decided they could re-open them. For now, every artery near the tragedy was closed. Frustrated people sighed and drummed on their steering wheels as the realisation they were going to be late for work sank in.

At the lights, an officer waved the car into Queen Margaret Drive. Barr got out and ducked under the blue and white tape stretched across the street. Two other police cars were already there and an ambulance sat with the engine running: the back doors were closed.

Andrew Geddes was waiting. His boss strode past him. 'What've we got?'

Geddes fell into step beside him. 'Middle-aged man hanging from the bridge. Life pronounced extinct by the medics. Been there a while I'd say. CSM's done his best to preserve the scene but it's impossible. Too public to leave the body where it was.'

The temperature still wasn't much above freezing. Barr rubbed his hands together and stamped his feet. DS Geddes wasn't sure he was listening. 'So, suicide. Okay, what else?'

Geddes read from a notebook. 'Jogger discovered it at seven-ten.'

'You've talked to him?'

The DS hesitated. Of course he'd fucking talked to him. 'Took an initial statement. Said we'd need him to give a more detailed one later today. Guy's pretty shook-up. Runs half a dozen miles every other day, come rain come shine. Even in a blizzard.'

'Mad.'

'Keen. Though maybe not after this. Bit of a shocker to come across before you've had your breakfast. Might need help to get over it.'

The DI was unsympathetic. 'Anybody who jogs in this weather already needs help. Where's the body?'

'In there.'

At the ambulance, Geddes touched Barr's arm – a friendly gesture and a mistake. 'Seen umpteen people hang themselves, but the first one, when I was in uniform, stayed in my head for months. As a way to go it's definitely not recommended.'

His concern wasn't appreciated. The DI shrugged off the warning. 'Get on with it, can we? Haven't got all day.'

Geddes signalled an ambulance man to open the door. Inside, a male somewhere between fifty and sixty lay on his back fully-clothed. The smell of whisky washed over the policemen; strong enough to make them gag. Geddes tasted bile in his mouth and watched the DI's reactions. If there was any, he didn't see it. Cold bastard.

Barr said, 'Sure he didn't drink himself to death?'

A purple mark at the dead man's throat proved there had been more to it than that.

'Who is he?'

'Credit cards in his wallet say Anthony Daly. We'll know more about him soon.'

Barr waved his hand through the alcohol fumes and gave his attention to the lines of traffic on Great Western Road. 'Let's get things moving.'

'What about the family?'

'Speak to them.'

'Me?'

'Yeah, you. Got a problem with that?'

Geddes did. 'Don't you want to interview them?'

'Why? You can guess what they'll tell us. Suffering from depression and recently something put him over the edge. Drinking heavily though nobody had any idea it was as bad as this.'

'I agree, except it assumes it was suicide.'

'And is there evidence to support another theory?'

'Nothing on the bridge. No footprints. That could be because he went into space before it started to snow.'

'All right. And the ligature?'

'A simple slip-knot. Photographed and on its way to forensics.'

'Then to assume he took his own life isn't such a giant leap – if you pardon the pun. Or am I wrong?'

'You're not wrong.'

Barr snorted. 'It was like a brewery. God only knows how much he had in him. And – one more cliché to add to the pile – they'll claim he didn't have an enemy in the world. Have I missed anything?'

He turned away. 'Clean this up. Talk to whoever you need to and let's get back to catching criminals. That is what we do, isn't it?'

Geddes didn't respond.

'In a couple of days the PM will confirm the cause of death and we can start looking for a Johnnie Walker. Last seen in every bar in Scotland.' He smiled a thin smile and pulled his coat around him. 'Job's hard enough, Geddes. Let's not kick the arse out of it, eh? I'll see you at the station.'

***

The information on Anthony Daly came minutes after DI Barr left the scene: the deceased had been fifty-two years old, unmarried and shared a flat with his sister in Bishopbriggs.

DS Geddes waved a young female constable to follow him. 'Come with me. I need you.'

They drove along a deserted Queen Margaret Drive – barred to traffic all the way to Maryhill Road – and turned left. The policewoman didn't speak; overawed to be in the same universe as the detective responsible for catching Richard Hill, the most prolific serial killer Scotland had ever seen. Every copper in Glasgow – probably the country – knew his name. Such a high-profile collar should've earned him promotion. It hadn't happened. The fresh-faced constable wanted to ask why. Word on the street said he was a first-rate officer who had a short fuse and didn't suffer fools. She was about to find out if it was true.

Maryhill was busier than usual because of the diversion and Geddes wasn't unhappy to have to wait. He wasn't in a hurry. This part wasn't nice: the reason DI Barr had landed him with it. He glanced at the constable in the passenger seat: twenty-five or twenty-six. Keen. Still believing she could make a difference. She'd learn.

'What's your name?'

'Lawson, sir.'

'Any idea where we're going?'

'No, sir.'

'Take a guess.'

'I'd rather not, if you don't mind, sir. No good at guessing.'

'All right. The guy on the bridge, you saw him, didn't you? Not pretty. Well, his name was Anthony Daly. And hard though it may be to believe, somebody loved him. We've got tell them they're never going to see him again. That's why you're here.'

'Yes, sir.'

'So, apologies in advance for picking you. That said, before we knock on the door and ruin a stranger's life let's understand a couple of things. This is tough for everybody but, when it's done, we'll go home. Whoever opens that door will have to get on with it.'

Lawson bit her lip to stop herself from speaking.

'We're delivering bad news; we don't get emotionally involved. It isn't happening to us. Don't forget it. Stay professional. Do the job. And if you feel you could do with a stiff drink, I'll be at your elbow.'

'Will you be buying, sir?'

In spite of the circumstances, Geddes smiled. 'You'll do, Lawson. You'll do.'

\*\*\*

Sandy Rutherford wasn't looking forward to the conversation he was about to have. Lachie Thompson had always gone his own way; how he would react to something like this was impossible to predict. Hanging Tony Daly in broad daylight was pure Jimmy. Very public. Very brutal. It had worked for the father and Rutherford had little doubt it would work for the son.

Thompson's first words told him he'd heard the news. 'That bastard. That murdering bastard.'

For a second Rutherford thought he was going to cry. 'Who told you?'

'It's on the news. The early report said a jogger found the body of a man hanging from the Queen Margaret Bridge. The police have confirmed the identity. I'm going to see Cissie later, once the initial shock has passed. Christ knows what I'll find to say to her.'

Rutherford gazed out of the window to where his car sat buried under snow. His head was filled with a lot of things; at that moment, sympathy for Tony Daly's sister wasn't top of the list. 'We need to meet, Lachie. Sooner the better.'

'Where?'

'Same as last time. Charing Cross.'

Thompson tempered his regret about Daly and thought about Joan and Annie.

'I'm leaving now,' he said, and hung up.

\*\*\*

Baby Grand was deserted. Sandy Rutherford took a seat at the back, ordered a cappuccino and a roll and sausage with mustard, and waited for Lachie Thompson to arrive. Despite the part he'd played in Tony Daly's death, Rutherford's appetite was unaffected.

The drive from his home hadn't been too bad. Getting onto the main road was a challenge; after that it was all right. At the far end of the bar, a television with the sound turned off played stock footage of the Queen Margaret Bridge, while a female wearing a scarf and gloves reported live from the scene; she looked cold. Over her shoulder two police vehicles blocked the road. In due course there would be a statement. Whatever they had to say didn't interest Rutherford; he knew more about what had happened than they did.

The TV camera scanned the small silent crowd, shivering and stamping their feet to keep warm; male and female; some young some old. Drawn by a need to be close to where another human being had suffered. Ordinary faces hiding twisted imaginations the councillor would never understand.

Fucking ghouls.

The breakfast waitress seemed familiar: in her early twenties, slim and black and very good-looking. Her dark eyes, fixed on her task, gave nothing away. Was she happy or unhappy? It was impossible to know. Faces were masks. Rutherford's proved it. Then he remembered. This was the girl who had asked if he'd wanted ice in his water and when he said no, brought it anyway. Today she'd forgotten the mustard.

He'd been right. Nobody listens.

Lachie Thompson hadn't listened. The threat to his family didn't dissuade him from believing he could go against Sean Rafferty and win. Fool. As usual, Tony had taken his side, driven by loyalty and Dutch courage. Thompson and Daly. Two for the price of one. Not anymore. Rutherford had called Tony Daly a sleeping partner.

He was certainly that now.

The door opened. Thompson came in, glanced up at the TV where a police officer was reading a prepared statement. The officer was young.

Lachie spoke to the empty bar. 'Where do they find them, eh? Got ulcers older than him.'

Rutherford tried to read his expression, hoping he was ready to see sense. Otherwise…

The waitress arrived, ready to take Thompson's order. He waved her away. Unlike Rutherford, he didn't feel like eating. 'Heard anything from Rafferty?'

'Not so far. He's made his move. The ball's in our court. He'll expect a reaction. We've got a decision to make, and we better make it quick.'

'Part of me wants to go to the police and tell them.'

Rutherford took a bite out of his roll. Crumbs fell to the table; he brushed them on to the floor. 'Tell them what, exactly?'

'For a start, he threatened my family.'

'Did he? "Sean says hello?" Doesn't sound very threatening to me.'

'Don't get cute, Sandy. You know what was meant.'

'I do, that's right. But when you say it out loud there's not a lot to it, is there? You're a public figure. Could be just a friendly message from somebody who hasn't seen you in a while. Plenty of guys called Sean in Glasgow.'

He leaned forward to make his point.

'Half the crowd at Celtic Park's called Sean. Try proving which one it was.'

Thompson hit back. 'If it's proof you want drop into the city morgue. You'll find it lying on a slab with a ticket on the toe.'

Rutherford wiped his mouth, drank some of the coffee and tried to take the heat out of the conversation. 'What I'm getting at is this. When you boil it down, it doesn't add up to much.'

'It adds up to murder, isn't that enough? Or was Tony just collateral damage?'

Rutherford's reply pulled no punches. 'No. Daly was an alki who hit his gutter and didn't come back up. A sad end to a sad life.'

'But they hanged him. Doesn't that mean anything to you?'

Sandy Rutherford was unmoved. 'Rather him than us. Or maybe you disagree, Lachie. Maybe you'd prefer to be the one swinging from that fucking bridge?'

'What I'd prefer is to never have met the Raffertys.'

'Except you did. We did. We took Jimmy's money and thought we could control him. Well we couldn't, and Sean's his son. You may not believe me but I am sorry. Tony didn't deserve to die like that. And neither do we. That's what'll happen unless we see reason.'

Watching Rutherford finish his breakfast, Thompson knew he was on his own. The fire in him went out. He sat back in his seat. Rutherford saw defeat in his eyes and pressed home the advantage.

'Rafferty wants an answer from us. What's it going to be? Are we in?'

Thompson suddenly felt old and tired; he nodded. He'd call Joan and get her to come back. In time, maybe, she'd understand and forgive him.

Rutherford was speaking. 'Good. You know it makes sense.'

'Does it, Sandy? Does any of it make sense to you?'

'Absolutely. With a man like Sean Rafferty, it's better to be part of the solution. Now we will be. I'll let him know. How soon can we get it through the council?'

'Soon.'

'That's what he needs to hear.'

Rutherford dropped money on the table and swirled the dregs in his cup. 'A shame about, Tony. He was a poor soul but I liked him.'

He stood, ready to leave. Thompson didn't move. 'You've been on his side from the beginning, haven't you, Sandy?'

'Not from the beginning. We made a mistake, Lachie.'

Thompson snorted contempt at their naivety. 'Just the one?'

'When Jimmy died we assumed we were shot of the Raffertys. We aren't shot of them and we never will be. I realised that on Hogmanay at the house. Best we can hope for is not to end up like Tony Daly, gagging on a rope. We don't have to like it, Lachie, but at least we're alive.'

\*\*\*

Cissie Daly's pink dressing-gown might have fitted her once. Now it hung off her shoulders over cotton pyjamas which could have belonged to someone else. Her uncombed hair stood out at crazy angles like a 1980s punk rocker. Geddes saw the bloodshot eyes and the trembling fingers and guessed that when the dead man settled down for a drinking session at home he had company. Cissie knew it was bad news the moment she opened the door.

Geddes coughed into his hand. He'd done this duty many times. Despite the speech in the car, it never got easier. 'Miss Daly?'

Cissie's eyes darted from the stocky man in the raincoat to the young constable beside him.

'Can we come in?'

'Why? What's happened?'

Geddes repeated the question. 'Can we come in? It would be better.'

She led the way into the lounge. In the corner, on the television screen, a reporter was talking to camera. The ambulance had gone but the police cars were still there. On the floor, at the side of an armchair, a half-full glass sat next to a dark green bottle with a familiar orange label. The Benedictine connection.

Geddes cleared his throat. 'I have some bad news, I'm afraid.'

No amount of training would make anyone good at this. There was no such thing as good. 'I'm sorry to have to tell you a man we believe to be your brother has been found dead.'

The woman folded her arms across her chest and rejected the statement. 'Tony's here. He's in bed. You've made a mistake.'

Officer Lawson shot a glance at the DS. Surely they hadn't got it wrong? Geddes remained calm; his expression didn't alter. 'Could I ask you to check?'

Cissie Daly's certainty was unshakeable. 'My brother's in bed. Tony works hard. He doesn't get up before twelve.'

'I understand. Can we take a look? Which room is his?'

She pointed to the end of the hall. Without needing to be told, Lawson eased past her and went to the door. The constable opened it, looked inside and came back. Over Cissie Daly's shoulder she shook her head at Geddes.

'He isn't there.'

Confusion and dread met on a face older than its years. 'Of course he is. What're you talking about?'

'Your brother isn't there. I'm sorry.'

Cissie moaned, staggered and almost collapsed. Stick-thin fingers tore at her hair. Officer Lawson guided her to the couch. Geddes stood in the middle of the room, powerless. The young constable put her arms round the woman and nodded to the DS. 'Put the kettle on.'

This time she didn't say, "sir."

Geddes did as he was told. When he returned with strong sweet tea, Cissie was curled in on herself, sobbing. He handed the cup to his young colleague and sat down. Lawson held it to Cissie Daly's lips. 'Take this. It'll help.'

She took a sip, then another encouraged by the policewoman. Like a child at bedtime she said, 'I have to go to the bathroom.'

Lawson's offer to go with her was refused.

'I'll be all right.'

When she was out of the room, Geddes lifted the Buckfast bottle and the glass and handed them to his constable. In the ambulance at the Queen Margaret Bridge, the smell of whisky had been over-powering. Here it was the sickly-sweet aroma of fortified spirits.

'Don't call it a family illness for nothing. Stop her having any more. Tastes like bloody cough medicine. How anybody can stomach it – especially first thing in the morning – is beyond me.'

'It's cheap.'

'Would need to be.'

Lawson had taken what the DS said in the car to heart. She'd been professional and kept her emotions in control. For a moment they got the better of her. 'Sad, isn't it?'

Geddes reply proved his reputation as a hard-arse was well deserved. 'It's life. Get used to it. You'll see a lot more of the same before you're finished. Told you. It's tough, but it isn't happening to you.'

'Sorry, sir.'

Geddes softened. 'You're doing fine. Stay with her. We'll pick you up when she's ready to identify the body and make a statement. Won't want to. There's no way round it. And she shouldn't be alone. Not tonight. Find somebody – a neighbour – who can come round.'

Walking down the path, Geddes could hear the TV drone: a terrible reminder of how quickly circumstances changed. Minutes ago, Cissie Daly had been drinking wine and watching somebody else's tragedy. Suddenly that tragedy was hers.

# Chapter Twenty-Three

Another day gone and not a word. The investigator had promised to let him know as soon as there was anything to report. David Cooper had wanted to believe him, but deep down he knew there would be no news. Law was gone and he wasn't coming back.

David closed the blinds, made himself a cup of tea and drank it in front of the television. With the carer's help he'd put Margaret to bed at four; with luck she'd sleep 'till morning. His choice of phrase amused him and he laughed a bitter laugh. Luck wasn't something they'd had any of recently. It wasn't luck Margaret hadn't died – he'd thought so at the time. He was wrong – it would have been better if she had. Better for them both, though he hated himself for even thinking it. There was nothing fortunate about the lingering half-life they were living.

New Year's Eve had been especially difficult. Usually, they'd have a party to go to with Margaret wearing a new dress, looking wonderful. They'd make sure they were together at midnight – not just a tradition, a symbol of their love – but like everything else, a memory better put behind him. There would be no more parties for the Coopers.

The last months had been hell and the nightmare played on. Some mornings, when he opened his eyes, the awfulness of it hit him and he was afraid he wouldn't be able to cope. Letting Margaret down terrified him most of all. Law offering to testify had given him a glimmer of hope, something to cling to in the darkest hours, but it was slipping away. The obstetrician had forgotten them. The whole world had forgotten them and David Cooper resented it.

The hoped-for improvement in Margaret's condition hadn't materialised, and though her husband continued to pray it would, lying to himself had become harder. David wasn't interested in money, only in what it could do for his wife. With the settlement they would have been able to afford the best care available. Margaret might have recovered – not fully perhaps, he accepted that – but enough for them to enjoy life again.

He swapped the tea for whisky and switched between TV channels – a man had hanged himself. Cooper envied him – then he went to the window and peered between the slats of the blind at the street outside. When he'd brought Margaret from the hospital, a few neighbours made it known they were willing to help in any way they could. Two or three had popped in to visit and David saw the horror on their faces as the women realised what Margaret had become.

One visit was enough, they didn't come back, and he didn't blame them.

He poured himself another drink, nursing it and the growing anger inside him as he remembered how the pompous director at Francis Fallon had washed his hands of them. And Wallace Maitland, the obstetrician who'd botched the operation, had hardly looked the road they were on.

David Cooper detested them all. And how could Law tell them not to worry because he was on their side then disappear? What kind of man would do that?

# Chapter Twenty-Four

The rape allegation against Gavin Law gave weight to the idea he had run off rather than face the consequences of his actions. And given his history with women, confirmed by the Malawian nurse, the lawyer representing Mr and Mrs Cooper, and the porters at Francis Fallon Patrick had spent my money on, it was an obvious conclusion to come to. Even Caroline Law's partner had suggested Gavin was a bit of a lad. My client – the sister who idolised him – was the exception.

Whoever was behind the accusation was still unknown. The hospital, in its own interests, was determined to keep it like that and avoid the publicity a charge of sexual misconduct would bring. So far they were in luck; the police weren't involved. Without Law it might never go any further.

But it didn't feel right.

The fundamental question of motive remained. Who stood to gain from Gavin Law's disappearance? On that score, Francis Fallon was out in front, followed by Maitland. I needed to speak to him.

The number Pat Logue had given me rang out until a wary male voice answered with a question. 'Yes?'

'Wallace Maitland? My name is Charlie Cameron. I'm working for Caroline Law. I would…'

The clipped tone told me his response had been considered long before I called.

'I have absolutely nothing to say.'

He hung-up. I tried again and got no reply. Clearly, the obstetrician didn't want to discuss anything with me. Patrick was downstairs on his usual seat. A guy behind the bar I didn't recognise pushed a pint across. Patrick grin his appreciation.

'Barman is an unsung profession, Charlie. To the untrained eye it looks easy. People don't understand. It takes skill; instinct and anticipation.'

He pointed to his drink.

'See this. Didn't even ask for it. He knew. He just…knew. Can't teach that. It's a gift. This man's a natural. Know what I'm talkin'?'

He was laying the groundwork for drinking on the slate.

'Where's, Jackie?'

'Not doin' so well. Called in sick. Lucky Tom's on the bench. Super-sub.'

'Maitland doesn't want to talk. Find out where he goes. Look for somewhere I can corner him. And I don't expect it to take three days.'

He downed the pint in one and wiped froth from his lips. 'Stand on me, Charlie.'

\*\*\*

As countries go, Scotland was small: drivable. Where I was headed wasn't far, but it was a world away from Glasgow.

On the other side of Biggar the road followed the valley floor between rolling hills covered, in parts, with forests of fir trees and the occasional white blur of a farm cottage on the distant slopes. A fast-flowing stream, bubbling over rocks, raced to join the River Tweed and unfamiliar names like Romanno Bridge and Dolphinton came and went. So did the rain, sometimes so hard the windscreen wipers couldn't cope and I had to pull in until it eased off.

I stopped to enjoy a long disused water mill at Blythe Bridge, then carried on, until the crumbling stones of Neidpath Castle told me I hadn't far to go.

In Peebles, I parked on Tweed Green and got out of the car. A chill wind made me catch my breath and drew my attention to a group of volunteers piling sandbags along the bank to prevent the river from over-flowing into the row of cottages facing it. The

Tweed was running high. Above the men, dark clouds said their work might be in vain.

McMillan had suggested we meet in the Cross Keys in Northgate – wherever that was – despite the weather, plenty of people were about. Two women, hurrying to get home, told me to take a left at the end of High Street. The hotel, they assured me, was easy to find.

When I got there, a bearded man poured the coffee I asked for while I read the history of the inn framed on the walls. The Cross Keys was built in 1693, and it had a ghost.

Behind me a deep male voice said, 'Meg Dodds.'

I turned to face whoever had spoken and found a tall man unbuttoning the camel coat he was wearing; the kind you probably bought once in your life. I was willing to bet the label on the inside would say Gieves and Hawkes, or Crombie. When it was new, it would've been a fine garment. Now it was scuffed at the arms and the nape on the collar ran in different directions. Like its owner, it had known better days. A flash of blue silk lining caught the light and was gone.

He gave a lop-sided grin. 'Our ghost. Sir Walter Scott used to drink in this very pub and modelled Meg Dodds – one of his characters – on the landlady, Marion Ritchie. Marion is supposed to have died in mysterious circumstances in the Cross Keys and appears now and again, on cue, to scare the tourists. My mother worked here as a cleaner in the mid-seventies. She saw her many times and had lots of stories about Meg.'

'Really?'

'Absolutely. One morning, a chambermaid asked about the queer old biddy on the stairs, muttering to herself and rattling a bunch of keys. The poor girl fainted when she told her there wasn't anybody else in the hotel. Apparently, if Meg took against you, you were in trouble, but if she liked you, she could be very kind. Back then, furniture being moved around in the middle of the night was common. Nowadays, her speciality is electrical appliances. Turns them on and off, so they say.'

'Interesting. Do you believe in ghosts?'

'My mother certainly did.'

'What about you?'

He glanced away and didn't reply.

I held out my hand and introduced myself. 'Charlie Cameron. Colin McMillan?'

'Good guess. What can I get you to drink?'

'I've got one coming. What would you like?'

'A large Glenfarclas, if you don't mind?'

It was half past twelve in the afternoon. We hadn't exchanged much more than a couple of dozen words and already he'd told me something. McMillan was a drinker.

He pointed to a table in the original building and we sat down. A waitress brought my coffee and I ordered for him. He called her back to ask for water and I got a look at him. He was tall, at least six feet. Striding through Francis Fallon on his way to theatre, he would have been an imposing presence. Most of his hair had gone. What was left was going grey. His skin was smooth and unlined. The traumas of his wife's death and losing his livelihood weren't visible. He seemed relaxed.

'I know what you're thinking. A large one at this time?'

I lied. 'Not at all. Depends on the mood, doesn't it?'

'Couldn't agree more.'

So what was his mood today?

He began, as strangers do, with small talk. 'How were the roads?'

'No problem. As long as you aren't in too much of a hurry.'

The waitress brought his water. He poured a little into his drink with his left hand, measuring the amount with his eyes. I waited. He was right to not want to spoil a great whisky. Finally he said, 'All right. How can I help you?'

'When we spoke on the phone, I told you Gavin Law had gone missing and his sister has hired me to find him.'

'I understood he was in the states.'

'That was the plan but he didn't get there.'

'Strange.'

'When was the last time you saw him?'

'I suppose that must've been when I went back to work.'

'After your wife's funeral?'

'Yes.'

'That would be, what? Two months?'

'More like ten weeks.'

'Did you discuss Wallace Maitland with him?'

'We didn't discuss anything, as I recall.'

'Though you knew he'd lodged a letter of complaint. The day after you returned to Francis Fallon you did the same. I assumed you'd talked about it.'

'No. It wasn't a joint thing. I'd been on the point of reporting Maitland more than once. With Joyce dying everything got pushed to the side. My best memory is we only ever spoke twice on the phone. He called me when I was suspended to say how sorry he was.'

'Had you given him your number?'

'No. He must've got it from somebody at the hospital. I told him to watch his back. But we weren't in it together; you mustn't think that.'

'Was it just coincidence that you complained about the same colleague at the same time?'

'Well, coincidence isn't the word I'd use. Maitland isn't competent. It's as simple as that. We acted as concerned professionals.'

'Independently.'

The suggestion annoyed him. 'Yes. Independently.'

McMillan lifted his whisky; some of it spilled. What I knew about being a surgeon wasn't worth knowing though I guessed a steady hand was important.

'When was the second conversation?'

'New Year's Eve.'

He caught my surprise.

'He phoned me.'

'At what time?'

The surgeon thought about his answer. 'Eight. Eight-thirty. Something like that?'

'What did he say?'

'He was angry. More than angry. Outraged would be a better description. He'd seen what they'd done to me and still believed he could take them on.'

'Brave.'

McMillan disagreed. 'Not brave. Foolish. He was never going to win. But the rape allegation made him realise what he was up against.'

'Law told you about that?'

'It was why he called.'

'What was your reaction?'

McMillan shrugged. 'Shock at first. Then again, I knew from my own experience these people will stop at nothing.'

'Who do you mean?'

'James Hambley and Wallace Maitland.'

'What did you tell Law?'

McMillan lifted his whisky with his left hand, took a sip and put the glass on the table. 'Don't be their enemy. I told him to withdraw his complaint and get a new job. He said it was too late to withdraw because the suspension letter had already been sent out and, anyway, he had an interview lined-up. In America.'

I was sceptical. 'You know, as an outsider looking in it's difficult to believe Francis Fallon would go to these lengths to protect itself.'

He sat up straight. I'd touched a nerve. 'Really? Listen to me. I've seen this from the inside. When I complained I went up against them. The very next day they find somebody prepared to swear I told them I was suicidal, and suspend me. What does that look like to you?'

'You're saying they framed you?'

McMillan tried to be patient and didn't succeed. Resentment got the better of him. 'Framed me? They finished me. Do you imagine hospitals will be queuing up to hire a man with a question mark over his emotional stability? They bloody well won't.'

'You're fighting this, of course?'

He played with his glass. 'The hearing's on Thursday. I'm challenging it but I don't kid myself. I'll lose.'

'Why so certain?'

McMillan threw the last of the whisky over and wiped his mouth. 'My wife committed suicide. Naturally I was depressed. Still am. They're using that to imply I'm unstable. Unfit to be operating.'

'What proof do they have?'

'An anaesthetist claims I admitted I wanted to take my own life.'

He let what he'd told me sink in.

'They're investigating it. Doesn't matter. The outcome is irrelevant. Mud sticks. They discredit you and they win. And that's what I said to Law.'

'I assume you agree with him about Margaret Cooper?'

McMillan glanced towards the bar. 'I had nothing to do with the case though I know what happened. Maitland's first duty was to save his patient. He ignored that and she ended up…the way she ended up. Law knew Maitland had got it wrong and reported him. In the normal scheme of things their little enquiry ought to have been the end of it. Except Law wouldn't let it go.'

McMillan shook his head.

'Knowing what they'd done to me, that was a mistake.'

'You reckon they've pulled the same trick twice, only with him it was a rape allegation?'

He signalled to the waitress for another round. 'They used Joyce's death to smear me. With him…'

He hesitated and changed tack.

'You have to understand how Francis Fallon works. Hambley thinks he's on his way to a knighthood and he's probably right. He won't allow anybody to put that in jeopardy. If it means destroying a career or two, so be it. Wallace Maitland is his brother-in-law. Unfortunately, though he's been able to climb the greasy pole, hard choices are beyond him, which means, as a surgeon, he isn't very good. Margaret Cooper was a tough call and he blew it.'

McMillan had avoided answering my question. I gave him a second chance. 'They used your wife against you, so they're clever. But with him, why rape?'

Before he could reply the drinks arrived. We sat in silence while the waitress set them on the table. McMillan thanked her and faced me. 'As an obstetrician, Law was pretty fair. There wasn't much they could attack him on professionally. His character was something else.'

'His character?'

'If you ask around the hospital I think you'll find plenty of nurses willing to talk about him. I'm sure his sister is a very nice person but I'm told her brother wasn't. No doubt Hambley had heard the rumours and came up with the rape allegation.'

'Another trumped-up charge?'

McMillan went into the ritual with the water again. I thought he wasn't going to answer, then he said, 'There's Hambley and Maitland, and there's Law and me. The only one I can definitely vouch for is me.'

His face was flushed. Anger or alcohol, I wasn't sure. May be both. Either way, the meeting was over. McMillan finished his whisky, put money on the table and stood. I hadn't touched my coffee. He didn't notice.

'Where are you parked?'

'I'm by the river.'

Outside on Northgate, he closed his coat around him and we started walking down Main Street. For the moment, the rain had settled to a steady drizzle. We didn't speak until we reached the green and McMillan made a stab at being the charming man who had educated me about ghosts.

He shook my hand. 'Drive carefully.'

'I intend to. Thanks for talking to me.'

He walked away. After a few steps he turned. Rainwater ran down his cheeks and off the end of his nose. His nice coat might never recover.

'The day they suspended me, I knew I was beaten. Officially, I still have a job, but Joyce killed herself and somebody is going to swear under oath on a stack of bibles I admitted I was thinking about doing the same.'

Unhappiness rolled off him. I saw it as clearly as his mother had seen Meg Dodds. Old ghost stories and large whiskies in the middle of the day hid the pain. For a while. But he was a broken man and I couldn't begin to imagine what he was feeling.

'There's another possibility we haven't discussed. One you might need to consider.'

'What's that?'

'If Gavin Law has disappeared just when David and Margaret Cooper need him, maybe it's because he's guilty.'

# Chapter Twenty-Five

Across Glasgow, DS Geddes stood on the pavement at the bottom of High Street, outside the city mortuary, waiting for Constable Lawson to bring Anthony Daly's sister to identify his body. To his left, the blue face and gold hands of the Tron clock told him it was ten minutes to three in the afternoon. The horrific scene at the bridge felt weeks rather than hours ago. It had been a long day, and it wasn't over.

Lawson had stayed with Cissie and performed well. Being near somebody who had lost a loved one was difficult but Geddes' cautionary words to the young policewoman had found their mark. The world could be an ugly place where people did terrible things to other people and to themselves. Learning to detach wasn't just a question of being professional; it was essential if you were going to survive in the job. On the phone, the officer calmly reported the early stages of grief and agreed to meet the DS at three. Geddes was impressed. Lawson was going to be all right.

In the car, Cissie Daly looked out at Glasgow and saw nothing. She'd stopped crying and sat silently playing with her fingers. The police car turned left at the cathedral, headed down the hill and stopped at the lights on Duke Street. Cissie Daly did her thinking out loud.

'I'll have to give his season ticket away.'

She turned to the constable.

'Do you ever watch football?'

'Not really.'

'Don't you have brothers?'

'No. Just sisters.' Lawson had two brothers; both Rangers supporters.

'So it wouldn't be any use to you?'

In the circumstances, it was a silly conversation to be having. Cissie was trying to make sense of life without Tony. At the mortuary, the constable helped her out and Geddes joined them.

'Sorry to ask you to do this today. It won't take long.'

'Has to be. Better to get it over with.'

DS Geddes had been to the city mortuary more times than he cared to remember. It wasn't the way they showed it on television. Nobody would be drawing back a white sheet to reveal the deceased. The viewing room was small, a few chairs in front of a screen set into the wall. Cissie Daly stood between the officers as it flickered and filled with her dead brother's face. Cissie tensed. For a moment she swayed. The constable laid a steadying hand on her emaciated arm.

'That's him. That's Tony.'

Geddes led them back to the car. 'Are you up to giving us a statement, Miss Daly?'

Cissie was confused. 'A statement? What about?'

'It would help us piece together your brother's movements prior to his death.'

She hesitated. 'I suppose so. If you think it's necessary.'

'We could go to the station and do it just now. Get you a nice cup of tea.'

Why did everybody keep giving her tea? She wanted to be left alone to come to terms with the fact that Tony wouldn't be coming home. And to search for the missing Buckfast. Lawson took her to an interview room and waited for the DS to arrive. Geddes began by establishing the background of their relationship before moving on to how the dead man had appeared recently.

'When did you last see your brother?'

'Yesterday. He left the house in the afternoon.'

'Did he say where he was going?'

'I assumed he was going to the City Chambers.'

'Was he worried or depressed? How did he seem to you?'

'No. He was fine. Heard him whistling in the bathroom. Tony always whistled when he shaved. It's my birthday soon. He told me he was going to surprise me.'

Daly had certainly delivered on that.

'So he was all right? No health worries? Money worries? Nothing like that?'

'He was a councillor so we did okay financially. I don't understand why he would kill himself. He was happy.'

'Your brother wasn't married. Did he have a girlfriend?'

She shook her head. 'He wasn't interested in women. Not since the divorce.'

'He was divorced? When?'

'Twenty years. More.'

'Any children?'

'Weren't together long enough. It was a mistake from the start. I don't see how this helps.'

'Was Tony a heavy drinker?'

The vagueness of the response told the DS what he already knew.

'He liked a drink; he wouldn't deny it.'

'We expect the post mortem to show your brother had been drinking heavily at the time of his death. That's why I asked if he had something on his mind.'

'He was fine. Just his usual. Easy-going. Playing his music.'

'What music did he listen to?'

'Country and Western. Real music, he called it.'

'Who were his friends?'

Cissie struggled to explain the dynamics of her brother's life. 'The council kept him too busy for friends. Sometimes meetings go on to all hours. Tony said it was a young man's game.'

'There must have been some. Other councillors?'

'He was pals with Lachie Thompson. Mentioned him a lot. Apart from that there was nobody. Except me. We looked after each other.'

She spoke to the constable. 'I'd like to go home now if that's all right.'

Geddes sympathised. Cissie was holding up well but it wouldn't last. He'd seen it before – a period of almost unnatural calm then grief arrived like a storm and blew the facade of normality away.

'Have you someone you could call?'

'Tony was all I had.'

Geddes didn't voice what he was thinking. An FLO – Family Liaison Officer – was only assigned when a murder had been committed. DI Barr was convinced Daly killed himself so his sister would have to depend on the kindness of a neighbour. Otherwise she'd be spending the longest night of her life alone.

'Okay. Give us fifteen minutes to get this typed-up then you can sign it and we'll organise a car for you. You've got my card?'

'Yes.'

'You might remember something about Tony. If you do, call me.'

Lawson took the woman's arm and led her to the door. Cissie straightened her back and held her head high in an effort to salvage some dignity. It was a good try.

The constable said, 'I'll wait with her 'til the statement is ready and see her home, if that's all right, sir. Get her settled.'

DS Geddes nodded and pulled Lawson aside. 'The wine. Put it back.'

\*\*\*

The drive back from the borders was uneventful. Late afternoon. I had the road to myself. On the horizon, dark clouds heavy with more rain scudded towards me. With luck I'd be in Glasgow before they arrived.

Meeting McMillan had been interesting. At one point, the bitterness he had to be feeling came through. Otherwise I'd found him remarkably candid. So far, the people I'd spoken to were either for Gavin Law or against him. McMillan struck me as being neither. Praise and criticism were offered in equal measure: Law was a pretty fair surgeon with a less than wholesome reputation as a womaniser that wasn't a secret.

Before I left, in almost the same breath, he'd made two suggestions: the rape allegation could be something James Hambley had invented to keep Law from causing trouble for his beloved Francis Fallon. Or, Law was guilty and had gone into hiding leaving the Coopers high and dry.

I liked Colin McMillan though I wouldn't want to be him. Whatever he told himself, he was drinking too much and, in the rain, on the banks of the Tweed, it was clear the man was dying of loneliness.

My mobile rang and a voice with an accent that wasn't from north of Hadrian's Wall said, 'Charlie?'

'Yeah.'

'It's Alile. Do you remember me?'

She couldn't be serious. It wasn't every day you met a goddess.

'I've been asking people around here about Gavin if you're still interested.'

In her, yes. In Gavin Law, not so much. This woman from Africa could be a movie star. I pretended my mind was on the case and tried to be cool. 'Sure. I can use anything you can tell me.'

'Good. Are you around? I'm finishing at four. Fancy a coffee?'

The clock on the dashboard told me it was three-forty-five. The city was thirty minutes away and rush hour traffic would swallow me up.

'Great idea. Where do you want to meet?'

'Was thinking of Sonny and Vito's in Park Road.'

'What time?'

'Four-thirty sound all right?'

'Perfect.'

'Okay.'

For the rest of the journey, my foot was hard on the accelerator while my brain processed images of a beautiful Malawian female who wanted to have coffee with me. At ten past the hour, I arrived at Newhouse and joined the motorway and the stream of cars heading into the city. The rainclouds I'd seen in the distance had taken a different direction – the sky was a brilliant blue – and

I almost persuaded myself I was going to make it. Then I hit Junction 16 and crawled my way past the Necropolis, the Royal Infirmary and on to Charing Cross, cursing my stupidity.

I could have suggested five o'clock. What difference would it have made? Instead, I'd chosen to make it difficult for myself and race like a madman across the country.

Alile was leaving Sonny and Vito's just as I turned into Park Road. When she saw me she smiled. 'They're throwing me out. They close at five.'

'Are you hungry?'

'I am a bit.'

'There's an Italian deli on the corner. Want to give it a go?'

'Why not? I thought you weren't going to show up.'

'Traffic.'

Inside Eusebi, a waitress took our coats and gave us menus.

Alile said, 'What do you recommend?'

'Everything's good here. If you like pasta, try the Yesterday's Lasagna.'

We ordered a bottle of Gran Passione Veneto Rosso to wash it down and launched into conversation that had nothing to do with missing obstetricians and everything to do with chemistry. Alile was the most beautiful creature I had ever seen: her dark eyes looked deep inside me and her smile made me want to kiss her and not stop. Eventually, with most of the red wine gone, the reason for meeting finally got mentioned. Not by me.

Alile ran a finger up and down the stem of her glass. 'I told you I'd checked Gavin out before I agreed to go with him to his sister's on Hogmanay. Some of the girls were against it. Said it was a bad idea. He had a reputation for being a bastard with women.'

'Yes. You thought he was brave because he'd made an official complaint against a colleague.'

'Did I say that?' She laughed a laugh that had more than a touch of Gran Passione about it.

'You did.'

'Then I suppose I must've felt it. But I hadn't heard about the rape allegation. After you left I asked a couple of nurses. None of them knew what I was talking about.'

'And what do you take from that?'

She turned her palms towards me. 'I think it's strange. You'd have to work in a female environment to get it. Everybody knows or wants to know everybody else's business.'

'It isn't just women who gossip. Men do, too.'

'But some women are on a mission. Secrets are almost impossible, and a secret like that... With the best will in the world, not a chance. Especially if a doctor was involved.'

'You're suggesting what?'

Alile shrugged. 'It would be a scandal. We'd have newspapers outside the main door and people queuing to sell the story. Even if they don't know anything they'd make it up because money was involved. That isn't happening.'

'So, in your opinion...'

She interrupted me. 'I don't believe it.'

***

Andrew Geddes was reading Cissie Daly's statement for the second time when DI Barr stuck his head round the door. The inspector flashed a smile which the DS assumed was an attempt at friendly. Geddes didn't return it.

'Just staying in touch with the troops. That go okay, did it?'

'As well as you'd expect. The poor woman's in shock. Doesn't know what's hit her. It'll be a few days before reality sinks in. Then she'll go to pieces. Seen it too often.'

'And – don't tell me – Anthony was a saint, am I right?'

Barr's cynicism annoyed his sergeant.

'Sinner or saint, he was her brother. The only relative she had in the world.'

Empathy wasn't Adam Barr's thing.

'By the smell off him and the look of her I'd say they were boozing buddies. So of course he'll be missed.'

'She loved him if that's what you mean.'

The rebuke bounced off.

'Wasn't worried about anything as far as she knew. Can't believe he'd take his own life. No relationship dramas. No money troubles.'

''Course not. He was a councillor. Up to his ears in brown envelopes.'

'She claims he wasn't a morbid drunk. Her brother was a happy guy.'

'Yeah. We saw him. Did he look happy to you? There's a line when the high becomes a low. Just how low depends on the individual and the amount, and that guy had had a skinful.'

'His sister knew him better than anybody. She could be well wrong but something about Tony Daly's death rings false.'

'Listen, Geddes. Happy people don't jump off bridges with a rope round their neck. This is simple. Write the report and move on.'

The door closed. The DS stared at it. Somewhere along the line Barr had skipped the class on the importance of considering alternative points of view. His mind was made up and had been from the moment he'd stepped out of the car on the Queen Margaret Bridge. The DI had the confidence of a man who didn't know what he didn't know. Barr was on a mission. Unfortunately for Cissie Daly, finding out what had happened to her brother in the early hours of a freezing morning, wasn't part of it.

# Chapter Twenty-Six

Caroline Law was due feedback from me. But what did I have to tell her? Opinion on the missing doctor was mixed and none of it matched her vision of the brother she had raised and clearly idolised. Even Alile, the Malawian nurse who was prepared to go out with Law because she thought standing up to the hospital was brave, admitted he had a reputation for being a creep.

A creep with a conscience. An attractive combo, apparently.

Colin McMillan saw his colleague differently and wasn't a fan. In the Cross Keys, he'd been at pains to stress his complaint about Wallace Maitland's competency was made independently. It seemed important to him. He'd been irritated when I'd suggested otherwise. Later, I understood why. While he was prepared to concede Law was a good enough professional, even admiring – at least initially – the stand he'd taken after Margaret Cooper's surgery went wrong, he hadn't liked him and said so. Chalk and cheese. Two very different characters arriving at the same conclusion about a reckless colleague.

Andrew Geddes hadn't come back on the credit cards used in London. I assumed because there was no new financial activity to report. And I'd fared no better on the seventh floor of Francis Fallon where James Hambley had been guarded and superior and told me little about Law but plenty about himself.

All in all, it boiled down to a whole lot of nothing.

Caroline Law wasn't a woman who let the grass grow under her feet; she'd proved it before and did again now. The door opened and in she came with Dean as usual lurking in the background. Whatever her weaknesses, lack of assertiveness wasn't one of them.

'I'm disappointed. I expected to hear from you.'

No apology for barging in. No 'Mr Cameron'. We were past that.

'Take a seat. I was just about to call.'

I may as well have said the cheque was in the post.

'We judge ourselves by our intentions. Unfortunately, the world judges by our actions. Are you any closer to knowing what has happened to my brother?'

'I wish I had better news. Any news even. But Gavin seems to have disappeared off the face of the earth.'

I brought her up to speed on everything I'd done, leaving out the criticisms she wouldn't want to hear. It wasn't enough to satisfy her. She wanted more and there wasn't more.

'So that's it? That's the end of it?'

'No, I'm still working.'

'The woman who accused him of raping her, who is she?'

'Francis Fallon won't comment.'

'And you accepted that? Surely I'm entitled to be told?'

'And you will be if it becomes a police case. We should be grateful it hasn't gone that far.'

Caroline was a difficult lady to please. 'Nevertheless, I'd prefer to know.'

We were off the point. I'd seen her in tears before; she was heading there again. Dean gently massaged her shoulders and whispered reassurance. Caroline couldn't see his face. Just as well.

'So what am I supposed to do? Pretend Gavin never existed? Forget about him?'

'I'll keep going. He might turn up. People do.'

'And in the meantime?'

I didn't have an answer for her.

She put her hand in her bag and threw something onto the desk.

'What's this?'

'The key to the flat. Got it from the cleaner.'

'I've already been there. We went together.'

'Go again. I'll come with you.' Caroline was back in the land of crazy expectations.

'Ms Law…Caroline…I don't think you understand.'

She wasn't listening. 'It's simple. Start again. From the beginning.'

'Look. I said I'd keep going. But…'

She didn't let me finish. 'This may be just another case for you. For me it's my whole life.'

Dean hadn't contributed a word to the conversation. I wouldn't be getting any help from that direction. It didn't stop me trying.

'Dean. Speak to her.'

He shook his head. I was on my own.

'If it's money, don't worry. We'll pay whatever it costs.'

'It isn't. It's about false hope. I'm not done with the case. There are still a couple of avenues left to explore. You have to accept I can't find what isn't there. I'm not a magician.'

'Yes, but…

'Gavin might not want to be found. Or he's on the run because the allegation against him is true. Maybe he did it. Are you ready for that? Ready to accept he's a rapist?'

I was trying to shock her and succeeded. Dean nodded approval. I was doing them both a favour and he knew it.

I lifted the key. 'Okay, but you're not coming with me. And I'm warning you to prepare yourself. Your brother may just show up or I might find him. Either way it could be the beginning of a new nightmare. What he's accused of is very serious and disappearing doesn't look like the action of an innocent man, does it?'

At that moment, though she was getting what she wanted, Caroline Law hated me.

'The hospital will protect its reputation at all costs. Don't forget, Gavin's the main witness for the Coopers against it and Maitland. Without him, the case will fail.'

Dean said, 'Do you think Francis Fallon has something to do with this?'

Owen Mullen

'Anything's possible. I'm pointing out how complicated it is, and – however it turns out – there might not be a happy ending.'

Caroline's expression wouldn't have been out of place on Easter Island. Suggesting her darling brother was less than perfect marked me as an enemy. 'I'm not a child. Please don't treat me like one.' She stood. 'Dean, take me home.'

At the door, she fired a final question, dipped in acid. 'Will I have to chase you for an update or will you let me know this time?'

'I'll be in touch.'

Two minutes later Pat Logue arrived. 'That the sister? Her face could curdle milk.' He drew air in through his teeth. 'Be a brave man who'd take a broken pay packet home to her. Bring her tea wallah with her, did she?'

'Partner.'

'Yeah. Junior partner by the look of him.'

He sat down and drummed his fingers on his knee, obviously ill at ease. Pat Logue wasn't backward at coming forward. I was used to these visits. Usually they involved money. An advance, as he liked to call it. This was a different Patrick.

'I need to speak to you. Got a problem.'

My guess was he'd tossed a coin – and I'd lost. 'Speak away.'

'It's personal. Man to man.' He hesitated, reaching for the words and not finding them. 'I'm havin' trouble.'

'Kind of trouble?'

'With…the one-eyed snake.'

At first I didn't understand what he was telling me. Then I did and held my hands up to stop him giving details that might scar a more sensitive mind. 'Hold it! When you said personal I thought you meant it was a secret.'

'It is.'

'Patrick, I'm not qualified to help with this. You need to see a doctor. You and Gail have been married a long time, involve her. She'll be sympathetic.'

'Gail doesn't know.'

I wasn't following. 'So if Gail doesn't know how is it a problem?'

'It's in the early stages.'

Very early, if his wife hadn't noticed.

'Want to nip it in the bud before it gets a hold. Thought I could talk to you…you know…maybe…compare things.'

'Whatever else, that won't be happening. If there really is a problem, my advice is to discuss this with somebody who understands. No need to be embarrassed. Sexual difficulties are common.'

'What will I say?'

'Explain what's going on. Describe the symptoms.'

He was brightening. 'Just say it?'

'Right.'

'In my own words.'

'Absolutely.'

'Reptile dysfunction.'

\*\*\*

Apart from mail on the mat inside the door, Gavin Law's flat hadn't changed. Based on the stale smell, nobody had been here. I opened a window to let air in and stood in the middle of the lounge, studying, for the second time, where Caroline's brother lived. On my previous visit the décor had struck as a deliberate attempt to impress. Laid-back and up-market. The kind of place young women might find appealing and, from what I'd heard, there had been plenty of those.

I wandered through the empty rooms, opening drawers and looking in cupboards, discovering nothing. Wasting energy on a dead end so I could tell Caroline Law I'd tried. Great detective work, it wasn't.

Ten minutes later, I was back on the street and heading to my car. It hadn't been a complete bust. The mail included two letters from British Telecom: phone bills. When Law left he'd taken his mobile, and although he wasn't answering now I was about to find out who he had spoken to in the hours before he dropped out of sight.

Pat Logue was halfway through a pint and gave a doleful nod when he saw me. Given his problem, I could have suggested he kicked the booze on the head for a while to see if it made a difference to his "reptile dysfunction." Somehow that little experiment hadn't occurred to him. Too radical.

In the office, I put Gavin Law's mail on the desk and took another look. There were three circulars from charities, an electricity bill, two from BT and a card with a nativity scene and South African stamps from somebody called Sonia that hadn't made it in time for Christmas.

I'd pass them on to his sister but not before I checked out the phone bills. The landline was unused – no calls had been made from it – the mobile was another story: a lot of calls though only to the middle of December. No bloody good. I buzzed the bar and asked Patrick to come up.

'Something to take your mind of things.' I passed the BT bills to him. 'We can forget the landline. It's the mobile traffic I'm interested in. Get me a record of every call between then and now.'

'Doesn't your pal normally do this for you?'

He meant Andrew Geddes.

'Andrew isn't in a good place right now. Better not to ask him for anything. You can handle it, can't you?'

''Course. Just wondered why you were coming to me.'

On his way out I said, 'And don't worry about that other thing.'

'Which other thing? Oh, you mean the horizontal hokey-cokey? All good things come to an end.'

'Doesn't have to be like that. Had an idea.'

'Yeah?'

'Cut back the drinking. Worth a try.'

He wasn't impressed. 'No offence, Charlie. I'm worried. So if you haven't got a serious suggestion, say nothing. Know what I'm talkin'?'

# Chapter Twenty-Seven

Andrew Geddes was at his desk when the call came through. The thin voice on the other end of the line was agitated, almost shouting. He struggled to make sense of the words.

'Rome! It was Rome. He was taking me to see the Vatican.'

Geddes recognised who was speaking and sat to attention. 'Cissie? Hold on. What're you talking about?'

'For my birthday. The surprise. I knew it. I knew it.'

The DS listened for the slur of alcohol and heard none. 'Slow down and start at the beginning.'

She breathlessly blurted out her news. 'Next week I'm fifty. Tony had planned something and wouldn't tell me what it was. Wanted it to be a surprise. It was Rome. Three days. The tickets arrived in the post. I've always wanted to go to Rome.'

'When did he book it?'

'I've no idea.'

'Which travel agent did he use? It'll be on the folder.'

Geddes heard her put the receiver down. Half a minute later she was back. 'Thomas Cook.'

'Gordon Street? Tell me the booking number.'

The DS guessed Tony Daly had protected his sister from the practical demands of living. The blind drunk leading the blind drunk, DI Barr might say.

'It's not here.'

'Look again.'

'Could this be it? TCRCB451121'

The DS wrote it down.

Cissie was satisfied with the reaction she'd provoked in the policeman. 'Told you he wasn't depressed. Maybe now you'll believe me.'

Geddes reply was gentle. 'I do. I do believe you.'

The manager at Thomas Cook was reluctant to discuss a client's booking over the phone until Geddes told him who he was.

'When was the booking made?'

'Two days ago.'

The same day Anthony Daly had hanged himself.

'Who dealt with it?'

'Let me check. Sharon processed it.'

'Is she there? I'd like to speak to her.'

'Yes. I'll get her for you.'

The DS explained to Sharon what he wanted to know. 'You must take a lot of business, especially at this time of the year. Do you recall anything about who made the booking?'

'As a matter of fact I do. His mind was made-up from the start. Rome or nowhere. The trip was a surprise for his sister's birthday.'

'He told you that?'

Her laughter came down the line. 'While I was doing the paperwork he threw in his life story.'

'Anything else?'

'Yes. I had to go over the details with him three times.'

'Is that usual?'

'No.'

'Then why do it?'

'Because he was drunk.'

'How drunk?'

'Not falling down. Happy. Started singing "the Celtic song."'

'He wasn't depressed?'

'Far from it, wouldn't shut up. Has something happened to him?'

***

DI Barr was in a meeting so Geddes waited in his office. Eventually, Barr breezed in looking pleased with himself. His smile faded when he saw his colleague. Barr had his own ideas on management and an open-door policy wasn't one of them.

'DS Geddes. What can I do for you?'

'There's been a development in the Anthony Daly case.'

'Hasn't come back to life, has he?'

'His sister called. She's just discovered her brother booked a weekend in Rome as a surprise for her birthday.'

The DI took his coat off, hung it up and sat behind his desk. 'So?'

'Daly made the booking with Thomas Cook somewhere after four o'clock on the eleventh. Approximately twelve hours later he went over the bridge.'

Barr stared at Geddes; he didn't want to hear this.

'They remember him.'

'Find that hard to believe. One guy arranging a city break and they remember him? Are they sure?'

'He was drunk. Not raging drunk but affected.'

'And your point is?'

'Well, sir. Don't you think it's odd? Booking a holiday isn't exactly the action of a man intending to do himself in. If the trip was just for the sister, okay. A grand farewell gesture. But it was for both of them.'

'I see what you're getting at. Because he was in high spirits in the afternoon it proves he didn't commit suicide.'

'That's how it looks to me.'

Barr leaned back in his chair and put his hands behind his head. Geddes felt a lecture coming on; he wasn't wrong.

'Didn't you just tell me he died approximately twelve hours later? Doesn't that raise the question of what happened to him in those twelve hours?'

'He was in great form. Talking his head off. Singing football songs.'

'That only shows how drunk he really was. And if that was him then, what state was he in later? We know he was blotto.

We smelled him, remember? Obviously his state of mind changed in the hours before his death.'

DI Barr was enjoying his display of superior reasoning. 'If you had even a shred of evidence foul play was involved I might consider it.'

'But sir, with respect…'

'As it is, we now have a witness who can testify that late in the afternoon, prior to his demise, Tony Daly was well on the way. The guy was an alkie. Emotionally unstable. Mood change is a symptom. High as a kite one minute, in the depths of despair the next. He offed himself. It's an absolute no brainer.'

Geddes realised he wasn't going to win. Better to let it go. That wasn't who he was. 'Nevertheless, those twelve hours are unaccounted. We don't know where Daly was, what he did or who he met. Anything that can help us answer those questions should be pursued.'

Barr focussed on a mark on the wall over the detective's shoulder; he was losing patience. The DS seemed to have forgotten just who the senior officer was. He had been given the opportunity to make his case and failed. Now he needed to accept it and leave.

'The PM is scheduled for tomorrow. I'm requesting a two-man job. One pathologist might miss something. Two won't. We owe it to his sister.'

Before Barr started on the fast-track career path he'd been warned about the resistance he was liable to meet along the way. Old-school coppers, stuck in a rut, disguising their resentment of younger smarter men behind phony objections to closing cases. Keen to drag every enquiry out no matter the cost in man-hours and money. The new breed of policeman in the twenty-first century realised resources were limited and used them accordingly. Evaluating cost against results. Geddes didn't understand that kind of logic. The guy was dinosaur. A plodder at best. The force would work more efficiently without his kind.

'I can tell you that's a non-starter. I'm prepared to go with the pathologist's recommendation but I'm not willing to second guess the autopsy and squander the budget on something as clear-cut as this case.'

DI Barr stood. He'd heard all he was going to hear.

'I'm well aware you don't approve of my appointment. In your position I'd probably feel the same. But know this, DS Geddes, as long as I'm in charge we'll be doing things my way, and that doesn't include throwing money around like fucking confetti. Your enthusiasm is appreciated and your objection has been noted. Now start acting like a policeman and, for Christ sake, get a grip. Request denied.'

\*\*\*

The sound of laughter followed Kim Rafferty from the lounge, where the clown was making balloon animals and giving them funny voices. The kids loved it. The adults – most of them mothers – were enjoying it too. Sean hadn't been pleased when she'd told him Rosie's first birthday party was on a Saturday afternoon; he liked to do as little as possible at the weekend, although it never worked out that way. Something always came up that couldn't wait.

At the study door, she hesitated, remembering the scene on Hogmanay. Since then she'd avoided physical contact with her husband. Sex she wanted, but not with him.

Inside, Sean, was on the phone – as usual – his feet on the desk. He smiled when he saw her and waved her in. He was drinking.

'So the pieces are in place, Emil. All we have to do is let it play out. Of course, you're welcome. I told you I wouldn't let you down. Speak soon.'

He hung up and spoke to his wife.

'How's it going in there? Is Rosie enjoying herself?'

Typical Sean. Paying was his contribution. He didn't know how to be a father. Hardly a surprise, considering where he'd come from. Kim had heard the stories about his family. Jimmy Rafferty had been a vicious man and a cruel parent. Living with him must have been a nightmare for his sons.

Her reply was tart. 'Why don't you join us and find out?'

'I will. Had to make that call.'

'There are children in our house and you stink of booze. You should be a part of it. You're spoiling our daughter's first birthday. She nearly didn't survive, Sean. We almost lost her. I never forget and thank God every day.'

Rafferty stifled his irritation. There was more to being grateful than ice cream and face painting. If Kim only knew she'd realise he hadn't forgotten. Taking care of business allowed her to do the nice things – like organise parties.

Lately, they hadn't spent much time together; that would change now the project was no longer uncertain. He'd been on edge. Pre-occupied. Impossible to be any other way with Emil Rocha on his back. For the moment, the Spaniard was satisfied. Reporting the obstacles had been removed put a smile on everybody's face. Sean Rafferty imagined a long and successful partnership with Rocha and it would happen, as long as he continued to deliver. Rochas' wealth, earned from drugs, was the key to turning Sean Rafferty into a legitimate operator. Respectable would take longer. One day people would hear the name Rafferty and not think of Jimmy.

One day. But not one day soon.

In the lounge, it was time for the cake. Kim lifted Rosie out of her baby-walker and held her level with the single candle, all the time encouraging her.

'Okay darling. Big blow. A big blow.'

The flame guttered and died. Everybody cheered and clapped. Rosie clapped too.

Kim took the cake back to the kitchen and sliced it. The other mothers put pieces on paper plates and carried them into the party along with cartons of juice.

Sean didn't appear for the photographs. Kim wiped cream off Rosie's nose and cradled her while the photographer encouraged the little girl to look at the camera.

'Say cheese.'

An hour later, the house was a battlefield and the birthday girl had fallen asleep. Kim took her upstairs to the nursery, put her down and sat for a while in the rocker. Sean was somewhere. She didn't know exactly where and didn't care. Rosie had had her party – the first of many – a miracle in itself. And her daughter wasn't the only one who was tired: Kim was exhausted.

She went next door, lay on the bed and closed her eyes. In seconds she was asleep. Hot breath on her neck wakened her. Whisky breath. Kim rolled away from it. A rough hand dug into her shoulder and pulled her onto her back. It was dark. She couldn't see his face but she knew what he wanted.

'No. No. No!'

Kim kicked out and heard her husband swear.

'You bitch! You fucking bitch!'

She scrambled to get away. Sean grabbed her hair. She screamed and clawed at the blackness around her. Her nails found his cheek and raked it. His turn to scream.

'Shouldn't have done that. Shouldn't have…'

'Please, Sean! Don't!'

He tore her blouse away, punched her and dragged her to the floor. She tasted blood. Somewhere in the distance Rosie was crying. He hit her again and again, kicking her until the pain was too much and Kim blacked out.

When she came to she was naked and alone. She stumbled to the bathroom and turned on the light. Kim's usefulness to her husband was her looks so he hadn't struck her face, but red welts marked her throat where he'd tried to strangle her. Bite marks on her breasts showed how out of control the attack had been. Yellow, blue and black bruises covered her body, and when she breathed, a sharp pain lanced her chest: cracked ribs.

She lay on the bed and the hellish images returned. He'd come after her and she'd refused him. This was what became of a wife who rejected a Rafferty. Kim was in shock – too numb for tears. Then she remembered Rosie had been crying. Moving was painful; instinct drove her. At the door she stopped.

The nursery was empty; her daughter wasn't there.

She heard Rosie's voice and struggled downstairs, every step an effort of will.

They were on the carpet by the fire, Sean pretending to be a monster and Rosie giggling when he made wild faces. Anyone who didn't know better would see a happy scene. Deep scratches ran from under his eye to his jaw.

Sean spoke to the child. 'Look, Rosie. Here's your mummy. Here she is.'

He beamed with pride at his happy family, as if nothing had happened and a terrifying realisation gripped Kim. There was no pretence here. She was married to a monster who got what he wanted and never took no. Even from his wife.

# Chapter Twenty-Eight

Patrick Logue knocked on my office door and came in. My first thought was the gee-gees must have pulled for him; he seemed pleased with himself.

'Finally managed to back two winners in a row?'

The bold Pat was unfazed. 'That day will come, Charlie. Stand on me.'

'If it isn't the horses, what?'

He handed a sheet of paper with four mobile numbers on it across the desk.

'Got this from the guy I know.'

I recognised Alile. The others weren't hard to guess: the hospital, Law's sister, and Colin McMillan.

Patrick said, 'The last three were called on Hogmanay. Since then, nothing.'

'And now it's unobtainable.'

'Yeah, but who doesn't have a mobile these days?'

An easy question to answer. 'Somebody who doesn't want to be found, or… What else have you got for me?'

'This Maitland character lives a strange life. Ask me where he was last night.'

'Okay. Where was he was?'

'Same place he was the night before. And for once, the beer wasn't bad.'

***

The sign on the exposed brick façade outside Blackfriars in Merchant City said "Free House," and promised real ale and good food. I got there at seven o'clock, ordered a bottle of Brooklyn lager – brewed in the "Vienna" style, whatever that was – and sat at a table against the wall. I'd heard plenty of talk about Wallace Maitland without ever seeing him. Patrick's description of the obstetrician – fifty, greying hair and bulldog jowls – fitted half of the men in the pub. When I asked him for something more, he'd shrugged.

'What can I tell you? Imagine a guy who claps when the plane lands and you won't be far away.'

'That the best you can do?'

'Likes to sit at the bar. Soon as he opens his mouth you'll know it's him.'

'He's well spoken?'

'No, Charlie. You're well spoken. He sounds as if he got his accent from eBay.'

The early evening crowd was made up of professional types, who preferred telling each other lies about how well they were doing to going home and guys who were picky about what they drank. In a corner, two men loudly argued politics next to a scruffy geezer wolfing down some kind of pie and scribbling on the back of a beer mat.

At twenty past seven, Wallace Maitland came through the door and took a stool at the bar. Patrick thought his voice would single him out. For me it was his walk: the purposeful stride of a man in no doubt about his place in the world. I pictured him marching along the corridors of Francis Fallon with a posse of eager young doctors trailing in his wake, hanging on his every word.

He was dressed as you'd expect someone making the money he was making to be dressed: charcoal grey three-piece suit, white shirt and a tie that had to be Armani. The obstetrician was tall, though the waistcoat straining against his belly told a tale of life choices not rooted in moderation.

He ordered in the deep plumy tones his parents had paid for by the term and Pat Logue found so objectionable. 'A large Chivas and a half of lager.'

No "please."

The woman serving put the drinks in front of him. He handed over a twenty- pound note and, if he thanked her, he must have whispered it. Maitland stared at his reflection in the mirror behind the gantry and sipped his Chivas. No one spoke to him, an arrangement his body language suggested he preferred.

I'd learned early to let other people squabble over the moral high-ground; some might have a legitimate claim. I hadn't met them. In this business, non-judgement was the only game in town, and while knowing you were on the side of the angels was a good feeling, innocent or guilty was somebody else's call.

Perhaps it was seeing what this guy had done to Margaret Cooper that changed my mind. Something had, because I disliked him before we'd even spoken. There was an air about him, a disdain that made me want to wipe the superior look off his face.

He was on his second double whisky when I slid onto the stool beside him and asked for another bottle of Brooklyn. Out of the corner of my eye, I saw him draw away. It couldn't be the beer – who could disapprove of a beer brewed in the "Vienna" style – it had to be me.

I watched him in the mirror. Surely he should be taking his wife to dinner or playing with his grandkids? But he wasn't. He was here. My previous attempt to speak to him had gone nowhere. In a public place it was harder to escape without causing a scene. The theory was about to be tested. At moments like this I envied Andrew Geddes his authority. If he wanted to interview someone it happened. This man could tell me to fuck off and there was nothing I could do. My best hope was the pressure he must be under.

I introduced myself and saw him tense. 'Mr Maitland. I called the other day. You hung up on me. Charlie Cameron. I'm working for Gavin Law's sister. As you're aware, her brother has disappeared.'

His reply was what I expected. 'Are you following me? You are, aren't you? I don't know and I don't want to know. I couldn't care less.'

'Really? I find that hard to believe. Law intended to testify against you and the hospital. You'd be finished in medicine. Might even go to jail. Without him you're in the clear.'

Over the years, I'd learned actions – in this, case reactions – were more revealing than words. Maitland had been caught off-guard. His eyes darted to the door and back to me. Close-up, his face was marked by broken veins and his posh voice rose an octave as he protested.

'Ridiculous! You know nothing about it! Gavin Law was a womaniser who crossed the line and sexually assaulted a member of staff. He ran away rather than face the consequences of his actions.'

'Did he? How convenient for you.'

Maitland's sneer didn't convince either of us. 'Convenient or not, it's the truth.'

Conversation in Blackfriars had stopped. Maitland pushed past and I followed him into the street.

'You'll have to talk to me sometime. Me or the police, Wallace.'

'Fuck off!'

He ran towards Candleriggs as if the hounds of hell were chasing him. I let him go. Caroline Law's brother was missing and I was no nearer uncovering where he was. But I'd learned something. Wallace Maitland was scared. As frightened as anyone I'd ever seen.

*\*\**

DI Barr wasn't in the habit of visiting his officers. When he wanted to see them, they came to him. The police, like the military, was founded on chain of command and Barr believed informality blurred the line. Today, he was making an exception.

His expression told the DS it wasn't a social call. Geddes was making a list of people he would interview if he was allowed to conduct a proper investigation into Anthony Daly's death. So far, it was a short list. Barr tossed a dark green folder on the desk – the PM report. Geddes pushed it away and kept writing. The DI swallowed his irritation and added the reaction to the catalogue of insubordination in his head. Unlike his DS, it was a long list.

Barr spoke as if he was making an important announcement. 'Death by asphyxiation and venous congestion.'

Andrew Geddes didn't lift his head.

'Weather conditions make an accurate assessment difficult but the pathologist estimates death occurred between four and six hours prior to the body being discovered. So somewhere between twelve midnight and two a.m.'

Geddes put his pen down and turned a blank stare on the detective inspector. Barr flashed a smile closer to a grimace, determined to press his point. 'I'll give you the highlights, shall I?'

'Don't bother. I'll take your word for it. Sir.'

The senior man was incensed by the dumb insolence coming back at him. It wouldn't be forgotten. He ran his finger down a page, stopping at a comment couched in language they would both understand.

"The ligature mark encircled the neck except for the area where the knot was located, resulting in a furrow in the tissue that had hardened and dried due to the abraded skin and corresponded to the material used; in this case, a rope."

He glared at Geddes. 'Need I go on?'

It would have been wiser for the detective sergeant to play the game. Barr hadn't come to tell him what they already knew; he was looking for confrontation. Geddes recognised the signs and could have defused the situation if he'd wanted to. He didn't.

'We seem to be talking at cross purposes. None of what you've said surprises me. My question has always been how he managed it, given the amount of alcohol he'd consumed. Said yourself he smelled like a brewery.'

DI Barr fought to keep his frustration in check. 'He was drunk. Of course he was drunk. Nobody in their right mind would do what he did.'

'Agreed. How did he get to the bridge?'

'A taxi could've dropped him off somewhere close.'

'With a length of rope underneath his arm? And nobody notices?'

DI Barr shook his head. 'You know, Geddes, I feel sorry for you. It has to be complicated. Dirty work at the crossroads or you're not happy. For Christ sake, the guy was out of it and decided to go for it. Maybe planning it for months but couldn't find the courage.'

'So he books a trip to Rome for him and his sister? I don't buy it.'

'At that moment, he was still sane. People swallow a handful of sleeping pills, go to bed and never wake up. During the day they take their kids to the zoo. A waitress at Pizza Express remembers them laughing and singing songs. From the outside, everything was fine. Everything was good. Except it wasn't.'

'Daly's sister told us he had no worries. Her brother wasn't depressed.'

Barr screwed up his face. 'Oh, please. We both saw her. She isn't sure what day of the week it is.'

'Not true. And okay. He brings the rope with him and has it ready. In the state he was in, how did he tie it to the lamppost?'

The DI leaned on the desk and towered over Andrew Geddes. He'd had enough. 'Listen. If it looks like a duck, walks like a duck and talks like a duck, it's probably a fucking duck. You're old-time gut instinct's over-rated.'

'Instinct doesn't come into. I'm asking questions that need answers. The TOX will show he was incapable. Which means somebody else was there.'

Barr waved his arms in the air; almost shouting. 'Let's call it like it is, Geddes. This isn't about some drunk doing himself in. You've resented me from day one. Don't deny it.'

The DS forced himself to stay calm. 'Again, not true.'

Barr thumped a fist on the desk, his face ashen with anger. 'You're setting yourself up to look like the dedicated detective railing against bureaucracy, while I'm the Uni pen-pusher, when in fact, you'd happily spend valuable police time and money on an obvious suicide instead of effective police work.'

Geddes sat back in his chair. 'You're right, I do resent you. But not for the reasons you think. My priority never changes. It was why I joined in the first place. I want to catch criminals. You're more interested in staying within the budget and getting a pat on the head from the DCI. Well done, Adam. Good boy. Tick.'

Barr stepped back as if he'd been slapped and Geddes realised he'd gone too far. A difference of opinion was one thing, insulting a superior officer was something else. 'I'm sorry. That was out of order. I shouldn't have said it. Can we at least wait for the TOX?'

The DI ignored him. 'We're waiting fuck all. Anthony Daly took his own life on the Queen Margaret Bridge between the hours of midnight and two a.m. Case closed.'

He lifted the PM folder, started to leave, and changed his mind. 'It seems you're a man who likes questions. Well, here's a question you'd better find the answer to pretty bloody quickly. Are you sure you're cut out for this job? Just because you've been doing it since Christ left Dumbarton doesn't mean shit. The world's changing and, from what I've seen so far, you're struggling to cope.'

He opened the door.

'You're a dinosaur, Geddes. And we don't need a TOX report to tell us what happened to them, do we?'

# Chapter Twenty-Nine

Jackie Mallon's voice was edged with concern. 'Charlie? Sorry to call you at home. Need your help.'

'What's happened? Are you all right?'

'I'm fine. More than can be said for your mate.'

'Patrick?'

'Andrew.'

'What about, Andrew?'

'He's drunk.'

'How drunk?'

'Drunk drunk. Fourteen out of ten on the Mankometer, as your other mate might say.'

'Don't let him drive. Take his keys off him. Get him a taxi.'

Jackie could come to those conclusions without me telling her. That wasn't why she was calling. 'It's beyond that. He's in the bar, giving everybody their character. I'm going to have to call the police. Last thing I want to do except we are trying to run a business. He's a good customer and all that but...'

She left the rest unspoken. Getting arrested for being drunk and disorderly wasn't going to do much for Andrew's career. In the background I could hear a man yelling obscenities

'That him?'

She sighed. 'That's him. And, pal or no pal, it can't go on. How soon can you be here?'

'I'm on my way.'

The drive through the city gave me time to think. Andrew hadn't been himself lately. I'd been aware the job was getting him down though I hadn't realised just how bad it had become. Geddes was a hard man to get close to; he only ever told you what he wanted you to know. Behind his gruff exterior was a grouchy bastard, waiting to get out, and he discouraged personal questions. I parked on Ingram Street and quickened my pace. Jackie could have called Sandra. Instead, she'd called me. Things must be bad.

And they were.

Andrew was standing in the middle of the bar and didn't see me come in. It was Saturday night; the restaurant was fully booked. He mimed pulling an imaginary pin from an imaginary grenade and lobbing it into the diners.

'Here! Share that amongst you!'

Jackie made a gesture with her hand across her throat that told me whatever goodwill Geddes had been travelling on, had been used up. Drunks could be an amusing distraction. By the look on the faces of the people in the bar, Andrew had stopped being funny.

I tapped him on the shoulder. He turned and I knew Pat Logue's Mankometer was going to need recalibrated. Manky didn't cover it. Geddes could hardly see. His eyes narrowed, searching for focus. When he realised who it was, he threw his arms round me like a long lost brother.

'Charlie! Charlie boy! What're you drinking?'

He dredged change from a trouser pocket and gave it to me. Half a dozen coins landed on the floor and rolled in different directions. Andrew didn't notice.

'Get whatever that'll buy you. And one for me while you're at it.'

The money wasn't enough for a packet of crisps let alone a round.

'You don't need any more. I'm taking you home.'

Not what he wanted to hear. In an instant his mood altered. He pushed me away, snarling and swaying unsteadily. 'What the fuck're you talking about? I'll go when I'm good and ready to go and not before. Who do you think you are?'

'Somebody who can see you've had enough.'

Andrew balled his fits. He wasn't a violent man but he was in a bad place and spoiling for a fight. His coat hung awkwardly, half on half off, the tie he'd been wearing probably lying in a gutter somewhere.

White foam gathered at the corners of Andrew's lips. He tried to wipe his mouth on the sleeve of his coat and missed. His voice slurred, hoarse with unhappiness, speaking to everyone and no one; a mix of rage and tears, unrecognisable from the tough-as-old-boots Glasgow copper who'd seen it all and survived.

The story came out in a spittle spray. 'Had enough? Tell you what I've had enough of – bastards telling me what to do. Sick of it. Sick!'

'Andrew, listen…'

He grabbed hold of a chair to save himself joining the coins on the floor. Angry eyes blazed; he had me in his sights. Friendships die on nights like this.

'Charlie. Charlie Cameron.' He grinned ugly and introduced me to the crowd. 'Charlie's a clever cunt. Smart arse extraordinaire.'

The booze was doing the talking and it had plenty to say. Tomorrow Andrew would be sorry. Now he was cruel and unstoppable. His next shot tested the years we'd known each other.

'Still looking for your sister, Charlie? Still looking for Pamela?'

It was time to end this. I moved towards him. He swung a punch that hadn't a snowball's chance of connecting but sent him off balance and knocked a table over. I caught him on his way down and hauled him upright.

Jackie was beside me. 'I'll send one of the waiters with you to get him home.'

'No need. I'll manage.'

'Where are you parked?'

'Outside.'

Jackie Mallon ignored me and with the help of two guys from NYB, we poured Andrew into the back seat, unconscious. On the drive to my place he slept. When we arrived in Cleveden Drive the fun began. Geddes was heavy. By myself it took twenty-five minutes to get him inside. At one point he tried to kiss me; for me, the worst thing he'd done all night. In the lounge I dropped him on the couch and sat listening to him snore, wondering what had inspired a blow-out this big.

I threw a quilt over him and went to bed. In the morning maybe he'd tell me what had inspired such craziness. When he'd lifted the first whisky, for sure, he didn't have good times on his mind.

Then again, it was Andrew – a guy who only told you what he wanted you to know.

I wouldn't hold my breath.

***

Noises from next door told me the barroom brawler was awake. The hiss of the kettle meant moves were being made. I could only guess at how Andrew was feeling and thanked God it wasn't me. Sometime after nine, the noises stopped and I tip-toed through to see how he was doing.

He wasn't in the lounge; he was in the bathroom. I knocked on the door. 'Andrew, are you okay?'

His bad tempered response reassured me the real Geddes was back. 'What do you think? No, I'm not fucking okay. I'm dying.'

Normal service had been resumed.

When he eventually made it back to the couch, I was waiting with coffee, water and Alka Seltzer. He'd aged about a hundred years: deep lines that hadn't been there before ran from his mouth to the end of his chin, matched by the ones under the sunken hollows where his eyes used to be. He gazed at me like a lost soul, put his head in his hands and tried to make some sense of how he'd woken up on my couch in my flat.

'Christ. Never been as bad as this.'

My lack of sympathy surprised him. 'Serves you right. Lucky you're not in the cells.' That got his attention. 'How much of last night do you remember? Honestly.'

He squinted at me, probably because looking hurt too much. 'Started early in a pub in Finnieston. Stayed there most of the afternoon then moved on to the BrewDog.'

'And after that?'

'Vroni's.'

'West Nile Street. Wine on top of whisky. Not wise. Then where?'

He dragged a hand across his face, pulling his features to one side as if they were made of Plasticine. When he let go they slowly reformed like a movie special effect and I was looking at Andrew's grandfather again.

Geddes was prepared to let me believe Vroni's was his final destination except I knew better. He didn't add another name to the pub crawl until I asked again.

'Then where did you go?'

He tried to bluster his way out of admitting he wasn't sure, pretending to lose it with me. Or maybe he wasn't pretending.

'Christ sake. What is this, the Spanish Inquisition? Can't you see I'm suffering?'

'Take the Alka Seltzer, you'll feel better.'

He took a sip and glared at me. 'You're a smug bastard, did I ever tell you that?'

'That and more, Andrew. After Vroni's, where?'

He kept his eyes on the carpet. Eventually he gave me the answer he didn't want to give. 'It's a blank but I'm guessing you're going to tell me. Did we meet in a pub or did I roll up here uninvited?'

I considered my reply. 'A bit of both.'

'See what I mean about smug?'

'It's a long story but you aren't well enough to hear it.'

I stood. If he wanted into NYB again, the whole sorry tale would have to come out. At the very least, Jackie was due an apology. I wouldn't bet on her accepting it. She was fiercely protective of what she'd built and, no matter what lay behind it, the scene last night had been unacceptable. Anybody else would be waking up in the cells this morning. Giving Andrew a blow-by-blow about what he'd done would be kicking a man when he was down. I satisfied myself with lesser tortures. Cruel but fun.

'So, breakfast?'

The thought was enough to turn his stomach. He groaned. 'Don't mention food. Said it before but this time I'm serious. I'm never drinking again.'

I'd seen Andrew Geddes low before. During his divorce from Elspeth he'd lost the place on occasion and tried to escape the bitter battle it became by drowning himself in booze. This was different.

'Hair of the dog any good to you?'

He turned his face away as if he'd been slapped, then thought better of it. 'Take more than the hair. I'm rough as a badger's. What've you got?'

'Can probably manage a whisky.'

'Make it a glass. A beer too, if you have one.'

So much for never again.

I brought him the drinks and watched the alcohol undo the damage it had caused. Eventually Andrew said, 'You didn't answer my question.'

He meant about where we'd met.

'Didn't I? I thought I had.'

He studied me, reluctant to push it, yet unable to hold his anxiety in check. 'Bad was I? Doesn't surprise me.' He shook his head. 'I was poison from the off yesterday. Heading for the rocks from the minute I got out of bed.'

'What's the problem?'

Geddes sipped the whisky and washed it down with beer. 'I've come to a decision, Charlie. I'm resigning from the force.'

I hid my surprise. 'Why would you want to do that?'

Andrew toyed with the amber liquid in his hand. 'Wanting to doesn't come into it. I'm past my sell-by date. Happens to the best of us if you hang around long enough.'

'Says who?'

'Says me. Never over-stay a welcome. I'm a dinosaur, apparently.'

'Yeah, but you were a dinosaur to begin with, what's changed?'

He didn't smile. 'The Service. More about politics than policing these days. I don't fit in so I'll leave it to those who do. Good luck to them.'

Being a policeman had been Andrew's life ever since I'd known him. He was a great detective. If he was a dinosaur, then Glasgow could do with a Jurassic Park-load. Something or someone had set him down a dark road where the consequences of acting in haste hadn't been thought through. Andrew needed the police force as much as it needed him. Without his job he'd be lost.

He finished the whisky and grimaced. I pointed to the empty glass. 'Same again?'

He hesitated. 'I'm starting to come round.'

'Is that a refusal?'

'See what I mean about smug. Can't help yourself, can you? Just a splash.'

'One condition. Tell me what's brought this on. And leave the self-pity out of it.'

'In that case, you better bring the bottle.'

***

I came back from the kitchen with his splash and what was left of the lager and waited for him to begin. For a while he stared at the floor. When he finally spoke the poor-me act was gone.

'You know about the body on the Queen Margaret Bridge?'

I nodded. 'Councillor found hanged. You're on that?'

'Yes and my boss is falling over himself to file it as a suicide and move on.'

'But you're not convinced?'

'I've no idea one way or the other. I'm absolutely convinced we haven't properly considered the facts. Barr had his mind made up from the start. At the scene, the smell of whisky off the dead man would've knocked you down. That was all he needed to call it suicide.'

'Is there evidence that says it wasn't?'

Andrew snorted. 'We may never know. Barr refuses to investigate anything that might put a hole in his conclusion.'

'Why would he do that?'

'Because he's determined to impress the powers-that-be by not wasting resources on open and shut cases.'

'So you're butting heads. Been there before, haven't you?'

Andrew finished the lager and read the label. 'Camden Hells. Trust you to have la-di-da beer.'

Not long ago, he hadn't been so critical.

'Remind me to have Tartan Special in for your next visit. Go on with the story.'

'The TOX report will show Anthony Daly was paralytic. So my question is: how does a man who can hardly stand get to the bridge and secure the knot to a lamp-post?'

'Had to have help.'

'Correct, Charlie. And get this. The same day, the guy books a weekend in Rome for his sister's birthday.'

'Just for her?'

'No. For both of them.'

'Then he wasn't thinking about topping himself.'

'But proving it would mean man-hours, so Barr wants it put to bed.'

Geddes paced the room, animated; talking with an intensity that had risen from nowhere; punching a fist against his palm as he reaffirmed his belief in why he's spent over twenty years of his life as a copper.

'Budgets are important. Resources are precious. But policing isn't a business and can't be treated like a business. It's about people. Not hitting targets and ticking fucking boxes.'

He sat down and covered his face with his hands. 'I interviewed the sister. She's heart-broken. Hard enough to look somebody in the eye when you're sure you've done your best. When you haven't…'

'So where has it been left?'

'Case is closed. Barr's a man in a hurry. Climbing the ladder. Christ only knows what his next half-arsed attempt will be.

Accused me of resenting him, can you believe it? I'm a dinosaur because I want to do the job the way it should be done. It's time to go time, Charlie, and yesterday I realised it.'

He waited for my reaction and I let him. 'Two things jump out at me, Andrew. First: Barr's right, you do resent him. His career is going somewhere and yours isn't.'

Geddes exploded. 'Resent him? He's a dick! Couldn't detect his way out of a paper bag.'

'Bottom line: he's giving the orders and you're taking them. Of course you resent him. Anybody would. He'll be in your universe for five minutes before he's off and another educated incompetent tosser takes his place. Unless you get motivated and go for promotion yourself.'

He glared at me but I had his attention.

'You're the man who caught Richard Hill. That should've taken you to detective inspector. It didn't because you don't want it. Until some rookie starts teaching his granny to suck eggs, then you want to throw in the towel.'

'What's the second thing?'

'If the case is closed the police are no longer involved, right?'

'Right.'

'Have somebody else investigate it.'

'Like who?'

'You're looking at him.'

'Thought you had your hands full with the missing doctor?'

I corrected him. 'Gavin Law. And he's an obstetrician. Hands full isn't how I'd describe it. Nothing else on the credit cards, is there?'

'Haven't heard anything.'

'Then it's going nowhere. Can't keep taking Caroline Law's money. So...'

Andrew threw his arms round me and hugged me so hard I couldn't breathe. I was back to being a long-lost brother. His hangover was on the run.

'Well make a start tomorrow. I'll come to your office and we'll go over it in detail.'

I stopped him. 'That could be a problem.'

'How?'

'Jackie will tell you when you see her.'

Andrew didn't understand; he soon would.

'My advice: buy the biggest bunch of flowers you can find and wear a suit of armour.'

\*\*\*

I closed the blinds in the spare room and left Andrew to die in peace. On my way out, I closed the door. I had a call to make and Gavin Law's sister wouldn't be happy with what I was going to tell her. The brother she blindly adored was still missing and I hadn't come close to discovering what had happened to him. Asking who had the most to gain with him out of the picture was a legitimate question. Of course, Wallace Maitland and the hospital weren't exactly heartbroken; they were off the hook. But, if the rape allegation was real – and if it was true – disappearing suited Law as well as any.

On the other end of the phone, Caroline sounded calm. More measured in her reaction than I'd expected. Some of the fight had gone out of her.

'I'm disappointed, of course, though I understand. You've done all you can, so it's over for you.'

The standard lines, meant to reassure, rang hollow even to me; they were all I had.

'The situation may change. Gavin might show up on your doorstep or call.'

She seized the straw and clung to it. 'At least I'd know he was all right.'

Before the conversation ended I gave Caroline something else to hold on to. 'For the record, I haven't found anybody at Francis Fallon who's even heard about the allegation against him.'

She reverted to type. Prickly, righteous and completely invested in the myth she'd created. 'I've been saying that from the beginning. Why doesn't anybody listen?'

# Chapter Thirty

David Cooper opened his eyes and stared at the ceiling. Night-time was the worst. But last night had been the worst of all. Margaret hadn't settled easily. It had taken almost an hour of holding her hand and whispering to her before she finally went to sleep. That and an extra pill. Three. More than advised on the dark brown bottle. More than the doctor prescribed.

But what was his opinion worth?

What were any of their so-called professional opinions worth?

The hours when Margaret slept were his. Sleeping himself would have been the best idea. David didn't sleep. He couldn't. He preferred to drive, though preferred wasn't the right word because he wasn't certain it was a choice. Perhaps in the beginning it had been. At any rate, he frequently found himself in the same place, often with no memory of the journey. Drifting between realities. Slowly becoming someone he didn't know, didn't recognise. It was stress, wasn't it? Had to be. Otherwise, what did that make him?

That wasn't the end of it. Taking care of Margaret took most of the day and, on the outside, David knew he must seem a dutiful husband, dedicated to looking after his invalid wife. Of course, it was true, he was.

Thank God they couldn't see inside his head. What went on in there was beyond imagining. Dark thoughts. But last night… last night they'd been close to being more than thoughts. Dark actions.

Gavin Law was a bastard who'd strung them along with his promise of support, then fucked-off out of it and left them – him – powerless against Francis Fallon and that other bastard,

Hambley. Cooper hated all of them though his deepest loathing he kept for the obstetrician responsible for turning Margaret into a vegetable.

Wallace Maitland.

Cooper didn't understand how the man lived with himself knowing what he'd brought about. Margaret was breathing but she wasn't alive. The woman he had known died on that operating table. In a different way, David had died there too.

Yet, the people responsible were walking around: living their lives, fucking their wives, while he changed nappies.

# Chapter Thirty-One

I recognised the coat before I recognised the man waiting to cross the road at the entrance to the Necropolis on Wishart Street. When I realised who he was I pulled in and opened the window on the passenger side.

'Colin. Thought it was you.'

He bent to see who was speaking and when he realised it was me he took off a glove and offered me his hand. His cheeks were flushed and his eyes were red and watery from the cold.

McMillan smiled. 'Charlie Cameron. What a coincidence.'

I leaned across to talk to him. 'What're you doing in this part of the world?'

'It's Thursday. Francis Fallon. Remember?'

I'd forgotten.

'Spent the morning there.'

'Of course? How did it go?'

He shrugged. 'As expected. They'll let me know.'

'Can I give you a lift? Where's your car?'

'Parked it and got a taxi. Didn't feel like driving.'

'Then get in.'

At the bottom of John Knox Street, opposite the imposing Victorian facade of the derelict Great Eastern, I turned right into Duke Street. Most of the snow had melted and the roads were wet. McMillan was quiet; more reserved than how he'd been in Peebles when he'd told me ghost stories. I guessed he was still recovering from what had to have been a painful experience in the West End of the city, and tried to cheer him up.

'What's the plan? Heading back to the borders right away or do you have time for lunch? My office is above an American diner. I can recommend the cheeseburger.'

'That's very kind of you. I haven't had breakfast. Not sure I could eat.'

'Something light, maybe?' I sounded like my mother.

'All right, I'll try. Nothing to be gained by starving myself to death.'

We left the car in the usual place and walked to NYB. Out of the blue, he said, 'I'm selling the house in Bearsden. Too many memories. It was always more Joyce's than mine. Peebles suits me better. There's nothing in Glasgow for me now.'

'You're assuming they'll find against you?'

He sighed and kicked a stone into the road. 'Certainty I imagine. Eddie Connelly – the witness who claims I told him I was suicidal – was very believable.'

Inside NYB, Jackie wasn't around. Pat Logue was. At the bar. Where else? In an uncertain world it was reassuring to know some things never change. A waitress gave us menus. McMillan ordered soup and I joined him. When we were settled I returned to the conversation.

'This witness.'

'Eddie Connelly.'

'What would be his motive?'

He considered his reply. 'Perhaps along the line he's fucked-up and this is the price for saving his arse. To be honest I don't care. All I can tell you is he'd read the script and delivered it word perfect. It was impressive.'

'Does this guy have an axe to grind?'

'With me?' He shook his head. 'Wouldn't have thought so. Hambley will be behind it.'

'I've met him.'

'Of course you must have. What did you think of him?'

It was a good question. 'Confident. Arrogant.'

'He's that all right. And ambitious, too. Further down the line he can hear the Queen saying "Arise, Sir James."'

'Is that a possibility?'

'Yes. If he keeps his nose clean, why not? Better chance of it happening if he wasn't tied to that brother-in-law of his. He's a ticking bomb.'

The soup arrived and for a few minutes we gave our attention to it. My companion found an appetite he didn't know he had and emptied the bowl. When he was finished, he took up from where he'd left off.

'Any luck with Law?'

'Not so far.'

'Apart from Hambley who have you spoken to?'

'His sister, of course. A nurse he was supposed to be going to a party with on Hogmanay and cancelled. And David Cooper.'

'So you've seen his wife?'

'Have you?'

'No, thank God.'

'Awful. Really awful.'

'And really sad. Law was determined to make Maitland pay for the suffering he'd caused the family. Admire him for that if nothing else.'

The implied criticism didn't escape me.

'How long will you keep looking for him?'

Another good question. 'Depends. Unless something turns up it's going nowhere.'

McMillan called the waitress over and ordered cheesecake and coffee. He'd been hungry after all. 'Prefer a large whisky but I'm driving. Don't want to lose the license on top of everything else.'

Hardly a consideration for a man on the edge of suicide.

Pat Logue passed on his way to the toilet. I introduced him. They shook hands. Normally Patrick had plenty to say, even to a stranger. Today he struggled with even the smallest of small talk, a Patrick speciality.

When he left, McMillan said, 'So it's true. Always going to be somebody worse off than you. Didn't expect to meet him today.'

I understood where he was coming from. Pat Logue's mood was bluer than the lining of his coat. I'd met Colin McMillan by chance and it had been pleasant enough. Given the stress he was under he was coping better than I would have.

He insisted on paying. 'The least I can do. Your shout next time.'

Out on the street, I remembered where he'd been when I ran into him. 'What were you doing at the Necropolis? Francis Fallon is miles away?'

He pulled his coat around him against the wind. The middle of the day and already the temperatures were heading south. 'Just walking. Needed to be alone.'

'Plenty of alone in there.'

He smiled. Almost. 'Wonderfully ornate tombs in there. Mini-architecture, really. Lovely sentiments on some of the headstones.'

Where McMillan was, the cemetery might offer him something. I nodded as if I understood, glad I hadn't a clue.

'When we were talking about the Coopers one of the inscriptions struck me as particularly poignant. "Save your tears for the living".'

'Appropriate.'

'Isn't it.'

We shook hands. McMillan seemed reluctant to leave. 'Look Charlie, I haven't been completely honest with you.'

'How so?'

'Gavin Law. I didn't much take to him. He was…let's say he wasn't like you.'

'I'm guessing that's a compliment.'

He pulled on his gloves. 'Clumsy, but yes it is.'

'Caroline thinks the sun shone out of him. From what I've gathered a few people wouldn't agree.'

'Maybe so. Maybe so.' He put his hand on my arm. 'Look, you stopped when you saw me at the Necropolis. I appreciate it. And for suggesting lunch. I feel better about things. Let me return the favour. Next week. Be an excuse to cook a proper meal. Not Glasgow. You come to me in Peebles.'

'I'd like that.'

McMillan walked away and the sad poetic inscription he liked so much came into my head. "Save your tears for the living." I'd promised to let David Cooper know if I found anything to give him hope. It didn't look like I'd be making that call.

# Chapter Thirty-Two

James Hambley stood at the window on the seventh floor of Francis Fallon with his hands behind his back and gazed out across Great Western Road. A cold sun shone in a clear sky. The hearing had gone exactly as he'd wanted. At first, McMillan responded calmly to the questions put to him; he seemed relaxed. But when asked about his wife the veneer fell away. His voice became quiet and Hambley had strained to hear the words. Listening to him relive the night he'd found her was difficult; watching him fight to keep control of himself made everyone in the room uncomfortable. McMillan's hands trembled and he was forced to pause mid-sentence more than once. The trauma of that terrible discovery was still with him physically. Before their eyes the colour drained from his face and he became pale and thin; the camel coat he was wearing might have belonged to someone else. By the end he'd looked defeated.

Surprisingly, with his professional future on the line, he'd chosen to appear without legal or union representation, flatly rejecting the accusation against him. His denial was convincing. Unfortunately for him, not nearly as convincing as the testimony of Eddie Connelly; the anaesthetist he had foolishly confessed his state of mind to. Connelly was neither an enemy nor a friend, just someone who happened to be there when he broke. His recollection of events was unclouded. Both men were scrubbing-up when McMillan suddenly became distraught. He'd put his head in his hands and started to cry, saying he couldn't go on. According to Connelly, he apologised almost immediately and pulled himself together.

But it was after they left the operating theatre that the real bombshell hit. McMillan apologised a second time, adding he didn't know how he was going to survive without his wife.

'I'm at the end, Eddie. I'm suicidal. I don't want to live anymore. Really I don't.'

There was no coming back from a statement like that.

Hambley told a silent McMillan he would hear from the hospital in due course though nobody was in any doubt about the outcome.

A bad day for Colin McMillan but a good one for Hambley and Maitland.

With McMillan discredited and Law missing, Wallace Maitland's decision to try to save Margaret Cooper's womb would stay unchallenged. He was in the clear. Francis Fallon was in the clear.

The knock on the door brought Hambley back into the present. Wallace Maitland smiled a weak smile and came in.

'How did it go?'

'Depends, Wallace. If it's your pathetic skin we're talking about, it couldn't be better though Colin McMillan and David Cooper might disagree.'

'You know what I mean, Jimmy.'

'Indeed I do. You're asking if it's alright for you to carry on putting the hospital and its patients in danger. And the answer is no it fucking-well isn't!'

Maitland blanched under the force of the attack and Hambley realised again that Martha's brother-in-law was a coward.

'You're off the hook. At least until they find Law's body. Credit where credit's due, Wallace. You're not good for much but killing people and hiding them seems to be a talent I wasn't aware you had. Not very useful in the normal run of things, then again, as you demonstrated on Hogmanay, you can never be certain when it's going to come in handy. No idea how you pulled it off. Or how long you'll get away with it.'

'Please don't joke. That isn't what happened.'

Hambley walked to his desk and sat down, enjoying Maitland's anxiety. Let the bugger stew; he deserved it. 'Isn't it? Sure about that, are you?'

'It isn't funny and I haven't.'

'See me laughing, do you?'

Maitland ran a hand through his thinning hair. Uncertainty had aged him. 'I still can't remember a bloody thing. But have a heart. Do you seriously believe I'm capable of murder?'

Hambley shot him a look. 'Perhaps Margaret Cooper's husband is better placed to answer that.'

'Oh, come on. The bleeding wouldn't stop. I was unlucky.'

Maitland was a self-absorbed child. Even now his concern was for himself. They both knew his mistake had left Mrs Cooper as close to a vegetable as made no difference.

'Unlucky? You really are a despicable bastard. You make me want to be sick.'

'That isn't what I meant.'

'Yes it is. Your only concern is how this is going to affect old Wallace. Everything and everyone else comes second.'

'I'm concerned. Of course I'm concerned. Who wouldn't be? But you've got your own motives. Francis Fucking Fallon! First, last and always!'

Maitland was shouting. Somebody would hear. It was time to get him out of the office. Hambley held up his hands to quiet the bloody idiot down. 'Listen. And let's not bullshit each other. Today went well for us. Without Law's testimony, the Coopers don't have a case against you or the hospital. McMillan isn't a threat. Nobody will be interested in anything he has to say. He's history. That leaves you.'

'Tell me what you want me to do, Jimmy. Tell me.'

'As far as the world is concerned, you've done nothing wrong. We're two doctors down. We need you on the list.'

Maitland nodded like a faithful dog. Hambley pointed a warning finger at him.

'But I meant what I said about the drinking.'

'I know. I've cut it way back.'

'Good. Now, fuck off.'

# Chapter Thitry-Three

The ten o'clock mass on Saturday was a celebration of Tony Daly's life – according to Father Scanlon. Those who'd known him could have told the clergyman it was a life of few pleasures, most of them from a bottle.

Daly had been a season ticket holder at Parkhead and in the packed congregation, half a dozen Celtic players mingled with the less famous. Glasgow City Council was well-represented. Seventy-five of the seventy-nine elected members were there, even if one of them was in a box. And on Clyde Street, outside St Andrew's church, hundreds of ordinary people gathered to silently pay their respects.

All things considered, not a bad turnout for a nobody.

Two rows from the front, Lachie Thompson had listened to trite anecdotes about how happy and fulfilled Daly had been and wondered who they were talking about. If you believed the waffle coming from the pulpit, Tony was a quiet modest man, devoted to his family. His selfless work on behalf of the community was talked up. No mention of the reprimand for over-charging his expenses, the two drink driving convictions that had cost him his license, or the years of alcoholism.

When he'd fallen from the Queen Margaret Bridge with the rope round his neck, he was intoxicated and, therefore, not able to judge his actions. A strange piece of good fortune. Mortal sin was avoided. Tony could have his big send-off.

Thompson was invited to give a eulogy but declined. Rutherford took his place and spoke movingly about the colleague and the friend.

Lachie Thompson wanted to be sick.

The priest circled the coffin, sprinkling holy water and incense that caught in Thompson's throat. Finally, the procession left to

The Fields of Athenry – a favourite Tony had drunkenly belted out from his seat in the Lisbon Lions stand in better times.

At Lambhill cemetery, the sky opened and they finished what an East End gangster had started in the rain. At the head of the grave, under a black umbrella, Father Scanlon read from a bible in a flat monotone, lost in the open air, as the casket was lowered into the ground. Solemn faces watched it disappear, wanting it to be over so they could get out of the miserable day.

'May his soul and the souls of all the faithful departed rest in peace. Amen.'

Throughout the service, Daly's sister had quietly sobbed. Now the realisation she would never see her brother again overwhelmed her and she broke down, wailing uncontrollably. Sandy Rutherford offered a comforting arm. Her fingers dug into him, drawing strength, unaware of the part he had played in Tony's death.

When it was over, mourners hurried to their cars. Sandy Rutherford held back to console the pitiful figure of Cissie Daly, shaking her hand and whispering empty words.

Lachie Thompson walked on. He didn't have the stomach to face her. Rutherford ran to catch up with him. Since their last meeting in Baby Grand, the two men hadn't spoken.

'Lachie! Wait! When?'

'Ten days. The next meeting of the full council.'

'Are we sure it'll go through, Sean wants to know?'

'So it's Sean now, is it?'

Rutherford didn't respond. 'He wants to know, Lachie. Have we got the numbers?'

Thompson pointed over his shoulder to two grave-diggers shovelling muddy earth into the hole in the ground. 'For our sakes we better have.'

Rutherford nodded; he understood. 'Nice service, wasn't it?'

Thompson spat his disgust. 'You're kidding, aren't you? It was awful. Really awful. The priest might believe it was a celebration of Tony's life, but – in case you haven't noticed – he's still fucking dead.'

\*\*\*

A bunch of flowers in a vase at the end of the bar told me Andrew Geddes had taken my advice and made peace with Jackie. It would've been good to have been a fly on the wall to hear the brusque detective throw himself on her mercy, though whatever he'd said had worked because he was at a table, reading the *Herald* and dunking a bagel into a cup of coffee, looking like he didn't have a care in the world.

I knew that wasn't true.

Today was the first I'd seen of Jackie Mallon since Saturday night and whatever reception I expected, I didn't get it. She gave me a tight smile that said I wasn't her favourite person and went back to doing what she was doing, leaving the distinct impression she somehow held me responsible for Geddes' behaviour. I'd saved the situation but maybe in her eyes that meant guilt by association.

Andrew's greeting was reserved and his colour was better, improved from the angst-ridden wreck throwing-up in my bathroom. It took a minute to realise it was an act; he was pretending to be okay when, in fact, he was far from it.

I started brightly; brightly and naïve. This was Geddes. On a good day with him the glass was half-empty.

'So you and Jackie are all right, then?

He sifted through the newspaper with trembling fingers and spoke out of the corner of his mouth without so much as a glance in my direction.

'Joking, aren't you? She's a woman. Once you step out of line it isn't all right ever again with them. If you'd kept your nose out and let her get me arrested I'd be barred and better off for it.'

'You don't want that. This is your second home.'

'*Was*, Charlie. *Was* my second home. I'll be on probation for the rest of my life in here. Grovelling doesn't suit me. I was drunk. It happens.'

Andrew was re-writing history with him as the victim.

'Well, you were out of order. I mean, really bad. Can't expect relationships to go back to normal right away; it takes time.'

Geddes looked uncomfortable and I soon understood why.

'Jackie told me what I said to you. I'm sorry I was really messed up.'

'We're good. What about DI Barr?'

'I'm still thinking of resigning. Haven't ruled it out.'

Self-pity was running riot. I nipped it in the bud. 'Yeah, you have. I'm going to Cissie Daly's house as soon as Pat Logue arrives.'

Geddes' expression hardened. He spoke with the authority of someone used to being heard and became DS Geddes, the scourge of Glasgow's criminal classes. 'You know how I feel about that guy.'

I wasn't listening. In my flat the previous day we'd agreed two things. First, I'd go where the policeman couldn't and investigate Anthony Daly's death. Second, I'd do it my own way.

'How you feel is noted, Andrew, now let me get on without jumping in, eh?'

'He's a scallywag. Kick his granny if the price was right. Don't trust him.'

'But I do and that's what matters. Or we can forget it. Up to you.'

DI Barr was in a different league to Pat Logue when it came to which of them Andrew disliked most. Patrick was a petty crook whose time would come; Barr was trashing everything DS Geddes believed in. He turned the focus back to the case in hand and put aside his reservations.

'Sure you've got a hold on this? As it stands it's an awful lot of nothing. Beginning to agree with Barr.'

'Don't do that. To be able to discount suicide we need to discover why somebody would want Tony Daly dead. Maybe his sister can tell us.'

Geddes sighed. 'Good luck with that.'

At a minute to eleven, Pat Logue strolled into NYB and sat on "his" stool at the bar. He'd ordered a pint before I could stop him. Patrick had a golden rule that allowed him to justify his excessive habit: he never drank on Sunday night. In all the years I'd known him – with a few exceptions – he'd stuck to it. The spring in his step and the light in his eyes told me the golden rule was alive and well; he seemed fresh.

When he saw me, he smiled. 'Charlie, how's your luck?'

I ignored his bonhomie. Some of Andrew's negativity had rubbed off. 'Before you get started, we've got a job.'

'An earner on a Monday mornin'. Lead me to it.'

'Leave the lager. It'll be here for you when you come back.'

Pat Logue wouldn't be rushed. 'Edge-up, Charlie. Got to start the day right.'

'Five minutes, then.'

'Takes five minutes when I'm in the mood to taste it. Hold on.'

The pint disappeared and we were out the door. Patrick fell into step beside me. We headed for High Street and my car with him hurrying to keep up.

'Where's the fire?'

'You're very up-beat. Take it your problem has resolved.'

'Absolutely. All systems go. Know what I'm talkin'?'

Glasgow was under a post-festive cloud that would last until Easter eggs appeared in the shops. By now, credit card statements carrying depressing news had arrived and jolted the Christmas over-spenders back to reality. Most people fitted that category. Pat Logue's eagerness to help his ailing finances was a shared wish.

On Maryhill Road, I gave him the background: the body on the bridge; Cissie Daly, the weekend in Rome and DS Geddes' frustration that brownie points had replaced a real investigation.

Patrick looked out of the window and listened. When he spoke his first consideration mirrored Andrew's. 'And your pal's okay with me stickin' my nose in, is he?'

I told him the truth. 'Okay isn't exactly how I'd describe it, but he hasn't a choice. We work together. If he wants me he gets you. But remember, his career could be on the line so he expects absolute discretion, naturally. That has to be a given.'

Patrick nodded. 'Let me understand. This DI Barr wants to shut the case down and move on. Your pal...'

'He's got a name, Patrick. Could you stretch a point and give it to him?'

We reached the outskirts of Bishopbriggs before he replied. The animosity wasn't all on Andrew Geddes' side. Pat Logue had every reason to be wary of the DS whose sworn intention was to catch him with a load of knitwear that had never seen the inside of a shop.

'...Andrew isn't satisfied and you've agreed to investigate on his behalf. That about it?'

'That's exactly it.'

'Then, in a roundabout way, we're helpin' the police with their enquiries.'

'Yeah. You could say.'

He bit his lip. 'Never thought I'd see the day. If this gets out...'

Pat Logue lived in a universe beyond my understanding, a place where people were measured by a different standard. It hadn't occurred to me it would be a problem for him. In the passenger seat he'd gone quiet, perhaps reflecting on the impact to his reputation of collaborating with the other side. I glanced across the car.

'You okay?'

He took his time answering. 'Tell you this, Charlie, and I'll tell you no more. Don't go him myself but he's lucky to have you as a friend.'

Silence was the best option. I took it.

His next question surprised me and raised an issue I hadn't thought of.

'We don't know what we're gettin' ourselves into. Could be dangerous. Will that be reflected in the pay? Just sayin'.'

Patrick always had an eye on the money.

'We can discuss it later.'

'Later as in when? Hangin' somebody is serious shit. This Daly could've been into anythin'. Then again, maybe there's bugger all and your ...Andrew... is over-reactin'.'

'Isn't his style, Pat. Geddes is harder to impress than anybody I've ever met. Seen just about everything there is to see. His gut feeling is telling him something isn't right.'

'Startin' with his DI.'

'Absolutely. A bookworm promoted beyond his competence. Classic example of the Peter Principle. Throws his weight around and refuses to listen to more experienced officers, then pulls rank when they insist on doing the thing the way it should be done.'

'In other words, an arse.'

'An arse that has Andrew Geddes considering packing it in. Whatever your opinion of him is, I assure you he's a top-notch detective. Ever find yourself in trouble you want him in the boat with you.'

Patrick smiled. 'Not the kind of trouble I get into.'

He had a point.

I turned the car into Cissie Daly's street and stopped outside her house. According to Andrew, Tony Daly had been buried on Saturday so what state his sister would be in was anybody's guess.

'What're we lookin' for?'

'No idea. Just keep your eyes and ears open. Geddes said she hasn't a clue why her brother would take his own life. The tickets he bought for the weekend in Rome on the day he died convinced her. Refuses to believe it.'

Pat Logue fingered the goatee that made him look like the fifth musketeer. 'Easy to understand where she's comin' from. Not what you do if you're thinkin' about takin' a long walk off a short pier.'

We got out of the car.

'Remember, this woman is as fragile as they come. Probably was even before. She was hitting the bottle when Andrew arrived to give her the news about, Tony.'

'Any other family?'

'No. She's on her own.'

'Tough.'

I knocked on the front door. Half a minute later I knocked again. Cissie Daly wasn't expecting us; if she had somewhere else to go she might not be home. The sound of footsteps coming downstairs told us she was. A chain rattled, a key turned in the lock and a small woman blinked at two strangers.

The way Geddes described her, at the very least, Cissie had a drink problem. More likely, she was an alcoholic. I saw no sign of it. Her hair was combed. She was dressed and though her eyes were red, I guessed it was from crying. For certain, she would've done a lot of that with plenty more to come.

I introduced myself. 'Miss Daly. My name is Cameron and this is my associate, Mr Logue. I wonder if we could talk to you for a few minutes.'

'Is it about, Tony?'

'Yes it is.'

'The policewoman said you'd be back.'

'We're not the police. I'm a private investigator.'

That wasn't what she was expecting and she hesitated. 'So why're you here?'

'To ask you about your brother.'

Patrick said, 'Wish the timin' was better.'

Her face showed her confusion. 'I'm not sure.'

Pat tried again. 'It could be important, Cissie.'

She started to warm to him. 'Who did you say you were again?'

'Investigators. I promise we won't take up too much of your day.'

Cissie pursed her lips. 'Then you'd better come in.'

Andrew Geddes had broken the terrible news to her about Anthony in this very room, but now it was different, and so was she. There was no bottle at the side of the chair. Cissie was sober in spite of her grief, dealing with her loss with courage and dignity. I admired her.

'I can make some tea if you like.'

'No thanks, we're fine.'

'Okay. Ask whatever you want.'

On Sunday at the flat – between bouts of retching and despair – Andrew and I had discussed how best to investigate the circumstances surrounding the death of Tony Daly and decided on the straightforward approach. Anthony Daly was officially a suicide so no longer an ongoing police case, which left me free to do my thing, preferably with the family's blessing. That meant getting Cissie's agreement to represent her.

'The investigation into your brother's death is closed. The authorities are satisfied he took his own life but the detective sergeant who interviewed you told me you were unhappy with that conclusion and thought you might appreciate having somebody else look into it.'

Surprise manifested in a frown. 'He's right, I'm not happy, though why would you get involved?'

It was a good question. And one I couldn't answer honestly. My job was to persuade Cissie she needed my help without mentioning her brother had been sold short. Charlie Cameron honest injun? Not today.

'Sudden death is hard to come to terms with. If there was a reason Tony killed himself I'm sure you'd want to know.'

'How could I afford you? I haven't any money.'

'Money won't come into it. I'll be doing it because I want to.'

The frown returned only this time it was heavy with suspicion. Andrew had found a woman in the throes of addiction; this lady had mined a strength she may not have realised she had.

'Mr Cameron. I've lived long enough to know people do very little that doesn't involve money. Why would you be different?'

'Tony killed himself publicly. I find that strange, don't you?'

Cissie's view hadn't altered from her statement. 'More than strange. I don't believe it. Do you know, on the day he died, Tony had booked a trip to Rome as a surprise for my birthday? Does that sound like a man thinking about dying to you? Because it certainly doesn't to me.'

'What if I can prove it?'

'The police have given up.'

Patrick said, 'Will you let us try, Cissie?'

If she'd been drinking I was certain she would've agreed right away. She wasn't, so she didn't jump at the offer and I didn't blame her. Tony wouldn't be coming back no matter what we found and reliving his death – maybe his murder – couldn't change that.

Against the odds, even this early, Cissie Daly seemed to be coping with losing her brother. Being dragged through the tragedy again, albeit in the name of justice, may not be in her best interests, and when I thought about it, the decision I was asking her to make had a lot of downside.

Instead of giving me an answer, she changed the focus. 'Are you sure I can't get you anything?'

Pat Logue had street talent: he understood people better than anyone I'd ever met.

'Wouldn't refuse a beer if you have one.'

'No beer. Could give you a rum. Tony loved his rum.'

A light went on in my head. 'Did he ever drink whisky?'

'Never, he hated it. Dark rum was his favourite. Can't stand it myself; the smell's enough. Probably end up down the sink.'

Patrick hadn't picked up on what Cissie had said, but I had. We did without the rum and moved on to her brother's friends.

'Tony never had friends. Being on the council didn't leave him a lot of spare time. Now and again, he'd mention names of people he met at the football. Apart from that...'

She chided herself for knowing so little about her only brother. 'I suppose Lachie.'

'Who's Lachie?'

'Lachie Thompson. Took Tony under his wing when he won his first election. He was at the funeral on Saturday. Most of the councillors were there. And a couple of the Celtic players.'

Pat Logue said, 'Always nice to see a big turn-out.'

Cissie nodded. 'Tony would be pleased.'

Patrick took a look round Tony Daly's bedroom and, at the door, I shook Cissie's hand and promised to be in touch. Deceiving her wasn't a great feeling, even for a good cause.

'I appreciate you coming, Mr Cameron.'

'Charlie.'

'Charlie. Nobody will ever convince me my brother killed himself. Just wait a minute, will you?'

Cissie disappeared into the lounge.

When she'd gone, Pat Logue said, 'Clean as a whistle. Apart from a pile of programmes at the side of the bed and a Celtic poster on the wall, nothing much there. And nicely done, by the way.'

'What?'

'Avoidin' the awkward questions. Should've been a politician like your old man.'

'Not my finest hour, Patrick.'

'I disagree. This is a bad time. You're helpin' her come to terms with her brother's death.'

Cissie came back with an almost full bottle of dark rum and handed it out to me. 'I'm trying not to drink. Take this away with you in case I'm tempted.'

'Keep it up. You're doing great.'

In the car, I asked Patrick what he thought. His focus, as usual, was on alcohol and Cissie Daly's willpower; he'd missed it. Monday morning, with just the one pint in him, wasn't his best time.

'The brother dies a violent death and she doesn't drown her sorrows. Amazin'. How on earth does one wee woman find that kind of strength? Couldn't do it. Wouldn't even try.'

'The body stank of booze.'

'So he was well away with it. Had to be to do what he did.'

'Except what Andrew smelled was whisky. Enough to knock you down he said. Turns out Daly only drank rum.'

Patrick was catching up.

'Somebody forced it down his throat. Tony Daly was murdered.'

*** 

The bottle of rum on my desk didn't look much, but for me, in terms of evidence, it was more significant than the dead man booking a holiday for himself and his sister on the day he died. Changing your mind was one thing; changing your drink was something else.

I called Andrew on his mobile. His gruff voice lacked its usual bite. He sounded down. What I had to report would cheer him up.

'I've got a new client. Cissie Daly's a go. And get this. She says Tony hated whisky. All he ever drank was rum.'

There was silence on the other end of the line while Andrew processed this nugget and realised its importance. 'The TOX deals in blood/alcohol level. Doesn't identify specifically what the alcohol was. Well done, Charlie. First day on the case and you've cracked it.'

Hardly. Though I didn't give him an argument.

'Added to his travel plans, it strongly suggests he didn't kill himself. All I have to do now is find out who did and why.'

'What's your next move?'

'His sister claims the council took up all her brother's time. Tony had no friends to speak of apart from some councillor called Thompson.'

'Lachie Thompson?'

'That's right. Know him do you?'

'Elder statesman. Been around forever. Could've been lord provost.'

'Why wasn't he?'

'Not interested. Prefers to stay in the background, I suppose.'

'Is he honest?'

Andrew laughed. 'He's a councillor, Charlie. What do you think?'

'Tell you after I talk to him.'

'How's Cissie doing?'

'Better than you'd expect. She isn't drinking.'

Geddes was impressed. 'Pleased to hear it.'

Glasgow City Chambers in George Square was round the corner from my office. I could walk there in two minutes but it made sense to check if Lachie Thompson was available. A female on the switchboard connected me. He answered on the first ring.

'Lachie Thompson.'

'Good morning, Mr Thompson. Sorry to break into your day. My name is Charlie Cameron. I'm a private investigator. I'd like to ask you about a colleague of yours. Tony Daly.'

The councillor hesitated. I gave him a prompt. 'I'm representing Mr Daly's sister. I understand you were a very good friend of her brother's.'

His reply was open and sympathetic. 'Known the family for years. My heart goes out to Cissie. Tony was all she had. Of course I'll help whatever way I can. Unfortunately, I'm tied-up all day today. I could meet you tomorrow. Say twelve o'clock, if that's any good to you.'

'Perfect.'

Thompson ended the call sounding like a friend. 'What happened to Tony was tragic. I blame myself. I should've seen it coming.'

*\*\**

The letters I'd picked up at Gavin Law's flat meant nothing. More interesting was the one from Francis Fallon informing Law of his suspension – it wasn't amongst them. Maybe it had been lost in the post if it had ever been sent at all; the person behind the allegation may have changed her mind about pursuing it. The alternative was the hospital had invented it to pull Gavin Law into line. Wild speculation at best. Everything about this case led in a circle. The letters needed to be forwarded to his sister. I tied them together with an elastic band, put them in an envelope large enough to take them all, and wrote Caroline Law's address on the front. In the middle drawer of the desk I found a book of stamps and stuck on three to be on the safe side. Jackie buzzed just as I was slipping the package into my inside jacket pocket. When I answered, she was her usual sarcastic self.

'There's a Miss Universe here asking for a Charlie Cameron. Surely she can't mean you?'

'Send her up.'

We hadn't arranged to meet, so this was a surprise – the best kind. Although Alile was dressed for winter she swept into the room like the first day of summer, wearing a beige raincoat over a cream roll-neck sweater, blue jeans and brown ankle boots.

'I was in the city centre and thought about you. Is this a bad time?'

'Absolutely not. Glad you're here.'

She unbuttoned her coat, shook-out her hair and smiled. 'Don't suppose you fancy taking in a movie?'

'You mean re-arrange my busy schedule at a moment's notice? Consider it done. What's on?'

'We've got a choice – a war movie, a romantic comedy or the new Dracula.'

'Mmmm.'

'And it's Humphrey Bogart week at the GFC.'

'What're they showing?'

'*Casablanca.*'

'Bogie and Bergman. No contest. When does it start?'

Alile looked at her watch. 'Ten to two. Plenty of time. But only if you're sure I'm not dragging you away from something important.'

'You aren't. Let's eat first.'

In NYB we started with minestrone then split a pepperoni pizza. While Alile ate, I watched her. She caught me.

'What're you thinking?'

'You wouldn't believe me.'

'I might. Take a chance.'

'Okay. Of all the gin joints, in all the towns, in all the world, she walks into mine.'

Alile laughed. It was a sound I could get used to. 'Why aren't you married, Charlie?'

'Just didn't happen.'

'Ever been close?'

'Not close enough.'

She moved the conversation on to safer ground before I could ask her the same question. 'Any luck finding Gavin Law?'

'None. He's disappeared. What's the chat at Francis Fallon?'

Alile made a face and still managed to look beautiful.

'Not a word. It's as if he never worked there.'

'And the rape allegation?'

The tapered fingers of an elegant hand gently brushed my question aside. 'The only one who's mentioned it is you.'

'Not anymore. Won't hear a peep out of me about it for the rest of the day.'

'Promise?'

'Cross my heart.'

'Then let's go.'

In the dark, halfway through the film, I felt Alile move closer. Her hand slipped into mine. I'd seen *Casablanca* a dozen times; that didn't matter. When Ilse got on the plane with Victor Lazlo, and left Rick on the runway in the rain, inside, I was still hoping it would work out for him. It hadn't the previous eleven.

That didn't stop me believing.

# Chapter Thirty-Four

A steady drizzle fell on the black Volkswagen Phaeton limousine as it turned off William Street and silently cruised to the main entrance of the Hilton hotel where a concierge, wearing a green cape and tartan trousers, stood ready with an umbrella to shelter the important visitor from the rain. The Lord Provost of Glasgow got out and was ushered through the foyer to a lift and on to an anteroom on the first floor.

The rebranding of an East End gangster could begin.

People were already there, drinking coffee and eating shortbread. On the surface, all very civilised. In a corner, Lachie Thompson shifted uneasily and avoided contact. The Lord Provost would be making the announcement and Lachie thanked God because he wasn't in a fit state to speak to anybody; the call from the private investigator had freaked him out.

Tony's murder and the threat to his granddaughter should have convinced him the only way he would ever be free was to go to the police. Unfortunately for the councillor, history was against it. Decades of corruption would come out. A long prison sentence was the best he could hope for, and, at his age, he wouldn't survive. More likely he'd finish up swinging from the end of a rope, like poor Tony, before he got anywhere near Barlinnie.

He needed to speak to Sandy Rutherford but the bloody idiot was in expansive mood, standing in the middle of the floor, chatting with a beautiful female. Sean Rafferty joined them and slipped an arm round the woman's waist: his wife. The suit and tie made him seem like a respectable businessman. Rutherford guided Rafferty towards the Provost and introduced him. They shook hands, no doubt congratulating each other on the project, and the benefits for the city.

Thompson caught Rutherford's eye and waved him over. The former shipyard firebrand smiled and put a friendly hand on his shoulder. His colleague brushed it away, barely able to contain his contempt.

'What's up, Lachie?'

'Tell you what's up. Tony isn't cold in his grave and you're making small-talk with the man who had him killed. Rafferty's a murderer. What does that make you?'

Rutherford glanced over his shoulder; somebody might hear. Lachie was losing it.

'Steady, Lachie, steady. Keep your voice down. It could just as easily have been me or you hanging from that bridge, and don't forget it.'

Thompson understood the self-serving argument and wasn't impressed by it. 'Say this for you Sandy, your flexible. Always land on your feet, don't you? Though if you believe you can trust Rafferty you're a bloody fool. He's a snake.'

'I agree, Lachie. Except, he's our snake. What the hell's got into you? We're home and dry with this thing.'

His colleague laughed a bitter laugh. 'Is that so? Then maybe you'd like to tell that to the private investigator who called me this morning?'

Rutherford tensed. 'Private investigator? What did he want?'

'I'll let you know. I'm seeing him tomorrow. He's working for Cissie so I expect we're not as home and dry as you think, Sandy.'

'Somebody should have a word with Cissie. Persuade her she isn't acting in her best interests.'

Thompson sneered. 'Yeah? Then you do it.'

Rutherford ignored the slight. 'According to the police, Tony took his own life. There's nothing to investigate.'

'So why is this guy interested?'

Neither man had an answer to that question. Five minutes ago, Sandy Rutherford had been flirting with Kim Rafferty then doing the introductions with her husband and the Lord Provost. He'd been enjoying himself. Now, fear crawled over him.

'What's this guy's name?'

'Cameron.'

'What do you know about him?'

'Not a thing. Might spend his time peeking in windows and taking photographs of people at it for divorce evidence for all I know.'

Rutherford breathed a sigh of relief. It didn't last.

'Although, I'd have to admit that wasn't how he sounded.'

Rutherford forced defiance into his voice. 'Well, I didn't kill anybody.'

Lachie Thompson's reply damned them both. 'Keep telling yourself that, Sandy. I do. Pity it doesn't help.'

\*\*\*

An artist's impression of Riverside with the slogan "Good For Glasgow," provided the backdrop to the model from Sean Rafferty's den, covered for the moment. At the entrance to one of the Hilton's fifteen meeting rooms, employees from the council's marketing department stood beside piles of press packs with instructions to wait until the end before issuing them. Nothing could be allowed to distract from the speech the Provost was about to make.

Invited guests, councillors, and reporters from newspapers and television – all anxious to hear officially the city's worst kept secret – filled seats laid out in rows. BBC Scotland and STV cameras trained on the Lord Provost as he made his way to the lectern. A photo-opportunity was arranged for the press. The city's most senior elected representative was there to introduce the ambitious public/private initiative to the world.

Lachie Thompson watched from the side. There was little doubt in his mind that the development would indeed be good for Glasgow and, as the Lord Provost was proving, anyone instrumental in making it happen would be popular. How it had been achieved made him want to retch. Beside him, Sandy Rutherford seemed relaxed, though in truth, it was an act; he hadn't regained his composure from Lachie's bombshell. Sean would have to be told and his reaction was impossible to predict.

The Provost patted the gold chain round his neck as if he was checking it was still there, and began with the history of the "'dear green place'", praising the vision of OTD and the project it was his honour to stand behind. In truth, he'd had nothing to do with it but credit was subjective: he was the main man. He talked-up the confidence the partnership showed and painted a picture of a prosperous future. When it was fully operational the city would be at the forefront of Scottish tourism.

He ended by inviting Kim Rafferty to unveil the model to applause. The next minutes were spent with the Lord Provost shaking hands with Rafferty, representing the city's newest partners, and posing for the cameras with Kim between them.

If it was a good day for the city, it was a great day for Sean Rafferty.

\*\*\*

Across the room, Kim had been kidnapped by a man with halitosis and terminal dandruff telling her a story she had no interest in, while over his shoulder she could see her husband playing Prince Charming with a willowy brunette from Scottish Enterprise. The stupid bitch fluttered her eyes, buying whatever bullshit Sean was selling. Kim didn't blame the woman; not so long ago she'd almost done the same.

Waitresses moved through the crowd offering champagne and canapés to the guests. Rutherford waited for an opportunity to pull Sean aside and give him the bad news. It wasn't easy because Rafferty was in demand. He was animated, enjoying himself; obviously pleased with how things had gone. The councillor gritted his teeth and edged towards him, nodding to familiar faces without stopping to chat.

When he got to him, he touched his elbow and whispered. 'Need a word, Sean.'

Rafferty disguised his annoyance, excused himself and followed Rutherford to the anteroom. Instinct told Kim something was happening. She made her excuses and went to the door. From inside, Sean's voice, full of contempt, carried to her.

'See your mates are managing to force the champagne down their throats. No surprise there. Always ready with their snouts in the trough. What does it say on the coat of arms? "Let Glasgow Flourish"'.

He laughed.

'"So Long As It's Free" would be more like it.' The smile disappeared. 'Okay. What do you want?'

Rutherford apologised. 'Sorry to drag you away but we may have a problem.'

'What kind of a problem?'

'A private investigator phoned Lachie this morning.'

Rafferty's expression hardened. 'What did he want?'

'Tony's sister has hired somebody to nose around. Cissie isn't convinced he killed himself.'

'Did Thompson tell him anything?'

'Of course not. He put him off 'til tomorrow, but I'm worried.'

Rafferty didn't like what he was hearing. 'This PI, what do we know about him?'

'Name's Cameron.'

Sean paused, suddenly wary. 'Charlie Cameron?'

'Yeah, I think so. Do you know him?'

Sean Rafferty kept his reply vague. 'Let's just say we've met.'

'So what do you want me to say to Lachie?'

'He sticks to the story and keeps it simple. Warn him not to try to be clever. He's an elected member of the council; clever doesn't come into it. Daly was depressed, remember? Been going downhill for a while. Too young. Such a waste. All that shite. Got it?'

Sandy Rutherford may have been a hard man, once. Not anymore. He panicked. 'You shouldn't have killed Tony. Not like that. Lachie would've come round quicker if you hadn't threatened his granddaughter...'

Rafferty grabbed Rutherford's lapels and threw him against the wall. 'Shut the fuck up. Nobody can prove anything unless somebody tells them. Pull yourself together or you'll be next.'

He slapped the councillor's face with the back of his hand. 'If you bastards had just taken your wedge we wouldn't be in this position and Daly would still be alive. Greedy gutless fuckers to a man. The folk who voted for you have no idea, otherwise you'd be out on your arses.'

Rutherford was afraid but something in the East End gangster's eyes had changed: the aggression was a front. Sean was rattled.

'How do know this, Cameron?'

Rafferty ignored him. 'Thompson keeps to the script and we all go home happy. For your sake, make it happen. You wouldn't last a day in the Bar-L.'

Outside the door, Kim savoured every word. She'd been prepared to wait for years if necessary. The opportunity had come sooner than she had expected. Her lips parted in a smile.

\*\*\*

The Maitland house was in darkness. Wallace turned the key in the lock and went inside knowing Shona was upstairs in bed pretending to be asleep. Since New Year, life had spun out of control and he'd spiralled into a black vortex of fear and paranoia. At the hospital, Jimmy Hambley refused to allow him into his office; every case he operated on was being scrutinised – he was sure of it – and when he spoke to patients, he imagined their reluctance to trust his diagnosis.

Wallace Maitland was slowly losing his mind.

But the hostile atmosphere at home was real. Shona hadn't exchanged twenty words with him since Hogmanay, and then it was to tell him the marriage was over. He was lonely. In his heart he accepted how badly he'd let his wife down but wouldn't acknowledge that, with Margaret Cooper bleeding out in front of him, he'd made the wrong choice. He hid behind good intentions while David Cooper pureed Margaret's meals and fed her with a spoon.

Maitland turned on the light, removed his jacket and pulled off his tie. Shona had poured the whisky that sat on the sideboard down the sink weeks ago. He hadn't bothered to replace it. Drinking depressed him and although he spent every night in a pub, it was merely a refuge from his wife's silent contempt. He hardly touched alcohol anymore.

A half-finished cup of tea, still warm, meant Shona had left it in her hurry to avoid meeting him. What had they become? He poured a glass of water, went back into the lounge and switched on the TV. Flicking through the channels told him what he already knew; there was nothing on except wall-to-wall rubbish. Maitland switched it off and listened to the house breathe as the central heating cooled. After a while he got out of the chair and wandered around the room that had been so familiar to him; a stranger in his own home.

At the window, he parted the blinds and peered into the street. A car was parked across the road with the silhouette of a man behind the wheel. Not doing anything; just sitting. Fear gripped Maitland's chest, quickly replaced by anger. He threw open the front open and ran towards the stalker. Immediately, the engine fired, and the car roared away, leaving him standing in the middle of the road, shaking his fist and shouting.

'Leave me alone! Leave me alone, you bastard!'

In the lounge, he got on his knees and dragged the contents of the sideboard onto the carpet with trembling fingers, scavenging like a homeless man in a dustbin, until he came across what he was looking for hidden behind a box of chocolates and a pile of telephone directories.

The vodka had been bought for a guest who had repaid the consideration by not showing up to drink it. Maitland brought a glass from the kitchen, filled it almost to the brim and emptied it. The clear spirit tasted vile and burned his throat; he didn't care; he needed to escape the hell he was living in. A second measure went the way of the first. Wallace Maitland put his head in his hands and started to cry.

Shona had heard the front door slam shut and, soon after, the anguished sounds of a soul in torment rose to the room above. She got out of bed and went downstairs. The Maitlands had been married for more than two decades. In that time, Shona had become used to her husband the worse for wear. None of it prepared her for what was waiting.

Wallace was on the floor, wailing like a lost child. Blood from his mouth had stained his shirt. His right eye was bruised and closing. Seeing her didn't stop him. He punched his face with his fist. Again and again, all the time weeping.

'Wallace…what…?'

'I killed him and I can't remember! I can't remember, Shona!'

Maitland's nose burst under the force of another blow. His wife knelt beside him, and cradled his injured head; he collapsed against her, sobbing.

'Help me. Please. Please. Help me remember Hogmanay.'

'I'll try, Wallace. I promise I'll try.'

# Chapter Thirty-Five

I woke earlier than usual and lay staring at the ceiling. I should have been thinking about Andrew and the hanged man on the Queen Margaret Bridge. I wasn't. I was thinking about a dark-skinned Malawian woman.

After the movie, we'd gone for a drink in Vroni's, of all places, where late on Saturday afternoon, a troubled DS Geddes had added wine to the whisky he'd already drunk and guaranteed the journey into oblivion ending with the ugly scene in NYB.

Alile told me about life in her country and how she'd come into nursing. The more she spoke, the more I appreciated what a special person she was. But at the end of the night, when the taxi pulled up outside her flat, I let her go inside by herself, no doubt wondering if she'd said or done something wrong. Of course, she hadn't; it wasn't her, it was me. In the wine bar, looking into her beautiful face, I could feel myself falling.

Given my history: not good.

Kate Calder's unexpected appearance with Big River on New Year's Eve had been a painful reminder of what we'd had. Without realizing it, I might be using Alile. She deserved better. Taking it slowly was the wisest course – although when had I ever done that? Trying to explain could mean it was over between us before it had even begun.

Chances were, I was complicating things, but it felt right.

My meeting with Councillor Thompson wasn't until noon so I gave myself the morning off and hung around the flat. By the time I arrived at NYB it was after eleven.

Jackie could be subtle when she wanted; today, she didn't want. 'How's it going with Miss World? Found you out yet, has she?'

'Has actually, Jackie. Tried to keep it from her, but you know what women are like. They wheedle stuff out of you.'

'And?'

'I'm Mr Wonderful. Her words not mine.'

Jackie fired back. 'And she seemed all right. Goes to show you just can't tell.'

Poor by her usual standards. She'd lost and she knew it. I lifted a copy of the *Herald* from the bar and headed for a table. 'Espresso, please, when you've got a minute.'

The small victory was short-lived. Inside the newspaper, on page four, a face I'd hoped never to see again, grinned at me under the headline "Good for Glasgow."

My mobile rang. DS Geddes.

'An old friend of yours has gone respectable, Charlie. Who'd have believed it?'

'Just looking at him, Andrew. Last time I saw him was at Edinburgh Castle with his psycho brother.'

'Well, now he's a pillar of the business community. According to the report, OTD, the company he represents, is in partnership with the city.'

'Good for Glasgow.'

'Yeah, right!'

'Close to Daly's swallow dive. Quite a coincidence.'

'Don't believe in them.'

'Me neither. Know anything about this OTD?'

'No. I'll start digging.'

I brought him up to speed. 'Got a meet at the City Chambers with Daly's friend, Lachie Thompson. Interested to hear what he has to say about the Lord Provost shaking hands with a gangster.'

'Probably used to it. Doesn't matter. Whatever's going on Sean Rafferty's up to his armpits in it.' He rang off.

Jackie came over with the coffee and surprised me with an apology. 'Sorry, Charlie. Shouldn't have said that about your girlfriend.'

'Don't worry about it.'

I'd stepped into the trap.

'Then she is your girlfriend. Wasn't sure.'

'You're putting two-and-two together…'

'…and coming up with romance.'

I filled the time before my meeting unsuccessfully trying to read the rest of the news. Concentration was impossible; anything Rafferty was part of could only benefit him and whoever he was in bed with. I took a last look at the Lord Provost of Scotland's second city and a gangster from the East End locked in a handshake, as a blonde model unveiled what was promised to be good for Glasgow.

I returned the newspaper – minus page four – to the bar on my way out and got a sarcastic thumbs-up from Jackie.

'All you need is love, Charlie.'

'I'll bear it in mind.'

***

Lachie Thompson was waiting for me at reception. Though I was aware he'd been a member of the city council for three decades and had to be in his sixties, at least, he was older than I expected: white-haired, thin and balding, wearing a blue suit that wasn't new. He shook my hand without making eye contact.

'Sorry to put you off yesterday. Busy day.' He didn't go into details and handed me a pass. 'Won't let you in without one of these.'

I followed him past granite columns, up a marble staircase to a small room on the first floor. When we got inside we sat at a wooden table, opposite each other. He didn't waste time on small talk and I realised we wouldn't be very long.

'You're here about, Tony. Okay, let me be honest with you, Mr…'

'Cameron.'

'I'd rather not talk about, Tony Daly.'

'Why?'

'It's too soon. Still too raw. Cissie's the only reason I agreed to see you. If anything can help her accept the terrible thing her brother did, then of course it isn't a choice. My feelings are unimportant.'

*Nice speech councillor.*

'I appreciate it.'

He nodded his head solemnly, as if we'd reached some profound understanding, and I resisted changing my first question from how well he'd known Tony Daly to his relationship with Sean Rafferty.

'Cissie Daly says you were one of Tony's best friends. What was he like, and did you notice a difference in him before he died?'

Thompson placed his elbows on the table and steepled his fingers: a man deep in thought. After a minute, he answered. 'Tony was one of the good guys. Completely dedicated to public service. Glasgow is the poorer for his passing.'

His eulogy sounded hollow and rehearsed. Or maybe I was having trouble getting round the picture in the paper. 'How long did you know him?'

'Sixteen or seventeen years. From when he was elected.'

'And you became friends?'

The councillor was used to answering questions harder than the ones I was asking. He relaxed and sat back in his chair. 'Tony was an easy guy to like and I did like him. Very much. But at the same time, if he disagreed with what you were saying, he wasn't afraid to tell you.'

'So did he?

'What?'

'Disagree with you?'

Thompson's eyes narrowed, suddenly wary. It wasn't possible to survive in politics as long as he had without being able to tell which way the wind was blowing.

'Not often, no. We tended to see things pretty much the same.'

I qualified my interest. 'I'll be straight with you, Mr Thompson. The police have written off Tony Daly's death as suicide. His sister believes – with good reason – it may well be something else. You were closer to him than most people, what do you think?'

He leaned forward, unimpressed with where the conversation was headed. 'You say you've been straight with me. All right, let me be straight with you. I can't imagine what Cissie's going through. It must be terrible for her. But clutching at straws isn't going to help. Somehow, she has to find the strength to put this terrible thing behind her and move on with her life.'

'Not easy when there are loose ends.'

He spread his arms. 'Loose ends? I told you Tony was a good man and it's true. He was also a flawed man.'

'Flawed as in?'

'He was an alcoholic.'

Thompson glanced away, reluctant to add more, though I was willing to bet he would. He drew on the table with his finger, hesitant and distracted, before continuing with a question of his own.

'The only way to say this is to say it. Obviously you've met, Cissie.'

'Yes.'

'Then you must have noticed she has a drink problem?'

'I didn't.'

He made a noise deep in his throat which cast doubt on my ability to investigate my way out of a wet paper bag. 'Take my word for it. You asked if I noticed a difference in him before he died. The answer is: yes, I did. He was depressed.'

'Depressed about what?'

He smiled sadly at my lack of insight into the human condition. 'Alcoholics don't need a reason, Mr Cameron. It's who they are. It's why they drink in the first place.'

'So Tony was...' Thompson's voice rose in defence of his dead colleague. '...a tireless worker on behalf of the people of Glasgow; that's how he should be remembered. Not as a man slowly drowning in booze. He deserves more. And certainly not as the defenceless victim of a dark conspiracy nobody, including the police, has even bothered to consider. What you're suggesting is murder, do you realise that?'

For thirty years, Lachie Thompson had been persuading the city's electorate to vote for him. It wasn't difficult to understand why. He could conjure passion from the air, while he remained a loyal friend saddened by another's mistakes. In the waters he swam in, an invaluable skill set.

The councillor studied my expression, expecting to find me convinced. It was time to knock him off-guard. I started slowly. 'Where did he stand on Riverside?'

Thompson – old stager that he was – took it in his stride. 'Riverside? Supported it one hundred percent.'

'Good for Glasgow?'

'Tony thought so, yes.'

'What about you?'

'As I said, we agreed on most things. I'm totally behind the project.'

There were no papers on the table. If there had been the councillor would have shuffled them. Instead, he made do with checking his watch. I'd had all I was getting. He finished on a compassionate note, assuming the meeting was over.

'Please tell Cissie I'll call soon.'

My question caught him unprepared. 'How well did you and Tony know Sean Rafferty?'

Thompson faltered. 'Sean Rafferty?'

'He represents the city's partner, OTD, on Riverside.'

The councillor shook his head. 'I've never met him and I doubt Tony did either.'

'Surely you met him yesterday?'

'Yesterday I was just part of the window dressing.'

'Making up the numbers?'

'Something like that.'

\*\*\*

Later in the day, Andrew phoned to ask how I'd got on with Thompson and to fill me in on what he'd discovered. I assumed his situation hadn't changed but, whatever frustrations DS Geddes was suffering, they weren't part of his conversation.

I replayed Lachie Thompson's reticence to speak ill of the dead before rushing to bad-mouth both the brother and his sister, all the time insisting he was a friend.

Andrew wasn't surprised. 'In his next incarnation, he'll be a lawyer.'

'Slippery enough, that's for sure.'

'So he hasn't a problem believing Daly did himself in?'

'Didn't commit one way or the other and kept to the official line – selfless public servant whose contribution will never be fully appreciated.'

'Typical politician.'

'According to him, Tony was all for the development though he isn't aware of any contact between him and Rafferty.'

'What did Thompson say about his own relationship with him?'

'Doesn't know him.'

Andrew snorted down the line. 'Not possible. In spite of the rise of the SNP, the Labour Party still holds a majority. As leader of the council, Lachie Thompson is a very influential guy in Glasgow politics. Probably the most influential. Apart from that, he's been around so long he knows everybody and everybody knows him.

'Knows him or owes him?'

'I'd guess both. Nothing happens he isn't involved in. No public/private collaboration could exist without his approval, especially something this high profile. It just isn't on.'

'But isn't the background of any outside company vetted to be sure they aren't crooks?'

Geddes laughed. 'Of course that's the theory. But in reality this city does business with shady characters all the time. So long as the right people are behind it, councillors will look the other way.'

He paused. Paper rustled on the other end of the phone.

'Riverside's a case in point. Been speculation about it for more than a year. Suddenly, out of the blue, it gets approved. Yesterday, we see who the City Fathers are in bed with and yes, it's true. The devil is in the detail.'

'Sean Rafferty.'

'Not Rafferty. The deal involves millions. Far too big for him to take on himself. He's only the frontman. I spent an afternoon digging into OTD and what I found won't come as a shock, Charlie. OTD stands for Orange Tree Development. Can you guess who that is?'

'No, but you're going to tell me.'

The sarcasm fell on deaf ears.

'Give you a clue. His father and grandfather were penniless orange farmers. That's right. None other than our old friend Emil Rocha.'

Geddes was wrong about the shock. Hearing the name sent a jolt of fear through me. In the past, my path and the Spanish drug lord's had crossed. I'd been lucky to survive the experience.

And Sean Rafferty was Rocha's man. It made sense.

Every ambitious criminal wanted to create legitimate businesses profitable in their own right that allowed them to wash dirty money. Win-win. On the sun-kissed Costas, Rocha was already a player in real estate, as well as one of the biggest dealers in cocaine, smuggled from Africa. Half the snow snorted in Glasgow had come from him, and been sold on the street by Rafferty.

'But there's more. The bold Sean hasn't let the grass grow. He's respectable these days; married with a daughter.'

'God help them.'

'Indeed.'

I brought the subject back to Lachie Thompson. 'Thompson and his friend Daly commanded a helluva lot of influence in the council and acted together on most issues. Though maybe the exception was Riverside. For whatever reason, Tony Daly wouldn't get on board, so they killed him. Does that make sense, Andrew?'

'Sense, yes. Enough to convince the procurator fiscal? Not a chance. It's a handy story to explain a violent death. It isn't evidence. Not even circumstantial.'

Geddes was right.

'Who else is there, besides Thompson?'

'It's hard to say. The vote to green-light the project was 47/32, which means the nationalists stuck together – they always do – and most of the rest approved it.'

'So who, Andrew?'

'Only other really well-known face is Sandy Rutherford. Old school trade unionist. Has a reputation for being a straight-shooter. Beyond that I don't know much about him. Can't do any harm to talk to him.'

Our options had narrowed and DS Geddes was realising it. He went quiet.

'Give my right arm to stick it to that bastard Barr. He's got us working on domestic abuse. Bumps up his numbers and makes him look like a policeman while serious crime gets ignored.'

'I told you what to do.'

'Don't think I wasn't paying attention, Charlie. Watch this space.'

# Chapter Tirty-Six

Councillor Sandy Rutherford was everything I expected a union fire-brand to be: a tall, barrel-chested man whose handshake was firm. Unlike his colleague, Thompson, he looked me in the eye. I took that as a good sign but if it was, it was the only one. Our conversation, in the same first floor room in the city chambers, was less than productive.

In a deep voice, Rutherford said his association with Tony Daly was cordial but distant; they weren't friends, and despite their years together on the council, hadn't met socially. Daly's death was a tragedy. Of course it was. Glasgow needed more of his kind. In short, the usual. No insight to advance what I already knew, which wasn't much.

When asked about Riverside, Rutherford freely admitted voting for it and parroted the benefits-to-the-city mantra; using the end to justify the means. Half-way through I switched off and filtered his baritone out until he finished whatever self-serving point he was making.

I'd heard rumours about the political elite, known as the Glasgow Mafia. Now I believed. Lachie Thompson was one of them. So was this guy. And probably the late great Tony Daly they cried crocodile tears over.

*Saint Anthony.*

To his credit, the councillor let the chat exhaust itself – "no places to go people to see" routine with him – and walked me to the front door. We stood for a moment watching the rain fall in sheets on a deserted George Square, waiting for it to ease. At the beginning, I'd been tempted to like Sandy Rutherford. His bluff, no-nonsense openness appealed. Since then, I'd changed my mind.

He talked different and looked different from Thompson, but there wasn't any difference.

He smiled. 'Never have an umbrella when we need one, do we?'

I turned my collar up and put out my hand. He took it in the same assured grip as before and was about to let go when I casually dropped a question into the conversation and sensed his fingers tighten against mine.

'How well do you know Sean Rafferty?'

He pursed his lips. 'Don't know him at all, really. Met his father a couple of times.'

'What was he like?'

'Jimmy? Unforgettable.'

Jimmy Rafferty had been that all right.

An orange and green corporation bus, racing to beat the lights, splashed through a puddle causing a mini-tidal wave to wash the pavement yards from where we were. Rutherford took his hand back and patted my shoulder, encouraging me to leave.

'I hope you can swim.'

'I hope so, too.'

*** 

Calling Sean with bad news was the last thing Rutherford wanted to do. He rehearsed what to say over and over and finally gave up on it because no matter what words he used, the message didn't change; the private investigator was still asking questions. Not a problem, until he'd mentioned Rafferty by name and Rutherford knew they were in trouble.

He left the council building at ten minutes to five and hurried across the square. In Queen Street, he stopped in a doorway and punched the familiar number on his mobile, hoping Rafferty wasn't there.

In his Bothwell home, on the banks of the River Clyde, Sean Rafferty was rolling around the floor, playing with his daughter. The interruption irritated him. Kim was right; he spent too little time with Rosie.

'Sean, it's Sandy.'

'What do you want?"

'Sorry to…'

'What do you want?'

The councillor blurted the unwelcome news. 'The private investigator came to see me.'

Rafferty exploded. 'The *what*? It was Thompson he was supposed to meet. How come you're talking to him?'

'He phoned. I couldn't put him off. It would've looked suspicious.'

'What did he say?'

'Asked about Daly. Where did I stand on Riverside. Stuff like that.'

'And you said?'

'What we discussed.' Rutherford heard fear in his own voice. 'A boost to tourism, jobs, retail income. Good for Glasgow, you know.'

Rafferty wasn't satisfied; he sensed something. For all his hard-man reputation, the councillor was weak. They all were and he despised them for it. 'Don't sound too sure. Tell me the rest.'

Two middle-aged women came into the shop. Rutherford moved aside to let them pass. When he put the phone to his ear, Sean Rafferty was waiting.

'Tell me exactly what Cameron said.'

Rutherford's voice dropped to an anxious whisper. 'He didn't say anything but I'm not sure I convinced him, Sean.'

Rafferty coaxed him. 'Of course you did. What makes you think you didn't?'

'He asked if I knew you.'

The silence terrified the councillor. Eventually, Rafferty spoke. 'And what did you say, Sandy?'

'Said I'd met your father once or twice.'

'Really? And how did that go down?'

'Okay. All right. He left.'

'So what makes you think he didn't believe you?'

'Can't put my finger on it. First Lachie. Now me. Just doesn't feel good.'

Rafferty's response calmed the councillor. 'I agree, but let me worry about it. Don't talk to Thompson or anybody else. Wait for me to contact you. I'll deal with it, okay?'

Rutherford gushed his thanks, relief rolling off him. 'That's great. Cameron caught me off-guard. Sorry, Sean.'

Rafferty had already stopped listening.

# Chapter Thirty-Seven

The tale Thompson and Rutherford had told was so similar they might have been twins, reading from a script. But – to use one of Patrick Logue's sporting expressions –fair play to them; they'd done a reasonable job. No surprise, given they were professional liars.

My meetings with them would've yielded nothing of interest if I hadn't already seen a Glasgow gangster in the *Herald*, convincing me beyond any reasonable doubt, they were involved in something, even before they opened their untrustworthy mouths.

Thanks to Andrew, we knew OTD was Emil Rocha, which made Sean Rafferty the front for dirty money. The lack of hard evidence didn't prevent me from being certain he'd murdered Tony Daly. As yet, I didn't understand why though it didn't take a big brain to figure the lucrative partnership with the city must be at the centre of it. Tomorrow I'd discuss it with Andrew. Tonight I needed to be free.

Alile came round to the flat and I squandered another opportunity to make love to her. She had to be wondering. All her life, men had fallen over themselves to get close to her and here I was acting like an emotionally stunted schoolboy. At best, the signals were mixed. Confusing for me as well as her.

Sitting on the couch with two-thirds of a bottle of wine inside us, she squeezed my hand and gave me the chance to explain. 'Want to talk about it?'

'Talk about what?'

'You're still in love with somebody, aren't you?'

Women know things; somehow they just do.

'Who is she?'

My first words damned me. 'It's over.'

She shook her head. 'No it isn't, Charlie. Whatever you're telling yourself, it isn't.'

I didn't disagree. Alile had opened Pandora's Box and it all came tumbling out. She listened while I told her about Kate Calder; how the romance ended and how it kicked off again – at least for me – when she showed-up unexpectedly on Hogmanay.

I left out the snakeskin boots.

*Too much information.*

Alile kissed me on the cheek; warm and soft. 'Thanks for being honest with me, Charlie. I'd like to go home now.'

We didn't speak in the car. When we got to her place she turned, took my face in her hands, and kissed me again. This wonderful woman was about to walk out of my life. The memory of wanting to be free came back to haunt me. They say be careful what you wish for; this wasn't what I had in mind.

'Honestly, Alile, it's over.'

The smile on her lips didn't reach her eyes. 'If it ever is, I'll be here. Just don't wait too long.'

At the flat I washed the glasses, poured the wine down the sink and called Kate's mobile. A female with an American accent told me the number was unobtainable. For a while – no idea how long – I sat on the couch where Alile had been and tried to picture Kate Calder the last time we'd been together.

I couldn't.

The next morning I felt ill and depressed.

Two glasses of wine will do that to you.

Not.

***

I parked, as usual, in High Street and walked to NYB under a sky that mirrored my mood; dark and overcast. Last night stayed with me. Turning a beautiful woman down wasn't an everyday thing and it didn't feel good.

He was waiting for me on the corner of the Italian centre: an extra from *Beyond the Planet of the Apes*. On another day, seeing him might have given me pause. Not today. I walked past and heard him fall into step behind me.

It was too early for the bar to be open. Pat Logue was letting a coffee go cold in front of him. Jackie started to say something when he tapped me on the shoulder.

'Mr Cameron? Mr Rafferty would like a few minutes of your time.'

What happened next surprised me as much as him. I grabbed his arm, pivoted and followed his graceless descent over my knee to the floor. He landed heavily on his back with me on top of him. The guy was mid-twenties and probably spent more time in the gym than most people spend at work. All for nothing when over-confidence takes your eye off the ball. And I was up for it. Punching somebody would be almost therapeutic.

I didn't punch him, though it was a close run thing. Instead, I dug my fingers into his throat and watched his face turn the colour of cooked lobster.

It had gone off so fast Patrick hadn't had time to move from his stool. Jackie lifted the telephone ready to dial. It wasn't necessary. The words came from a bad place; I spat them out like orange pips. 'Tell your boss I'm not going anywhere. If he wants to see me, I won't be hard to find. Now fuck off.'

I let him go. Back at the ranch he'd have some explaining to do. Rafferty would pay by results and the thug might find himself suddenly out of the intimidation business.

Patrick kept his admiration on a tight leash. 'This the new way you start your day? Impressive. And if that's what you get for wantin' to speak to you, bloody glad I didn't ask for a sub. Who is he?'

'Long story.'

'The Clint Eastwood CD box set you got at Christmas got anythin' to do with it? Seriously, who sent him?'

Jackie's expression had blame written all over it. Telling Patrick Logue the biggest gangster in the city was back in my life wasn't going to get a good reaction. She ignored me and went to her office under the stairs.

'Our old pal, Sean Rafferty.'

'You're jokin'?'

'Wish I was.'

'How come I haven't heard?'

'As I said: long story.'

'In case you've forgotten, Charlie, the Raffertys tried to kill you.'

I didn't need to be reminded.

'Maybe this time they'll have better luck. Told you before. Don't mess with these bastards. They're premier league bad guys. Do whatever it takes to get out of their way. Although, looks like that advice is too late.'

'I didn't plan it. Getting threats from killers isn't me living the dream.'

He searched my face for answers he wasn't going to find. 'Hate to hear myself say this, but if you need any help…'

'Don't worry; you'll be the first to know.'

\*\*\*

Jackie Mallon had never been happy with me in the office above NYB. I knew where she was coming from. She managed the place yet her office was a cubbyhole a fifth the size of mine. Alex Gilby's promise I could have it as long as I wanted was solid. But in truth, however much a city centre address suited me, it wasn't appropriate anymore. The business I was in attracted all kinds of people: the thug Sean Rafferty had sent was an example. After what had just gone on, Jackie had a case. It was time to acknowledge it.

She kept her eyes on the computer screen when I opened the door and a glance at her desk, covered in post-it notes and the walls lined with sheets of paper, was enough to convince the selfish part of me that would've held on to my gig upstairs.

I began with an apology. 'Sorry about that. Shouldn't have happened.'

'We agree on something.'

'Again, sorry.'

Her voice was low and steady, holding the anger and resentment in check. It wasn't easy for her. The resentment was old; its roots were deep. 'First the scene with Andrew Geddes. Now this. It's not on, Charlie.'

Jackie was forgetting I'd helped her out with Andrew.

'Excuse me?'

'I said it's not on.'

'Really? Correct me if I've got this wrong, but didn't you call *me* when one of *your* customers got out of order? I also remember I wasn't slow to help.'

She fired back. '*My* customer and *your* friend. I gave you a chance to stop him getting arrested for being drunk and disorderly, which was what he deserved. How does that entitle you to do what you like in here?'

'It doesn't.'

'Then what about that little scene just now?'

Arguing wasn't going to improve things.

'You know what, Jackie, forget it. I'll speak to, Alex.'

'You do that.'

She lifted an envelope from her desk and passed it to me; it was sealed. My name was printed in blue Biro on the front.

'When did this arrive?'

'A kid delivered it last night.'

I turned the white rectangle over in my hand. 'What did he look like?'

Jackie wasn't in the mood to answer questions. 'Like a kid delivering a letter.'

I stormed upstairs to the office at the heart of Jackie's resentment, more angry at her than Sean Rafferty's gorilla. Andrew Geddes out of his face and the tussle with the heavy weren't connected. Trouble had come to me. I hadn't gone looking for it. Clearly, with Jackie at least, I'd over-stayed my welcome. It was time to move on.

Inside the envelope a small piece of paper with a single sentence written in the same blue ink brought me back to the case Andrew's DI wouldn't allow him to investigate, and I forgot everything except proving an innocent man had been murdered.

## ASK LACHIE THOMPSON
## ABOUT HIS GRANDDAUGHTER

With few exceptions, every case needs luck; this might be it. What I was holding could bring Sean Rafferty down. My pulse quickened. I reread the words, willing them to tell me more until, slowly, the truth dawned. It was unlikely Thompson would add anything to what he'd already said. Speaking to him would be a waste of time. So was speculating about who had sent the note. Another councillor crossed my mind. Glasgow council had seventy-nine less Daly, Rutherford and Thompson, leaving seventy-six.

As Pat Logue would say: Su perb.

Thompson wasn't the author. It was about him and where his granddaughter fitted in was anybody's guess. I called Andrew and caught him in a rare good mood.

'Charlie. Just thinking about you.'

I didn't fill him in; that could come later. 'Lachie Thompson's granddaughter. Find out about her.'

'Didn't know he had one.'

'Apparently he has.'

'Sounds as if you're on to something.'

'Maybe. Maybe not. Just get the information. I'll explain when I see you.'

The door knocked. Patrick came in and sat down. I tossed the note across to him and watched his reaction. When I hung up he said, 'Who's this from?'

'No idea'

I brought him up to speed on my meetings with the councillors which didn't take long.

'So what's the next move?'

*Good question.*

'Let's see what Andrew comes back with.'

Patrick changed the subject. 'You and Jackie, what gives?'

'She's upset about this morning.'

'Can't blame her.'

'I don't, but that isn't all of it. She's never been happy having me here so time to go time. I'm moving out.'

'No complaints. You've had a good run. Where will you go?'

Before I could answer him my mobile rang. James Hambley was too important to spend even a minute of his day on the likes of me; at least, that was his opinion. But here he was.

'Stop trying to intimidate my staff.'

'What?'

'You heard. Leave Wallace Maitland alone.'

'I'm sorry. I don't know what you're talking about.'

'Don't lie, Cameron. You've been following him. He saw you.'

'No, he didn't. Speaking to him once in a pub hardly constitutes harassment.'

Hambley dismissed my protests. 'This is the first and last opportunity you'll be getting. Stay away from him or I'll bring in the police.'

The line went dead.

Patrick was smiling. 'Not a fan, is he?' He glanced around and returned to our conversation. 'Hate to admit it, but Jackie does have a point. Couldn't swing a cat in her office.'

'I agree. I'll speak to Alex and tell him I'm leaving.'

Patrick yawned and apologised. 'Up too early this mornin'. Got a wee deal goin' on over at the fruit market. They start work in the middle of the night. Needed to inspect the goods.'

'Everything okay?'

'Peachy. So if you're lookin' to score some bananas...'

He got up.

'If there's anythin' you want me to do, make it quick. As soon as I've made the right connections, I'm out of your life forever.'

'Then let me wish you good luck.'

'Cheers. And changin' your address might not be the worst idea in the world. Might stop you ending-up dead. Seriously. By the by, drivin' back from the market, I saw your pal.'

'Who?'

'What's his name? The guy with the coat.'

*Colin McMillan.*

'Where?

'Comin' out of the Necropolis.'

# Chapter Thirty-Eight

David Cooper shaved and showered while Margaret was asleep. In their bedroom, he put on the suit she'd got him the previous Christmas – the black one with the wide pin-stripes – a luxury from before they knew she was pregnant and decided to tighten-up their spending. Babies were expensive. Life was about to change and every spare penny would be needed.

Choosing a tie wasn't an easy decision; eventually, he went with the blue one. When he was ready, he inspected himself in the mirror. Not bad, considering. Margaret would like it. That was the only thing that mattered.

Downstairs, he picked his way through their CD collection until he found what he was looking for. "The Four Seasons" – her favourite piece of music – and put it in the player. They'd bought it after a concert in Sainte-Chapelle in Paris, where a young female Japanese violin virtuoso moved them to tears with an unforgettable performance. They'd held hands and gazed at the stained-glass windows, while Vivaldi's famous work filled the historic room that had once been the private chapel of the king of France. It had all been so wonderful and David Cooper had n ever been happier.

That was then. Now, his wife's eyes were empty. She might not even be hearing it.

David combed her hair, tied the plastic bib round her neck, and put a spoonful of chocolate ice cream in her mouth, moving her jaw with his hand to help her swallow, speaking to her as if he was expecting an answer. Old habits.

They'd been great talkers. And great friends.

He pulled a chair next to the wheelchair so they were side-by-side and opened the photograph album. A younger Margaret

Cooper stood in Trafalgar Square, laughing at the camera with a pigeon on her head.

'Remember that? Our first trip to London. Walking at night through the streets back to the hotel. I wanted us to move down but you said it wasn't somewhere for children. Too big and too busy. Not the place to bring up a family.'

He looked at his wife's dead eyes.

'Of course you were right. I was always a dreamer. You were the practical one. We would've trailed round the world like a couple of hippies if it was up to me. You insisted on planting roots.'

David dipped the spoon into the ice cream, and tried again to get her to take it. Dark rivulets of melted chocolate dripped from Margaret's chin onto the bib. He pointed to photographs of them in Rome and Barcelona, chattering over his tears.

The woman who had been the light of his life went back to sleep. Margaret Cooper didn't know it, but she'd had a good day.

Her husband gently slipped the pillow from behind her and laid it on the floor. He couldn't do it. Not yet. He wasn't ready. He put his head in her lap and let the music run to the end. When it finished, he kissed his wife, and gripped the pillow in both hands.

# Chapter Thirty-Nine

The buzzer broke into my thoughts. I lifted the receiver and heard Jackie, terse and distant, on the other end of the line.

'Somebody for you.'

Three words more than she wanted to give me. When I went downstairs, she was behind the bar taking stock. Painted fingernails, dripping hostile indifference, fluttered in the direction of the back wall, while she concentrated on her work. If Jackie hadn't pointed out the guy over near the Rock-Ola, drinking coffee and reading the *Herald* on the table in front of him, I would've walked past him. On cue, the stranger raised his head and I was staring at a face I'd last seen on the battlements of Edinburgh Castle. Back then, Sean Rafferty had been the second son of the notorious East End gangster family; now, he was the boss, and the man responsible for Tony Daly's murder.

Just hearing him speak brought the memories flooding back.

'Charlie. Long time.'

Not long enough.

The voice was the same, but the rest was different; very different: light suit, white shirt and short fair hair. You could've been sitting next to him at the Royal Concert Hall without suspecting this was, arguably, the most dangerous man in Glasgow. When he lifted the cup to sip his Americano I noticed his nails were buffed. He folded his arms and waited for me to join him. We didn't shake hands; that would've been too surreal.

'How's tricks?'

'Tricks is fine. What're you doing here?'

Rafferty spread his arms. 'You turned down my invitation to come and see me so I thought I'd come to you.'

The visit from the knuckle-dragger wasn't ever going to be the finish of it but I hadn't expected the main man to show-up in person half an hour later.

'What do you want, Rafferty?'

'Oh dear. Got out of the wrong side of the bed this morning?'

'Why're you here?'

'To talk to you.'

'We don't have anything to say to each other.'

'I disagree. Want to bring you up to date. You're living in the past.'

The second time I'd been told that in twenty-four hours.

'You hear the name "Rafferty" and immediately think of old Jimmy. Understandable, given your experience, but I'm not my father. Take my word for it.'

I wouldn't.

'These days I'm a legitimate businessman. All the other stuff's in the bin.'

'All of it? Don't believe you.'

He smiled to keep me on-side. 'Well, most of it. All right, some of it.'

Sean Rafferty, honest injun; the gangster was stealing my act.

'You're about to tell me it's good for Glasgow, aren't you?'

He brushed a speck of dust from his sleeve. For him to bother with this charade meant he had to be seriously worried. Killing me was the easy option, except I might have discovered something and passed it on. That uncertainty was the reason I was still alive.

I kept hearing how good Riverside was for Glasgow. It certainly hadn't been good for Tony Daly though, as yet, nobody was connecting his suicide to it. Rafferty was afraid I would.

'That's exactly what I'm going to tell you, because it's true. Riverside is the most important development in the west of Scotland in years. How many cities can boast a complex like it? Marina, hotel, casino, restaurant and retail. Is it good for Glasgow?

Of course it is. Jeopardising it puts thousands, probably tens of thousands, of jobs at risk.'

Rafferty's eyes bored into me, unblinking.

'People are depending on it.'

'People like Emil Rocha?'

His face registered nothing. He straightened his tie. 'I came to emphasise the damage you're doing trying to connect a suicide to a project that will positively impact the prosperity of this city. And you should know any attempt to derail it will have consequences.'

The note in my pocket gave me courage. 'Like?'

Rafferty sighed, unwilling to spell it out. 'It won't end well.'

'Is that a threat? Should I call the police?'

He smiled indulgently at the sarcasm and drummed the table. 'I don't make threats, Charlie.'

'You had Tony Daly murdered.'

The friendly-chat approach disappeared; the gangster, hiding in a sharp suit, fought to come into the light, and I knew I was right.

Rafferty's voice fell to a whisper as he hissed his reply. 'You got lucky the last time, Cameron. Wouldn't count on it happening again.'

'I'm still here.'

He shook his head at me. 'Never learn, do you? I'm trying to be reasonable. Why do you always have to go the long road, Charlie? Take a telling, and stop making a nuisance of yourself. This is the third time you've been a pain in my arse. Having you in the world is becoming too expensive.'

Sean Rafferty stood and pulled on leather gloves. 'Know your problem, Charlie? Too clever for your own good. Shame, really.'

It was tempting to produce the note with a magician's flourish and announce that the police had already been informed. If I did I wouldn't see tomorrow.

He threw money on the table and pushed past me. 'Can't help yourself. I blame it on all that expensive education your old man paid for selling drugs.'

'Whisky.'

'Same thing.'

'Speaking of whisky, your goons filled the guy on the Queen Margaret Bridge with it before they threw him over the edge. Big mistake. He was a rum drinker. Dark rum. Hated whisky.'

Jimmy Rafferty had been a gutter gangster; his son was evolving into something much worse. Malice rolled off him. If he could he would've killed me right there. Yet he rose above my reckless baiting and held it together because the prize demanded it. Emil Rocha demanded it. Patrick Logue came in clutching a pink betting slip; Rafferty bumped into him on his way out.

'Was that who I think it was?'

'Yeah.'

'Hardly recognised him. Looks like a man with somewhere to go and something to do when he gets there. Didn't know he made house calls?'

'He's making an exception.'

Patrick wagged the first four favourites at Newmarket at me. 'Not funny, Charlie. Not funny at all. If you poke a snake with a stick don't be surprised when it bites you. One word from that guy and it's over for you.'

Patrick's warning hit home; he was right. The satisfaction of provoking Rafferty had made me careless. Stupid would be a better description. I'd put myself in danger and now he knew what I knew, which wouldn't give him sleepless nights. Daly drank rum, so what? Rafferty and his corrupt cabal were still free and clear.

\*\*\*

Based on my previous experience, I wasn't hopeful of getting anywhere with Lachie Thompson. With his off-the-peg suit and record of public service, he should have impressed as a man you could trust. That wasn't what I'd taken from our conversation. His stoic insistence on not discussing his deceased colleague hadn't lasted. In minutes, he was dragging Tony and Cissie Daly's dirty laundry into the open under no pressure from me – alcoholics both, according to him – while his praise was over-rehearsed and poorly delivered. It left a bad taste in my mouth. With friends like him…

In spite of that, he was a polished performer – par for the course from a guy who'd spent decades telling people what they wanted to hear – and at the end, when I threw the Sean Rafferty bomb at him, he'd fielded it like a pro.

But a liar, even a good one, is still a liar.

On its own, the note was intriguing though not much else. If, as was likely, Thompson stuck to his story, it wasn't the breakthrough the anonymous author supposed. Nevertheless, I took heart from knowing somebody who was no friend of the gangster was watching from the wings.

I called the council chambers and, to my surprise, got put through right away. Thompson wasn't hostile – in fact, he was pleasant. I asked a couple of inconsequential questions which he batted back with saintly patience. When it seemed as if I had nothing more, I pulled the rug from under him.

'By the way. How's that granddaughter of yours?'

For the first time, he faltered. '…She's very well.'

'Good. I'm pleased. Because I heard she'd had some trouble.'

Thompson's reply was stiff and unconvincing and told me I was right. 'I'm afraid I've no idea what you're talking about, Mr Cameron.'

# Chapter Forty

The car wasn't in the drive at the Cooper house. That surprised me. Margaret's level of disability was severe, taking her anywhere was impossible, and anyway, what would be the point? She spent most of the day sleeping, and when awake, she didn't know where she was. Life had been reduced to a one room limbo on the ground floor. For David and Margaret the world outside didn't exist.

It was a crime. Yet nobody had admitted to it.

Since my last visit, especially in the wee small hours, the memory of Cooper tending his wife would come into my head, and for a few harrowing moments, I'd relive their tragedy and pity them. Witnessing what Margaret had become must have torn David apart. At times, he'd be forgiven for seeing her as his mute, helpless and relentlessly demanding jailor.

James Hambley's irritated phone call, his groundless insistence I was hounding Wallace Maitland, had struck a warning note I was unable to articulate, even to myself. But it was enough to bring me here.

I got out of the car and walked up the path. David's routine would run parallel with his wife's. Time meant little to these people now; they might both be asleep. For a second I hesitated. The front door was open.

In the hall, I called his name. 'David? David, are you there?'

No one answered.

Shadows from the street fell across the lounge and, as my eyes adjusted, I recognised the stand-by on the hi-fi, glowing red in the corner. The sound of my breathing was the only sound. My fingers scraped the wall, searching for the light switch, aware this was someone's home and I was an intruder with no right to be here.

If the Coopers weren't home, where were they? Where would a quadriplegic woman and her husband be on a winter's night in Scotland?

I reached for options – maybe the wife's condition had taken a turn for the worse and she was back in hospital. Maybe it was an emergency and, in his hurry, David hadn't closed the door behind him. Maybe they...

I turned on the light and froze.

Margaret Cooper was exactly as I remembered her: in her chair, eyes closed, head slumped forward on her chest. A spoon and a carton of ice cream lay on the floor beside the plastic bib; her hair was combed and a pillow rested on her lap.

People say peaceful when they mean something else. Margaret was certainly that.

She looked younger. Her features had lost the intensity her condition had imposed and there was a softness to them, a beauty I hadn't noticed before.

And she was dead.

Suddenly, James Hambley's accusation made sense though his certainty it was me stalking Wallace Maitland was off the mark. I retreated into the hall, took the mobile from my pocket and punched Andrew's number. When he answered, I barked an address at him and ran to the car. I could be wrong, though I knew I wasn't.

The drive across the city passed in a blur and ended with mounting the pavement outside Maitland's house. The blinds were drawn. Two voices carried as far as the gate; one crying, one angry. Instinct took me to the back door. It was open. I crept into the kitchen and peered into the lounge.

Wallace Maitland knelt in the middle of the room, naked from the waist up. There were cuts on his face that didn't look new. His hands were tied and blood ran from wounds carved criss-cross on his bare chest. David Cooper was standing behind him holding a knife in his hand. He caught Maitland by the hair, dragged his head back and whispered in his ear. Whatever he said made the obstetrician beg.

'No. No. No!'

Cooper noticed me and laughed. 'Just in time, Mr Cameron. I take it you didn't find, Law? Doesn't matter now.'

He waved the knife in the air and I noticed its short blade: not a knife, a scalpel.

'This bastard's about to tell us something he should've said at the beginning.'

The irony of the weapon was clear: it traced a path to Maitland's left nipple, leaving a thin trail of sliced flesh in its wake. Maitland moaned and Cooper grinned, unrecognisable from the gentle caring husband I'd met. He was ready to kill, though he wasn't a murderer; he'd cracked. Margaret may have died unexpectedly. In her condition, that was always a possibility.

I didn't believe it.

The ice cream, the combed hair – and perhaps the most telling detail of all in that macabre still-life, the pillow on her lap – helped me guess what had gone on. A decision to bring the hell they were living in to an end had been taken. Out of love, David had smothered Margaret, and stepped over an invisible line into madness. All that remained was revenge. And here it was. I was looking at a man with nothing left to lose.

Cooper deftly flicked his wrist and the nipple parted company with Maitland's torso. A red rivulet flowed down Maitland's pale skin; he screamed. The obstetrician was minutes, at most, from a violent death. If DS Geddes was coming, it better be soon or it would be too late.

Cooper inspected the scalpel, satisfied with its work, and spoke to me, smiling. 'Doesn't like it, does he?'

I moved cautiously into the room and tried to reason with him. 'David, this isn't the way. This isn't what Margaret would want.'

He snapped and turned his anger on me. 'How do you know what she would've wanted? How would any of you know? All he had to do was admit it was his fault and he wouldn't.'

Terror distorted Maitland's face. His eyes darted wildly as he mouthed please help me, over and over again.

Cooper yelled at him. 'Say it! Say it!'

Maitland confessed to save his life. 'Yes. I did. I did it.'

Cooper yanked his head back and shouted. 'Say what you did!'

'I killed her.'

Cooper relaxed his grip but held on. 'At last,' he said. 'At last the truth.'

Before I could get to him he drew the blade across Maitland's throat. White became crimson. A jet of blood splashed the carpet in a long red line and Maitland fell to the floor, making a noise like a rubber bag releasing air. There was nothing anyone could do for him, and whether Andrew came mattered less than it had a minute ago.

'Put the knife down, David.'

Cooper talked to himself. 'Say it. That was all he had to do. Just say it.'

'David…David…'

What happened next was more sickening to witness than the execution, and would stay with me for the rest of my life. Cooper raised his head and looked straight at me. I doubted he even recognised who I was anymore. The blade came up and he slit his own throat. Blood spurted onto the carpet and the light went out of his eyes; he stumbled forward and fell on top of Wallace Maitland.

I was riveted to the spot; my feet were lead, unable to move. It had been so fast. A car door slamming in the street barely registered with me. Andrew Geddes arrived with uniformed officers and stopped in his tracks. The DS thought he'd seen everything. But he hadn't seen this. He edged round the pool of blood and the bodies on the carpet and touched my arm.

'Christ Almighty. You all right, Charlie?'

I did what Maitland, Hambley and Francis Fallon had never done – I told the truth.

'Not really, Andrew. Not really.'

# Chapter Forty-One

A fair-haired constable took an initial statement from me in a police car outside. I'd give a fuller account of what had gone on tomorrow. For now, the Maitland house was a crime scene. I was numb with shock so they let me go. Being alone tonight was a bleak and unappealing prospect. Too many pictures in my head. I almost called Alile, then, with the mobile ringing in my palm, changed my mind. That would be using her. In the end I drove home and poured myself a large one. Around eleven o'clock I had an unexpected visitor.

Andrew Geddes stood in the doorway; he looked tired. 'Thought you might appreciate company.'

'Good thought. I think.'

I got him a whisky. He handed it back.

'If you're worried about my licence, Charlie, forget it. Got a taxi, so stop pissing about and give me a real measure, will you?'

I topped mine up, too.

'Barr showed up at the cow's tail. Always at the front of the queue when they're dishing out prizes.'

'Success has many fathers.'

'And failure is an orphan. Too true, Charlie.'

'Imagine he's pleased.'

Geddes gulped his drink; he was in the mood for a session. 'Pleased as fucking punch. Can't be sure about Margaret Cooper 'till the autopsy comes back but it looks like she'd been smothered. That would make three murders and a suicide thrown in. All nice and neat. Lovely stuff. Just the kind of police work Barr revels in.'

'The easy kind.'

'For him, the only kind.'

He sat forward, warming to his new hobby of bad-mouthing his superior officer, who by the sound of him, thoroughly deserved it

'Don't expect credit. Won't happen.'

From where I was there wasn't much to take credit for. Nobody had survived.

'You mentioned three murders. You mean two, don't you?'

Geddes smiled. He had news and he wasn't in a rush to tell it. 'No, I said three and I meant three.'

'Margaret Cooper, Wallace Maitland and…'

He emptied his drink, wiped his mouth on his sleeve and dangled the glass in mid-air. 'Stick another one in that for an old friend.'

I ignored him. 'And who else?'

Andrew got out of the armchair and organised a refill. His I-know-something-you-don't-know expression told me he was enjoying this. 'Gavin Law.'

'Law? Cooper killed Law? That doesn't make sense. He was going to testify for the Coopers. Their star witness. Without him, their case collapsed.'

'Not Cooper…Maitland.'

'What? When?'

'Hogmanay.'

He'd lost me.

'Mrs Maitland was visiting her sister when we finally tracked her down. Devastated of course. Between them we pieced it together. Maitland showed up at Hambley's in the early hours of New Year's Day, incoherent and covered in blood. The next morning, he couldn't remember where he'd been, or what he'd done.'

'A couple of million people were in the same boat.'

'There's more. His own wife says he was convinced he'd killed Law.'

'Why would he?'

'Because Law put in a formal complaint against him and was ready to testify he'd made a pig's ear of Margaret Cooper's operation. His reputation would be ruined. Might even be struck off.

Hambley confirmed his brother-in-law was in a terrible state. He'd been drinking heavily, was very confused, and looked like he'd been involved in a car crash.'

Andrew caught the scepticism in my eyes.

'Law spoke to his sister on Hogmanay, then he disappeared. We think Wallace Maitland killed him sometime later that night.'

'We? Is this Barr's theory or yours?'

Andrew bristled. 'A missing person and a guy with blood on him who thinks he killed somebody? Not such a stretch.'

I disagreed. 'How do you explain the credit card withdrawals?'

Geddes shrugged. 'A party animal comes across Law's wallet and the year's off to a great start. Oh happy day.'

'Cash was taken out in London. Explain that?'

'Simple: a wee holiday before they get cold feet and stop using them.'

It wasn't enough.

'Where's the body?'

'It'll turn up. Barr's over the moon. Loves nothing better than a result that doesn't get in the way of counting the paper clips.'

'Have you spoken to Caroline Law?'

'Not yet. We'll interview Shona Maitland and the Hambleys again tomorrow and see where we are.'

Geddes went quiet and played with his glass; he'd expected a different reaction. I hadn't bought into his version of events. He made one last attempt to persuade me.

'You're a great investigator yet you haven't come close to finding Law. Doesn't that tell you something?'

I shook my head. 'Killing in a blackout, sure. Happens every day of the week. But a drunk man hiding the body? Not for me. You didn't believe Tony Daly was capable of hanging himself, what's different with this?'

'This one confessed to his wife.'

'Confessed, or couldn't remember?'

Andrew finished his drink; the session hadn't materialised. He stood, and buttoned his coat. 'There are loose ends. I don't deny it.

But when everybody dies what else can you expect? We may never know the whole story.'

I threw him a bone. 'Three out of four isn't bad.'

He put a friendly hand on my shoulder. 'And to answer your question: it's Barr's theory. Racing to conclusions – his trademark. Ten minutes in the door and the case is solved.'

'You were testing me?'

He grinned. 'Yep.'

'So how did I do?'

'Like you usually do, Charlie. You passed. It's bullshit.'

\*\*\*

Weak sunshine on the road to Peebles seemed almost tropical compared with the weather of late. A long way to go to have lunch with a man I barely knew, but after the hellish scene with David Cooper and Wallace Maitland, the city felt oppressive; escaping it wasn't unwelcome and I did my best to enjoy the trip.

At Neidpath Castle, I got out on the high ground and studied what remained of the ruined tower house close to the River Tweed, imagining what living here must have been like. The sun chose that moment to dip behind a cloud and brought the obvious conclusion. Bloody cold. I got back in the car and drove on.

Sometime today, the police would give Caroline Law the news about her brother and she'd been right about something bad having happened to him. I'd have to speak to her as well and wasn't looking forward to it. What I had to say wouldn't match. She'd be in enough pain without me raising a question mark against the official version, flimsy though it was. Andrew had floated his DI's flawed reasoning and got the reaction he was looking for. Yet, something he'd said rang true – we might never know the whole story. Both of my cases had run into a dead end. Caroline and Cissie Daly were going to be disappointed women; there were a lot of them about. Alile had been gracious and understanding about Kate Calder, more than could be said for me. I was all over the place.

I arrived in Peebles after two o'clock to find Colin McMillan waiting where I'd parked on my previous visit to the town, still wearing his expensive coat. When I turned down Port Brae to Tweed Green he waved. In the car, I followed his directions and drove up Main Street, past the Tontine hotel. McMillan seemed in good form for a guy whose whole life had gone down the toilet.

'At least it isn't raining.'

'There's always that though it's cold. I stopped at Neidpath Castle for five minutes and nearly froze.'

He laughed. 'Tell you about the castle later. Remind me.'

'Another ghost story?'

'Fraid so.'

'You should write a book.'

He let the idea settle. 'Maybe I will. Take the Innerleithen Road. I'm about half a mile away. Is pasta okay? Thought I'd keep it simple since I'm out of practise. Or we can always go somewhere. I won't be offended.'

'No need, pasta's fine.'

A couple of hundred yards further on, we stopped at a cottage set back from the road. It was old and uncared for.

McMillan read my mind and explained. 'This was my mother's house. Considered selling it after she died. Glad now I didn't. Doesn't feel like home, but then, nowhere does.'

He led us inside, took my coat, and hung it up behind the door. In the lounge, the remains of a wood fire burned in a hearth that had probably been new in 1935 and filled the room with smoky air that caught the back of my throat. Noises from the kitchen told me my host had already started on our meal.

He shouted to me with forced joviality, like someone not used to having company who was trying too hard. 'Got the water on. Won't be too long.'

'No rush.'

'And sit down for God's sake.'

I didn't sit down. I wandered round, taking in my surroundings. A cottage in the country sounds romantic; this was anything but.

The low ceiling made a small room smaller, and I guessed the heavy furniture, set against the white-washed walls, had belonged to McMillan's mother. It reminded me of old times and hard times. There was no television, stereo, PC or magazines. Nothing of him.

How did he spend his time? What did he do at night?

On an ugly chest of drawers that might have pre-dated the First World War, a photograph of a blonde woman holding an infant lay beside the envelope it had come in. The woman was kissing the child's forehead. Underneath the inscription written in an assured hand read "One year on and going strong. Thanks to you."

McMillan came in and saw me studying the picture.

'Not bad, eh? Another satisfied customer. Only thing I miss about it.'

He knelt down and added wood to the fire from a wicker basket, grinning.

'These old places don't hold the heat. No joke this time of year I can tell you.'

'Can imagine.'

'What'll it be?'

'I'm good. And I'm driving.'

'Don't mind if the chef indulges himself, do you?'

'Not at all.'

He disappeared into the kitchen and came back with a whisky the size of three pub measures; the obstetrician wore it well but he was still drinking heavily. We sat by the fire watching tongues of new-born flames devour the logs, not speaking, until McMillan broke the spell.

'Any luck with Gavin Law?'

'As a matter of fact there is.'

'You've found him?'

I told him about the night before and he listened in silence. When I reached the end he poured himself another drink. The story affected him; the hand holding the drink shook though his voice was steady.

'Sorry, Charlie, don't believe it. I knew Maitland— not well – though I knew him. His incompetence might have hurt people, but he wouldn't kill anybody.'

'How can you be sure? Law had him in a corner. He must've hated him.'

'Even so, it doesn't compare with David Cooper. His wife had been taken from him. Over the years, Maitland's done well enough financially. Being forced to retire early isn't the worst thing in the world.'

He sipped his drink and got up to set the table. Out of the blue he said, 'So what did he do with the body?'

I gave him the answer Andrew had given me. 'It'll turn up.'

McMillan was smart; smarter than DI Adam Barr – how hard was that? 'Hasn't so far. Shouldn't that concern the police?'

Not when closing a file was more important than the truth. His voice reached me from the kitchen. 'Hope you've brought your appetite with you.'

A minute later, he appeared holding two plates of spaghetti. 'Careful, it's hot.'

He opened a bottle of red wine and offered me a glass. I refused.

'Sure? Just one? All right. More for me.'

The pasta was cooked to perfection and the meat sauce hadn't come from a jar.

'Don't stand on ceremony. Dig in.'

McMillan spoke through a mouthful of Bolognese. 'What happened to the rape allegation Law was so worried about when he spoke to me?'

*Good question.*

'The woman won't come forward. So Hambley says.'

McMillan paused. 'I wonder if there ever was an allegation. Wouldn't be surprised if he invented it to shut Law up. He'd realise no hospital would employ an obstetrician without a reference. Believe me, I know.'

He changed the subject.

'I've decided to go away for a while. Take a villa for six months and live like the locals then move on to somewhere else.'

'Where?'

'Haven't decided. The Greek islands. The South of France. Sit in the sun and watch my lemons grow.'

'Nice idea. Won't you get bored?'

He smiled across the table. 'I expect I will.'

'When are you leaving?'

'Soon. I'm done with Scotland. Glasgow especially. Won't be going back there. The agent can sell the house and everything in it for all I care.'

Colin McMillan sounded low. The adventure he was describing didn't excite him as much as he made out. His eyes were hooded and his cheeks were flushed, and in the firelight, he looked old and unhappy. He refilled his glass, missing me out. He hadn't been joking about more for him.

'So I suppose what I'm saying is, this is goodbye.'

'Drop me a postcard from the Promenade des Anglais, or wherever.'

'I will. And don't stop searching for Law. The answer is probably staring you in the face. All you have to do is see it.'

At the door, he said, 'You're a smart guy, Charlie. I like you.'

'I didn't hear the ghost story. Neidpath Castle, remember?'

'What? Oh, yes. Some other time. Take care of yourself.'

On the drive back to the city, it started to snow. Night closed in and although it was only five-thirty, it could have been ten o'clock. At one point, it was coming down so fast the wipers struggled to clear the windscreen, and I was glad I'd left the drinking to him. Colin McMillan was decent company but he was heading for trouble. The shaking revealed how much booze he was getting through. A new beginning took courage. McMillan could be going through the motions, making a geographical change, or he might be opening himself to the future.

I wished him well.

At a BP station in Biggar, I stopped, still thinking about the obstetrician and what he'd been through. I'd been through some stuff, too: from discovering Margaret Cooper dead in her wheelchair to standing helpless while her husband executed Maitland and turned the knife on himself. And I hadn't once thought of Kate Calder.

My text was short, two words: *it's over.*

Alile's reply matched it: *I'm at home.*

I got into the car, turned off the forecourt, and put my foot on the gas.

\*\*\*

The door opened before I reached it and Alile stood with light at her back. There were no words. We tore each other's clothes away until we were naked and fell against the wall. She buried her face in my shoulder, crying and moaning before she climaxed. I carried her upstairs and in her bed, we finished what we'd started. Slowly and deliberately this time, but we finished it.

# Chapter Forty-Two

I lay quietly watching Alile sleep, tracing her perfect features with my eyes and wondering how I'd ever considered letting her slip away.

The night before had been wonderful and, for the first time since Kate got on the plane, I was at peace. Love was strange. David Cooper was proof of that. Smothering his wife – if indeed he had – was courageous and unselfish. The final act of devotion. To care so much for someone was an awesome thing and when the balance of his mind wasn't disturbed, he'd felt the same. I'd seen it.

On the way to Francis Fallon, bright sunshine and blue skies made it seem like summer had arrived early. But it was bitterly cold, and snow from yesterday piled in drifts on the pavement. I was wearing my coat. I would need it. Alile was from Africa; no snow there. She stared at it and didn't speak, maybe trying to decide if she'd made a mistake with Scotland and with me.

As she was getting out she said, 'Will I see you tonight?'

'Tonight and every night.'

It was the question and the answer we both had to hear. She kissed me and smiled. 'I'll look forward to it.'

In NYB, Jackie Mallon set aside our differences to grill me. Jackie was a sharp-eyed cookie. Apart from that, she was a woman, and as soon as I stepped through the door, she spotted a change in me. Resentment about office space was no match for gossip straight from the mill.

'So when're we going to meet her, then?'

'Don't know what you're talking about, Jackie.'

She laughed, and started making the cappuccino I hadn't asked for. 'Read you like a book, Charlie. You're like the cat that got the cream.'

'And you're a silly romantic, Jackie.'

She set the coffee in front of me. 'It was cappuccino you wanted, wasn't it?'

'As a matter of fact, it was, yes.'

Her fingers pressed her temples, closed her eyes and went into a mock trance. 'Magda know all. Magda see all. So shove your denial chat. You and Miss Universe are together.'

I lifted the *Herald* from the bar and headed to a table and sanctuary. Jackie could be a scary woman, but I'd miss her. The paper was full of speculation about how bad Brexit was for the country and not much else until an item on page five caught my eye. Leader of the council, Lachie Thompson had resigned. His colleague, Sandy Rutherford, was quoted saying how much he regretted the elder statesman's sudden departure – which, of course, he respected – and praised his contribution to the city. The report didn't touch on why Thompson had chosen this moment to go. I thought I understood. Out of politics, Sean Rafferty had no more use for him, and, given what I'd seen, it was probably one of the councillor's easier decisions.

As for Jackie, she was teasing me. I didn't mind. Over the years her car-crash love life had put her in the firing-line. My turn now and a small price to pay for Alile. I thought about the lady from Malawi, then focussed on what was certain to be a difficult day. By now, Gavin Law's sister would have been told DI Adam Barr's flimsy fantasy, where Wallace Maitland murdered her brother. It would destroy her, but in time, some kind of acceptance might be possible.

And she had Dean. Cissie Daly had no one. I hoped I could find the words.

Normally, it would too early for Pat Logue – the bar wouldn't open for a while – yet he was here, drinking a coffee with his head buried in a book. He acknowledged me with a distracted nod and followed it with a question.

'Could use a lift if you're going out again, Charlie.'

'Where to?'

'The fruit market. Got a deal on.'

'It'll have to be soon.'

'Ready when you are.'

'Then let's go.'

On the way to the car, he offered un-asked for insights into his mid-life crisis. Pat Logue lived in bookmakers and shady transactions.

'I'm at a stage where I need to decide where I want to go.'

We swept up High Street, passed Barony Hall, as far as the traffic lights opposite the St Mungo Museum, and rolled to a halt. In the passenger seat, Pat Logue stayed in entrepreneurial mood, exploring the pros and cons of his business model – whether I was interested or not. He recognised a captive audience when he had one. Patrick stroked his goatee and loudly invited me to consider the world of business, giving his newly acquired language an airing. For the moment, what was going to win the two-thirty at Wincanton didn't figure in his thinking. Joining the ranks of the Rothschilds did, although, when he searched for an example to illustrate a point, the sport of kings was there to help.

'Low risk investments bring low returns which is why, with the gee-gees, bettin' the favourite won't get you much. Perishable goods are high risk, Charlie. And decidin' on a stop-loss position in case it all goes Pete Tong, that's where the skill comes in.'

How much risk could there possibly be in five dozen boxes of bananas?

I threw my tuppence-worth in. 'Stop-loss? Isn't that for the stock market?'

Patrick wasn't fazed. 'Stock market. Fruit market. Comes down to the same thing: makin' money or losin' money.'

We moved on, into Castle Street, as far as the Cathedral and waited while a steady stream of people, likely coming from the Royal Infirmary, crossed in front of us. I'd successfully filtered Patrick out and was drumming the steering wheel and remembering Alile when I saw him. Without his distinctive coat, he would've been just another face in the crowd.

Colin McMillan walked purposefully, and Pat Logue's description of Sean Rafferty came into my head: a man with somewhere to go and something to do when he gets there. Less than twenty-four hours ago he'd told me he wasn't coming back here.

*I'm done with Scotland. Glasgow especially.*

Yet, here he was. The jigsaw puzzle came together in my head. 'McMillan! Bloody McMillan!'

Patrick hadn't seen him. Before I could act, the lights changed and I was forced to go with the traffic instead of turning right onto the motorway and Blochairn. I swung left.

Patrick started to protest. 'Wrong way, Charlie. The market, remember?'

I didn't explain; there wasn't time. A minute later, we were back where we'd started, facing the Royal Infirmary and Cathedral Square. There was no sign of Colin McMillan. I pulled into the kerb and jumped out.

'You'll have to drive, Patrick. Park and find me.'

Pat Logue didn't understand what was happening. 'Where will you be?'

I pointed. 'In there.'

McMillan was going to the Necropolis. The Victorian graveyard on a hill over-looking the city, originally intended to be Glasgow's version of the famous Pere Lachaise cemetery in Paris. And it was big - thirty-seven acres. The man I was after could be anywhere.

I raced towards what I later discovered was the Bridge of Sighs and found my way barred: the heavy black and gold gate was locked. Through it I saw McMillan, already on the higher ground, surrounded by tombstones, unaware he'd been spotted. I charged back the way I'd come – took a left, then down the hill another left, across from Cathedral House hotel – and arrived at the main entrance. Further away, the path McMillan had been on rose to the heart of the cemetery. There was no sign of the obstetrician and I stopped to get my bearings, out of breath, amid more frosted reminders of mortality than I could count.

On every side, paths led to more paths. Footprints in the snow helped me decide. I followed them and ran, until, in the distance, I saw the camel coat, and McMillan standing at the foot of a grave with his hands clasped in front of him. For a second, I thought he was praying. The last interment had been before he was born. Who did he know here?

When I reached him he smiled his sad lop-sided smile at me and didn't offer to shake hands. 'Charlie! Wasn't expecting to see you again.'

In the cold light, his face was lined and tired, older than he'd seemed in Peebles. He kept his eyes on me, waiting for my reaction. We'd shared pasta and ghost stories and I had liked Colin McMillan. In other circumstances we might have become friends.

That wouldn't be happening.

I found my voice. 'It was you. All along, it was you.'

He shrugged an apology. 'Afraid so. No choice. Sorry if you're disappointed in me.'

'Why?'

He studied the rock-hard ground.

'You never met Gavin Law, did you? Take it from me he was a bastard, especially with women. Callous. Used them, and threw them away. Joyce met him at a party when our marriage was in trouble; they had an affair. We could've got over it. We'd agreed to give it a try then he convinced her he was serious about her. Instead of getting back together, Joyce moved out. Five weeks later, he dropped her. I tried over and over to get her to speak to me. She wouldn't even meet me. She was a good person and she was ashamed and humiliated by what she'd done. But it wasn't her it was him.'

The memory overwhelmed him.

'Ending the affair was one thing but treating her the way he did was unforgiveable. He shunned her and she took her own life.'

'How do you know that's what happened?'

'She left a note explaining everything. I kept it. And that night, I swore Law would pay for the suffering he'd caused.'

'So you killed him? How?'

The surgeon seemed keen to unburden himself maybe because he felt he owed me the truth.

'We weren't friends and never would've been. But, because I complained about Wallace Maitland, Law considered us allies; on the same side. Thought I didn't know he was the man Joyce was having an affair with, and confided in me. After the harm he'd caused he telephoned on Hogmanay to tell me about the rape allegation, and I knew this was the chance I'd waited for.'

'You set it up from the beginning. The anaesthetist was telling the truth. You told him you were suicidal because you knew Francis Fallon would suspend you.'

McMillan sighed. His breath drifted on the air. 'Gavin Law was cruel, and so obsessed with himself, he didn't realise what I was doing. It was all about him. My wife – his lover, a woman he'd persuaded to leave her husband – was only two months' dead, and he'd moved on.'

I asked again. 'How did you do it?'

'I drove to Glasgow and went to his flat.'

'Wasn't he surprised to see you?'

McMillan laughed. 'His ego was so big, the fucking idiot assumed I was concerned about him. We talked. I said he should go to his sister's party. I'd give him a lift if he wanted.'

'And?'

'I killed him in the car.'

The world was suddenly over-run with people telling fairy stories – James Hambley, DI Adam Barr and now, Colin McMillan.

I shook my head. 'Nice try Colin, but you didn't kill anybody. It was Sean Rafferty.'

The lop-sided smile reappeared. 'I'm lost, Charlie.'

No he wasn't.

'When I saw you heading here again, I realised who the woman in the photograph is. The satisfied customer. It's Sean Rafferty's wife. His daughter almost died. You saved her life, and Sean owes you. Am I right?'

McMillan dropped the pretence and applauded; slowly and deliberately. 'You're a smart guy. No doubt about it. Rafferty warned me to be careful round you. Well done. But how will you prove it?'

The grave was modest compared with some. Wind and rain had eroded the name of whoever was buried here. The inscription survived and I'd heard it before. He'd quoted it to me in NYB the first time we had met, when he was describing the attraction of the Necropolis.

*Save your tears for the living*.

I tapped the frozen earth with my foot and took out my mobile. 'That won't be a problem, Colin.'

We waited for DS Geddes and the uniforms to arrive. McMillan didn't try to run. He seemed resigned, pleased even.

'You and a murdering thug like, Rafferty? I don't get it.'

McMillan stuck to his script. 'I've admitted I did it and told you why and how. Beyond that...you're imagining things, Charlie. Settle for what you've got. I have.'

\*\*\*

Putting handcuffs on him was unnecessary; he wasn't going anywhere; they did it anyway. Andrew Geddes kept his distance and let Barr have the glory. The DI didn't acknowledge me, and, at a guess, my contribution wouldn't feature in his report. When they'd taken McMillan away, the grave was cordoned off and an officer placed on guard until permission was granted to open it. I had no doubt about what they would find.

Patrick should have been back by now. The sight of so many policemen might have scared him away. He'd turn up with a story the length of the street and probably true.

I walked the steep incline to the John Knox monument, with virgin snow sighing under my feet, passed the elaborate final resting places of tobacco barons and their moneyed neighbours. Knowing you can't take it with you hadn't prevented some people trying.

From the top, in the extraordinary light, the cathedral was a doll's house dusted in icing sugar, and the sounds of the city barely a whisper. For a spot to spend eternity, it would be hard to beat. If it mattered.

"Save your tears for the living" had spoken to Colin McMillan. David Cooper would have understood only too well. Caroline Law and Cissie Daly would appreciate where he was coming from.

# Chapter Forty-Three

NYB had been my second home for longer than I wanted to remember. Leaving would be hard but, as Pat Logue liked to say, it had to be done.

Jackie wasn't around when I arrived. I guessed she'd heard I'd asked Alex Gilby to see me this morning and would be dancing on the tables at the thought of getting my office and quitting her shoe box under the stairs. Not so.

She said, 'Alex told me you're moving out. Never thought I'd hear myself say it. I'm going to miss you, Charlie. You're a good guy.'

Now she tells me.

Pat Logue was in bad shape, and looked as if he'd spent the night in a barn. His usual hail-fellow act was beyond him. Patrick was hungover. I'd last seen him at the Necropolis on his way to the fruit market and his deal.

He spoke to me from behind his hand. 'Any chance of a sub, Charlie? I'm potless.'

'Thought you were geared up to take on the world?'

He tried a smile that didn't make it. 'Business is a cruel world. It's dog eat dog out there.'

I'd heard. So far, nobody had paid me. Patrick's need was greater than mine. I gave him a large photograph of the queen.

'Thanks. Take it off my next wage.'

He handed the money to the barman and took a pint in return.

'Come up and tell me what went wrong.'

'Will do. By the by, the jungle drums are sayin' today's the day you're offski, that true?'

'Yes. Time to go time.'

In the office, I started clearing my stuff; not much to show for the years I'd been here.

Alex Gilby found me emptying the desk drawers. He seemed subdued. 'Sorry you're going, Charlie. Sure you won't change your mind?'

Generous, except we both realised it was for the best. The arrangement with Alex had been great for me but it hadn't been intended to last indefinitely.

'Had a good run. No complaints.'

'Where will you go?'

'Don't know yet.'

He fished a set of keys from his pocket and threw them on the desk. 'A place round the corner in Cochrane Street belongs to me. Could use a coat of paint and it's small. It's yours if you want it.'

'Cheers, Alex. I'll take a look.'

Half an hour after he left, Andrew Geddes poked his head round the door. 'Still here? Thought I might've missed you.'

Those jungle tom-toms were loud.

DS Geddes did a line in solace few could match. And even fewer survived. He sat across from me and gazed around, preparing to conjure up good old days that had never happened. I braced for comforting words which would have us both in tears.

Andrew sighed. 'Sad, Charlie. Has to be said.'

No it didn't. I was moving offices not going to Patagonia. I nipped it in the bud.

'What about Colin McMillan?'

Geddes took the hint and let it go. 'He's confessed to murdering Gavin Law on Hogmanay. And you were spot on; he didn't change his story. Claims to have driven from Peebles to his flat, and killed him. In the snow? Remember how bad it was?'

'You were worried about getting a taxi to take you a couple of miles home.'

'Hard to argue with a guy who's determined to take the credit. Barr's as happy as a pig in shit. Loves it. Getting a reputation as a can-do copper.'

'Except it would be impossible for McMillan to do it by himself. Doesn't Barr get that?'

Andrew shrugged. 'Doubt forensics will find much. Even if he did do it, the one thing a surgeon understands is contamination. Barr's got a signed confession from a guy with motive – Law seduced his wife then dropped her. She committed suicide. More than enough for most people.'

'Unless they're interested in finding out what really happened.'

'Barr isn't.'

'Then he must be deaf, dumb, and blind, because the physical logistics don't add up. The Necropolis was closed, so how did he get in? Even if he somehow managed that he'd have to drag the body to the other side of the cemetery, dig a hole and bury it. Way more far-fetched than Tony Daly. It would take a Sean Rafferty to make those problems go away. And the cash withdrawals would be easy for him to organise.'

'Nevertheless, as a place to hide a body, the Necropolis is hard to beat. And while McMillan's protesting his guilt, it isn't up to the police to prove he isn't telling the truth. According to him, the phone call from Law gave him the opportunity.'

'What he isn't saying is he never left Peebles. He called Rafferty and told him about the rape. And that Law was on his own.'

'Yes. Killing him was the plan from the beginning. Complaining about Maitland was a ruse to make it look like he was on the same side as Law. Same with admitting he was suicidal to another member of staff. Knew he was putting his career in jeopardy, and didn't care. Difficult to argue against.'

'Can only imagine how angry and bitter he was to sacrifice his career for revenge'

'Not really. Did you notice his hand shaking?'

'Assumed it was the booze. Anytime I was with him he was drinking for Scotland.'

Geddes shook his head. 'It isn't booze.'

'Then, what?'

'Parkinson's. His days in theatre were over.'

'So what about his connection to Sean Rafferty?'

'Denies there is one. The Rafferty baby almost died. McMillan saved her life. Just doing his job.'

'Again, not true. Rafferty owed, him or thought he did. He'd heard what Law had done and offered to square things. There's a photograph of Rafferty's wife with the daughter in his house in Peebles.'

'That's when you sussed it?'

'No. I couldn't place the woman's face until McMillan crossed in front of the car, heading towards the Necropolis. Then it hit me along with something Rafferty said. He told me I'd been a pain in his arse three times. Thought he'd made a mistake because I only counted two: the last time I crossed his path and Daly. He was talking about Law.'

I handed Andrew the picture I'd torn from the *Herald*: the Lord Provost, Sean Rafferty and a blonde woman unveiling a model of Riverside.

'It was too crazy. The day before McMillan had told me he was finished with Glasgow – pretty definite about it, too – and suddenly, there he was. It didn't feel right. And, unlike your DI, I didn't believe Wallace Maitland had done it. Pat Logue saw him coming out of the Necropolis and I'd already run into him on the street there as well. Three times was too much of a coincidence. Spun a yarn about how fascinating the architecture was and quoted the inscription on the gravestone.'

'"Save your tears for the living." Was he giving you a clue?'

'You'd have to ask him that.'

'I will. And before you start feeling too sorry for him, remember, Rafferty might've been the instrument but McMillan was at the centre of it, even if he didn't actually do the deed. That makes him a murderer.'

'How did Law actually die?'

'Asphyxiated.'

'The same as Joyce McMillan. Poetic.'

Geddes laughed. 'Fucks Barr's fairytale about Maitland killing Law right up.'

'But it doesn't explain how Maitland came by his injuries on Hogmanay.'

'You've called it so far. What's your best guess?'

'I'd put money on David Cooper. The guy must've been going under even then. Went to talk to Law and ran into Maitland. Stopped short of killing. Later on he snapped and finished the job. Anything from Francis Fallon?

'No. Though you can't get near the place for reporters. Hambley's knighthood's out the window.'

'Couldn't happen to a nicer guy. He's still getting off lightly.'

'You did great work on this, Charlie. Great work.'

A compliment from Andrew was a rare thing. I would savour it.

'Yet the real killer is getting away scot-free. Sean Rafferty has murdered two people and nobody knows it.'

'Whoever sent you the note about Thompson's granddaughter knows. Hope they find more courage next time.'

'If there is a next time. Rafferty's on his way to becoming respectable.'

'He'll never be that, and there's always a next time with scum like him. We'll get another chance. Sooner or later he'll run out of luck. They all do.'

Geddes stood and took a last look round, on the point of going maudlin on me, then changed his mind. 'Oh, just so you know, I've put in for promotion.'

'Not before time. Pleased to hear it.'

'Barr will be asked to input, so don't hold your breath. I'll play the game his way until I can play it my way. No more meltdowns. You won't have to rescue me again.'

'Can't keep a good man down, Andrew. Don't forget it.'

The unbeliever in him never slept.

'Been doing a pretty fair job so far.'

My mobile rang. Andrew waved, and left. On the other end of the line, Caroline Law was understandably subdued, but all right.

'I wanted to thank you for finding Gavin. Without you, I would've lived the rest of my life not knowing, and blaming myself.'

I identified with that feeling.

'Send me your bill, and thanks. I really mean it. Thanks.'

Pat Logue must have been waiting, because no sooner had DS Geddes left than he appeared. The money I'd given him had done its work. Whatever his business reversal had been, he'd put it behind him and was his breezy self again, though it wasn't all down to the alcohol. Now and then, the storms of life raged and threatened to drown him, but he always surfaced; Patrick was a survivor. Seeing him back on form made me smile. Some things should never change.

He clapped his hands. 'Right,' he said. 'Where's this Eskimo woman you want me to wrestle?'

# Epilogue

Kim Rafferty sat in the rocking-chair with Rosie in her arms; the toddler was almost asleep. Today had been a big day; she'd said her first word: mama. As usual, Sean wasn't around to hear it. Kim hadn't seen him for two days; he hadn't come home. Probably with one of his whores. She didn't care. Being in the same room with him made her want to be sick. Their child was the only good thing to have come out of the marriage. All that ever would come out of it.

Rosie's eyes flickered open and closed again. Kim smiled down at her daughter and whispered. 'Mummy's note wasn't enough. But we'll get him, won't we, Rosie? Daddy's a bad man but we'll get him. Just you wait. You wait and see if we don't.'

# Acknowledgements

For me, the biggest surprise in writing has come from the encouragement and support of people; many of them strangers. Their generosity has been a humbling experience. The debt of gratitude is so large it is difficult to know where to begin, but perhaps a mention to all the book clubs and their members is a good place to start. Also, the reviewers and bloggers who tirelessly work to help a novel reach the maximum audience deserve to be recognised. If they weren't there, I would be whistling in the dark. Naming them individually is a recipe for missing someone out and offending them, so I won't go there. It isn't necessary; they already know who they are. Thanks, everybody.

In bringing the story to the page, I again credit DS Alasdair McMorrin of Police Scotland CID for keeping me within the bounds of reality, Heather Osborne, my editor, and Betsy and Fred at Bloodhound Books for their faith in me.

Putting a book together is like making sausages; a process it is better no one witnesses. In that regard, my partner, inspiration and guiding light is, as always, my wife, Christine. How fortunate to be married to such a creative thinker. It means I am never stuck for long because she sees possibilities I am blind to. Her vision is unsurpassed and, without her input this book would not exist.

Owen Mullen
Crete 2017